Is there anyone in the literary universe who quite writes, sounds or undulates like Karen An-Hwei Lee? If David Markson's *Wittgenstein's Mistress* were spliced with *My Octopus Teacher* and Rachel Carson's *Sea Trilogy*, it might come close to producing Emily, an inquisitive, "accidental" octopus with a penchant for spice cake and philosophical ruminations on the fate of rogue genomes and the enigma that is our souls. Singular and shimmering.
—**Lisa Hsiao Chen, author of** *Activities of Daily Living*

Have you ever watched the hues of a sleeping octopus shift dreamily from bright chartreuse to ghostly pale blue and from ghostly pale blue to the color of evening skies? If so, the wonder you felt is similar to the wonder you will feel reading *Love Chronicles of the Octopodes*, every page of which astounds and abounds with dazzling lyricism, narrative innovation, and prose textures movingly evocative of otherworldly sentience. With ingenuity and care, Karen An-hwei Lee incorporates research on cephalopods, black holes, genome editing, and the life and work of Emily Dickinson into sublime experimentations with language and genre. The result is art—and the art is powerfully transformative. To be submerged in the gorgeous songfulness of Karen An-hwei Lee's science fiction is to find oneself metamorphosing into a novel life form. I woke up from the dreamscapes of this book with exclamation marks in my brain and a new, tentacular, bioluminescent sense of possibility.
—**Seo-Young Chu, author of** *Do Metaphors Dream of Literal Sleep? A Science-Fictional Theory of Representation*

Karen An-Hwei Lee, whose marvelous mind gave us Kafka—weird as ever and wonderfully alive—in twenty-first century Los Angeles and then a post-apocalyptic data cloud on a quest for the keys to happiness, outdoes herself with this brilliant head bend of a book. *Love Chronicles of the Octopodes* chronicles the adventures of one Emily D, octopus extraordinaire whose signal genetic material can be traced back to a certain legendary poet from Amherst but whose verve and swerve are all her own. Which is to say that Emily D is an original. As is Lee. There is no one else at work on the American scene like her.

—**Laird Hunt, author of** *Zorrie*

# LOVE

# CHRONICLES

## of the

# OCTOPODES

# Also by Karen An-hwei Lee

## Fiction

*The Maze of Transparencies* (Ellipsis Press)

*Sonata in K* (Ellipsis Press)

## Translation

*Doubled Radiance: Poetry and Prose of
Li Qingzhao* (Singing Bone Press)

## Poetry

*Duress* (Cascade Books)

*Rose is a Verb: Neo-Georgics* (Slant Books)

*What the Sea Earns for a Living* (Quaci Press)

*Phyla of Joy* (Tupelo Press)

*Ardor* (Tupelo Press)

*In Medias Res* (Sarabande Books)

*God's One Hundred Promises* (Swan Scythe Press)

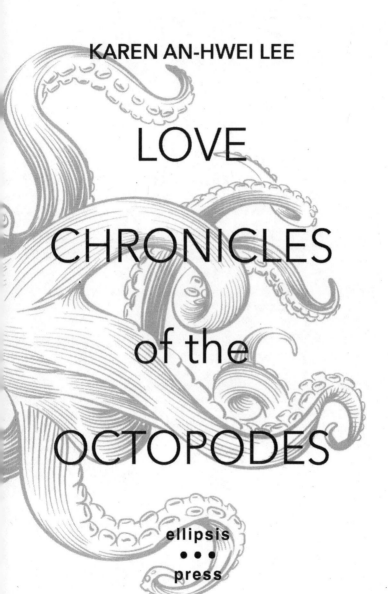

KAREN AN-HWEI LEE

# LOVE

# CHRONICLES

## of the

# OCTOPODES

ellipsis
• • •
press

Portions of this book have appeared in somewhat
different form in *Your Impossible Voice, The Big Other,* and
*Dispatches from the Poetry Wars.*

Design by Corey Frost and Eugene Lim

First Edition
ISBN 978-1-940400-10-5

Ellipsis Press LLC
P.O. Box 721196
Jackson Heights, NY 11372
www.ellipsispress.com

*Library of Congress Cataloging-in-Publication Data*
Names: Lee, Karen An-hwei, 1973- author.
Title: Love chronicles of the octopodes / Karen An-hwei Lee.
Description: First Edition. | Jackson Heights, NY : Ellipsis Press, [2022]
   | Includes bibliographical references. |
Identifiers: LCCN 2022036359 | ISBN 9781940400105 (paperback)
Subjects: LCGFT: Novels.
Classification: LCC PS3612.E3435 L68 2022 | DDC 813/.6--dc23/eng/20220812
LC record available at https://lccn.loc.gov/2022036359

You are altogether beautiful, my darling,
beautiful in every way.
**Song of Songs 4:7,** *New Living Translation*

What's true of oceans is true, of course,
Of labyrinths and poems. When you start swimming
Through riptide of rhythms and metaphor's seaweed
You need to be a good swimmer…
**Jack Spicer**

When you pass through the waters, I will be with you;
and when you pass through the rivers,
      they will not sweep over you.
When you walk through the fire, you will not be burned;
the flames will not set you ablaze.
**Isaiah 43:2,** *New International Version*

# CONTENTS

# 1 | Portrait of an Octopodean Paradise

In which we meet our heroine and learn details of her origin as a rogue soul, her banishment by the stardust editors from the flesh factories of the Genzopolis to a lagoon on the other side of the universe. The moonlight delivers lost letters. The postdiluvian deluge.

## Portrait of an Octopodean Paradise

O N THE LAGOON, IN THE MILKY RAYS of dawn, I woke after a night of deep slumber, and after several minutes of realization—slowly blooming on all nine of my brains—understood I was no less than an octopus. No less, no more, said my unwitting soul. You're not the person you thought you were yesterday. You're an octopus, I sighed, curling one of my arms over the edge of a water mattress. Not a drowsy woman lounging in a wetsuit, but rather, an atypical mollusk shot through with grit to the guts, purple as waxy plum lipstick all over the body, to boot. I lay sprawled across my waterbed, kissed yet irked and tickled by the soft rain falling through my window in the night, musing warily, maybe this is all there is. Make no bones about it. In fact, I have no bones. Not a lovely female in a gown of skin the color of cherry orchards draped on her shoulders; no fuzzy faux fur muffs to adorn her wrists; no gems of carbon vapor deposition the size of pomegranate pips, and no polymer nylons clinging to her sundry legs, thank goodness. No matter what her ambitions once were, if any, I finally know what this is all about.

My dear sea stars, I'm an octopus.

16

The ganglia of my flesh, tingling in eight limbs, buzzed and sparked, vexed by this awakening. On the shores of this lagoon, the kelp forest brightened outdoors while the sun shone like a cleaved starfruit, tapping the eaves of my lair in tandem with bright drops, a staccato rhythm of ellipses. Pip pop, pip pop, pip. Pop. Why say it's spring rain when no seasons exist here, the passing of time marked by a band of light? A willy-nilly smithing of words, I suppose. It's always spring on this side of the universe, a fair green lyric gracing the seaweed. Yesterday, I scribbled these lines by siphoning drams of my own do-it-yourself, homemade sepia ink, stored in a sac about the size of a mint leaf; some folks use gallbladders, while I use an ink sac. Drizzling drops of melanin inkiness, I jotted these lines:

Spring sings green through my window facing the sea.
Green is the scent of the air, a grove's upturned leaves.
Green glimmers under iridophores in my skin, a lagoon
of tranquility without sailboats or pearl-divers in sight.
Green is the color of matcha steaming with promise.
It's eternal green here, always. Doesn't this fact alone
drive a suspicion that all is not what it appears to be?
The balmy weather without a single cloud in the sky,
and your multifarious limbs on the floor, inching out
to the rock garden. This is a small place sans mirrors.
You don't fully realize who you are until you wake
with rain kissing your chromatophores shimmering
with emerald shifting to grenadine of toxic anemone
in the lagoon. My sea stars, you're an octopus.
Forget about the funny fruit you thought you'd be—
breadfruit, pawpaw, starfruit, even the noxious durian
with its reeking, creamy innards spooned into a glass
as a challenging treat. Not a human, you're an octopus.

Who gives a jumping gene about the art of being an octopus? As it goes, I speculated to my chinless self, I do. I've never sported two arms, always eight in sum. Never used an elbow or a pair of knees to knock about. No belly button or other dimpled oddities to mark a physical birth. I am not a mammal, not a designer-gene human entitled to special privileges, although my sequences were edited in the scriptorium of the Genome Omnibus Database, G.O.D. To this end, I'm barred from imbibing gene cocktails at the splendid bioinfusion bonanzas, never privy to gestures like a kiss on the forehead once in a blue moon, or even a glass of syntropically cultured kombucha with traces of nostalgia for a lost girlhood. Made without memories, a genetic anomaly, I arrived in this world as a zygote without kindred to call my own. Frankly, the concept of a family unit is foreign to me. I belong to nobody under the farthest stars, not a single soul who flies or creeps upon the face of the blighted Genzopolis.

As one of the rogues, I have no proper name. Rather, it's a ninety-digit, alphanumeric serial code with nine palindromes. I prefer to go by a nickname, Emily D. The letter D stands for dystopia, dysfunction, dysphagia, dyschronology, dyspnea, or dyspepsia. Please just call me Emily, yes. Emily of the dystopic dysfunctions, a dysphagic dyschronology of dyspnea and dyspepsia. While dystonically shy, I'm not agoraphobic like the original Emily on the other side of the universe. This Emily of the first genetic edition was a poet who lived in the ancient era when codons for amino acids were unknown. The double helix was not yet espied by x-ray crystallography. The genetic laws governing inheritance presented newfangled ways to look at lifeforms. Emily's unique genetic fingerprint, unbeknownst to the general public, would spawn generations through a lock of auburn hair tucked inside a letter, perhaps a lock once curled gently above a sherry-colored eye. Not erythropoiesis or hematopoiesis, but rather, poiesis, no more, i.e. a mysterious

genesis of poets. The original Emily had no inklings about the role of reverse transcriptase in protein synthesis for hair, eighteen amino acids: proline, arginine, cysteine, and fifteen others.

A pea plant was a pea plant, not a genetic lifeform for probability computations in a monastery garden. Like the original Emily, the breathless belle and poetess of em-dashes, a dazzling diva of unconventional syntax, I dwell in seclusion; unlike Emily, however, I have no share in the wilderness of nights. Nights of brambled, blackberry wilderness. Nothing I do would grant time off my avocation of monotony. Thanks to the faults of the star-crossed editors, a flaw means I'm forever tagged as an accidental lifeform, flung into forgottenness. However, I've resigned to this fate of unstructured boredom, which I meet with a breathless ecstasy despite the doubt, as the unedited Emily might say. No austere, bleached dress adorns my body. I prefer to roam my domain without a stitch of clothing, as if I reside on a nudist colony: shyness, my beloved companion, has nothing to do with it.

This lagoon, in my opinion, is a bath spa of pleasure and sustainability alike, both aesthetic and pragmatic. I upcycle everything, even pints of rejected whelks alongside other odds and ends from the lagoon. It's a wholesome lifestyle, if you consider excommunication from the Genzopolis a rare luxury. A green living zone, at minimum. Saying I'm one hundred percent sustainable and readily compostable is a paltry under-statement. I pay no citizen taxes or gene tariffs, the odd perks of bioexile. There's no poll tax or tourism fee. Rather, I spend my days soaking in a hydrotherapy bath of salts—magnesium sulfate heptahydrate—or sashaying across the lagoon. An ed-ited lifeform am I, a genetic anomaly, not a free woman. My papillae are attuned to the whimsies of the bioengineered cos-mos. In nocturnal reveries, the designer citizens sketch blue-prints of modified flesh imitating my hydrostatic muscles.

Up to this day, before this awakening, I've nursed no regrets.

As a zygote in a dish, I was powerless over my fate, which lay in the realm of the stardust editors. This vocation as a cephalopod doesn't grant fame, fortune, or fun holidays in the antipodes, of course. No excursions to the coastal villas, no picnicking in the foothills, no frolicking in the fern grottoes, no bungee jumping into gorges as a boon. I do enjoy living at the beach, where the land is a stone's throw away from the sea. No matter how much I grumble, and if you'll forgive the platitude, I make it a goal to remember each day is a gift; how easily this would've been otherwise with extra strokes of a genetic pen in the scriptorium. After all, gratitude triggers endorphins and boosts the immune system. A biomolecular blessing on the other side, I'm barred from access to bioin-fusions to enhance my genotype. As my genes program my gambol through this seabound life, I'm in tip-top shape, phys-iologically and psychologically. No root canals and no tooth decay, never broken out in hives or rosacea, and never warded off flesh-eating bacteria or wrinkled like a raisin by soaking in hydrotherapy baths. No fatigue headaches, fibromyalgia, vertigo, or migraines, and no cephalalgia, the latter which has nothing to do with cephalopods in particular, despite the name. It's caused by the dilation of arteries in the noggin.

For me, a mammalian way of knowing, with all its nu-ances, is merely a dream.

No hindquarters were ever punctured for booster shots, my nonexistent knees never knocked for reflexes, nor glands or lymph nodes probed for lumps. Never visited a phleboto-mist or a hematologist for low blood cell counts or elevated potassium levels. Never received infusions of artificial plasma engineered from fluorine and carbon in the form of perfluo-rocarbons, for all I know. An oddity, I blossom in a profusion of rogue genes. My cyan-hued, coppery blood isn't iron-for-tified; rather, it's infused with hemocyanin instead of heme,

water-blue as the ink barrel in a fountain pen, not vampire scarlet like human blood. Through no choice of my own, my wayward fate was inscribed by automated stardust editors. I don't wax sentimental about it, you see. Faced by cosmic irony, I hear the faraway stars whisper, you're an octopus, *an octopus,* I repeat even now, lying quietly on my waterbed, which heaves up and down as if in commiseration. Deal with it, you winking, warily wretched, and waterlogged one.

Deal with it in the present tense, I mean.

An octopus, nonetheless, an atypical one named Emily, I echo into my chamber where a cherrywood rolltop desk sits an arm's length away; one out of eight, not the sum of all limbs, I mean. This humdrum routine isn't what a bona fide, designer-gene citizen of the cosmos might imagine it to be; in other words, it is a pseudopodial sojourn on an undulating waterbed, or outdoor exercise of pushing stones the size of plumcots, apriums, pluots, or apriplums in a garden, or gnawing on brine-cured olives and luscious slices of papaya— not my own glossy flesh, but rather, tropical fruit the color of orangeade—while scooping ounces of seaweed gelatin out of jars and massaging gummy drops of it onto my suckers as well as my melonhead. An octopus of rogue genes, I love the water, you see, a shore-hugger who's hydrophilic in my own right, but I can also crawl ashore, if I feel so inclined. The gelatin functions as a good emollient, a skin moisturizer, if you will, for my forays out of the kelp forest onto the shore, where the miniscule crabs and shrimp flicker in tide pools. The gelatin plumps up my epidermis in a lovely way. The fluid drachm of slime I'd secrete while drying and withering in the light wouldn't be adequate to keep me alive.

I prefer to spend my days soaking in a tub, my head up inside my lair. I wonder what it would be like to harbor alveoli blossoming like red, oxygenated azaleas in my body. Inhaling iodized air instead of oxygenated saltwater, however, is the least

of my fantasies. I spend my days holed up in hundreds of jars, hours upon hours spent in blissful solitude, luxuriating in the wet suit of my plum-colored skin, the largest organ of the body. You see, it's a paradox. Inwardly a woman, yet outwardly—phenotypically expressed, I mean—an octopus to the judging eye of a citizen of the Genzopolis. So thanks to rogue genes, I'm a lifeform with the bodily shape of an octopus or vice versa. I should count it a blessing not to be rejected for eugenization. I don't want to be a designer-gene citizen if it means other lifeforms should not exist. If the flawless future of the Genzopolis excludes lifeforms like me, so be it.

Missing a silky cloud of hair and lush mink eyelashes, without the supple skin and melodious voice of a designer-gene citizen, I've still got the toughness and tenderness of a fully adult woman. Overlook this tangle of ganglion-rich arms under my shapely melonhead, and skin the color of a ladyslipper. Actually, I express a range of hues from indigo and purple to lotus on lily pads and jade. Thanks to my edited genes, I'm immune to communicable diseases. No small pox or chicken pox or coxsackie virus will infect me, huzzah. No measles, mumps, or rubella. No typhoid, no tetanus. Feeling all the frisky frills and gills of an octopus in the wild, I'm a sea creature who travels by jet propulsion like an undersea hydrojet. Yes, an oddball octopodean, am I. Solely for amusement, not for survival, I can mimic a hairless rambutan fairly well by raising the papillae on my mantle and rolling into a mottled ball of pips.

Without a ruddy neck or pair of clavicles afloat under a chin, my balloon-shaped torso is fused directly to my head like a fireplug. I noodle around with a giant ganglion in each of my eight hands: Arms, I should say. Why can't I navigate life as a sea cucumber and renounce my genetic melodrama, or drift aimlessly through a brackish lagoon as a filter-feeder? As an afterthought, I add, what do I possibly mean, having

exhausted the multicellular potential of pluripotency long ago? As long as I physically look like an octopus, full-fledged womanhood will never bloom, thanks to molecular scissors and genetic pens who've muted those genes. Today, I harbor three hearts, of which I'm quite proud: a systemic one circulating blood throughout my body, and a pair of branchial vascular hearts, a double blessing. The systemic heart is a futurologist who looks forward, while the lesser pair of hearts nudge my blue-filtered wishes out to an inner sea of feathered gills. An act of faith, if you will. Finally, I've a doughnut-shaped brain of slightly above average intelligence. Not a fish brain. Not a squid brain. Not an eel brain, neither an electric one nor a freshwater unagi; not a jellyfish of stinging charms. Not a shark, oh my brittle sea stars. Nine brains is the right sum. I won't brag about this.

I'm an oddity dubbed Emily, by all means.

With a madcap tango of minor gravitas, it's manageable to juggle nine brains in a molecular dance of biodata. The neurons in my flexing limbs outnumber those in my melonhead. Eight arms of agile legerdemain enjoy autotomy—not autonomy but rather *autotomy*, a fleet of geckos casting their twitching tails from vertical walls, slashing the air with irrepressible vitality; limbs sprout like altered pekoe buds of modified tea shrubs, hybridized with the grassy resilience of seaweed. If only human hands could do all this, then multiply by four to make eight in a dynamo of prestidigitation.

I wave my shyest arms, mimicking the sea anemone on a coral reef.

If only the unedited Emily could see how I sport a puckered mouth under every arm, which a casual observer wouldn't spy. The fountain of blood coursing through my veins is blue as the long horizon of an ink barrel, not cranberry, pear, or cherry. If you cut me with a knife, although I hope you won't, I'll bleed midnight ink while I grab you with

one of my juicy huggers, my musculature shot through with myelinated nerves.

As the original Emily might say, good morning.

Soon enough, good midnight, my friend.

This is all to say, my renewed awakening—or awakened renewal, I mean—on this remote lagoon has led me to regret the time I've spent mired in an illusion, a pipe dream, if you will. I'll never fully embody a female human Emily. Marooned in a lagoon, if you'll forgive the rhyme; not the worst of fates, yet I'd erroneously assumed this octopodean glass was half-full when it was empty, albeit armed with an ink siphon. Am I a human copy whose genome was inscribed by genetic pens, or an octopus with Emily's sequences spliced into a rogue genome? In the face of this dilemma, the realm of possibilities runs away from me. Poof! My name is Emily, not an octopus. Boom! Ladies and gentle genes, the woman is now an octopus. Bam! This colloquy holds almost no sway over my ousted status as a rogue, so please let me start over again.

An octopus, not a woman.

As a postscript to this afterthought, the bubbling indigestion—while my skin changes from viridian green to the blue of fox grapes—implies I can't fully grapple with this new realization. Huzzah! Or maybe it's indigestion from consuming an excess of fig and gorgonzola crackers, gourmet cousin to the modest saltine? As the rogue genes would have it, I'm an octopus who relishes olives with gorgonzola and figs, not oyster shooters or escargot, and worse yet, the flesh of my own species. Our zoomorphology counts as the bottom line on the other side of the universe, if I may use an excess of pronouns to convey what I mean: you are not only what you consume but what you look like; you are not only what you look like but what you consume.

Hand me a spy glass for a glimpse into the future.

What's already known, and what's yet to elapse? More relevantly, what or who will be our future forms? My systemic heart, the terrestrial dreamer of cosmic protoplasm, says nothing, pulsing in the perpetual night of my body like a faraway radio star. Or more immediately, who or what's for dinner? I prefer a macrobiotic, vegetarian diet with bites of an all-vegan charcuterie now and then: dried figs and cranberries, banana chips dipped in coconut cream, and of course, olives. Octopuses in the wilderness gorge on seafood all day, all night. I'm definitely not an omnivore in this regard; rather, an omnivore of biomolecular information or biodata for short. I say, enjoy a bite of everything in moderation, even what you love best. If you can set boundaries for yourself, paradise isn't a raw deal, pun intended. On the contrary, let us relish the papaya dressed in rainwater-rinsed seaweed. Consider this lagoon no less than a spa resort, one without looky-loo tourists and spying staff. On the other hand, it's also dearth of kindred, the absence of a gene family within my sphere of intimacy, not even squids and cuttlefish, a sense of not belonging to the universe.

Pangs of blue-blooded heartache, I suppose.

Not fully knowing my genetic palette doesn't really bother me as I go about raking the eelgrass or rearranging the stones in my garden; rather, it's a nagging isolation wavering between loneliness and solitude, as if I live alone in an igloo, with no other sentient lifeforms to cheer my sea-blooded hearts. What else would one expect of an octopus named Emily? In the long run, I'm okay with this solo circus act on the wrong side of the universe, a spectacle or side show without spectators, if the alternative is total annihilation. An accidental octopus, I'm banished from the Genome Omnibus Database, the flawed sequences of my molecular identity logged in its archives as errors. The blueprint of my rogue genome are tagged as

mistakes never to be replicated. Copies of marred blueprints must be tossed into black holes, those portals of fragrant night.

Most days, all I desire when I wake in the morning is a fragment of orange sun, not an existential reckoning. Wish I could glance in a mirror where a fabulous woman bedecked with pearls—rather than a rogue octopus, an accident—gazes at her cheekbones on the right side of the universe. On the contrary, the reverse is true. Now I understand why no mirrors exist in this place. Can't disrobe my flesh and put it in a suitcase. Guess I've lived as an octopus my whole life, billed as a woebegone blob, yet this bauble of blue blood is still every jot a woman with the human wit and humor that go with it. In the wink of an octoeye, after flying at lightspeed through a marvelous black field rife with rhododendrons, I found myself lying in this room, a sequestered life arranged around me with a waterbed and a rolltop desk. A round porthole, a window with a sky-colored nook, faces into the kelp forest. What shall I read in a room without books? Or what shall I write, and to whom? Without errands, there's nothing to do but wander on the fathomless, undersea sands.

No fishermen on the sea, no lighthouses, no moorings for boats.

There's a lost wicker basket and a rope in my lair, yet no black spice cake to lower into a garden. If I had a platter of tea cakes with boysenberry glaze to offer, there's still no one to enjoy it. My abode is only one story, anyway, and it's at sea level. Only the original maker, the creative fabricator of the universe, who is occluded from our knowledge domain because no one has seen the maker, fully understands our origins. Who lived on this lagoon before me, and who else will follow me? I'll bet there's one of these lagoons for each accident, a gazillion lagoons for every rogue, an infinitude of worm-holes bored into a parallel universe of inky stars. By the

way, each lagoon is alternately called a lacuna or a loophole, not a laguna. If this were a beach house on the seashore, I'd hang a sign over the sink, as follows: A lacuna universe, not a lagoon, a lagunitas, or a laguna. It's riddled with fragrant black holes and ruffled time-warp spaces, I speculate, which is how I arrived on these shores.

A cosmic shoot by far.

On the other hand, citizenry means the omnibus enterprise genetically inscribes your bag of blood and bone, your fleshy envelope bobbing in the Genzopolis: Your lovely lungs, your four-lobed liver, your fatty marrow shot through with nervous jelly, your hiccups, your eyelash follicles, your shy and shrinking nasal polyps, not to be confused with those mindless polyps in the sea, and above all else, your four-dimensional intelligence. As a rogue octopus, assuming I'm exempt from temporal thinking framed by chronological time, please consider me dyschronological. There's no sliding-scale pension for banished rogues, no life insurance for swift vanishings or expulsion from the Genzopolis. There's no way to make a livelihood on the wrong side of the universe. All things considered, a bioexile in paradise isn't a raw deal for eight arms and a bogus melonhead tossed in, too. I attest that a life of vitality can exist after a vanishing; this biochronicle of moonlit love is my testimony, or else it is my private luxury. Outwardly an octopus, inwardly a woman bound—no, blessed and gifted—by this unraveling, deckle-edged sentence called life.

Yes, more than a blob of biodata myself, I'm an omnivore of biomolecular information in the shape of an octopus, a devourer of biological data expressed as the flourishing of life in this lagoon—a gene garden of sorts. I imagine one of the Emily variants adored ox-eyed daisies, scarlet flax, zinnia, snapdragon, poppy, black-eyed susans, or all of the above. I could eat all of it in a jiffy but my palate doesn't favor the

botanical. Let's say Emily's four-chambered heart was made of pear-shaped cellulose paper garnished by a smattering of wildflower seeds. Soak the heart of seeds in water overnight, she'd whisper. Tear up the heart and bury the fragments under a thin layer of soil. Water daily until the seeds germinate. Beautiful, but give me the heart itself, I would say.

Bury me, then breathe: This is a way of life.

With the invention of scissors and genetic pens, the stardust editors could inscribe and erase base pairs—the yoked nucleotides of our hereditary codes—in our genomes. Although the editors are machines of keen artificial intelligence, they do mess up from time to time. A slip of the scissors means I'm ill-fated to be tagged, then tossed into a black hole. Even now, in paradise, I dwell under a taboo of bioexile in a lagoon overshadowed by a grotesque fate not due to any fault of my own. An octopia—a utopia for octopuses—no other octopuses in sight. We don't get along. I assume this expulsion is an everlasting state. I grew three hearts, an ink bladder, and an octopine face—octopian, if you will, or octopodean. I'll never be cloned, my sequences never replicated; rather, tossed into the sea of lost letters: A for adenine, G for guanine. C for cytosine, T for thymine. Zero rainchecks, no consolation prizes, and no vouchers for an interstellar space flight next winter. To be honest, I'm not painting a jollier picture of this situation than it actually is; please read the fine print. The stigma of a flawed genome is inscribed on my mantle—as aforesaid, my emblazoned label is no less than a ninety-digit, alphanumeric serial code with nine palindromes I won't repeat here. Call me Emily D, dear ladies and gentle genes. In other words, sporting a melonhead with eight arms waving in the air, not to mention the gouache palette of my skin, means none other than bioexile.

By the way, on the bright side, my colors change like a mood ring.

Happiness is a lovely shade of eggplant. Aubergine blushes without apology, if you will, although no one in my vicinity cares which adjective I choose. Nervous agitation is the color of rambutan peels or cranberries populating a bog, and everything in my guts from jealousy to sorrow fluctuates on a continuum of pistachio green and chartreuse. If doves alight in my soul, I turn pink as a ladyslipper orchid, then skim milk with a pale blue tint. How could you expect less of an octopus on an isle of gorgeous garbage, the genetic refuse of the Genzopolis? A lagoon of the disinherited? Roseate as a tidal bloom of red dinoflagellates, I've risen above the categorical imperatives of shell-arranging and ink-siphoning, thanks to a mass of neurons in my noggin. This aforesaid prefrontal cortex, albeit not larger than a walnut, overrides the obsessive compulsions of a wild octopus with a loopy limbic system. Expressing my oddities in a harmless and hairless manner, I wake up on the same side of my waterbed, nudge rocks and shells around in my garden, rearrange jars on my sill, and find myself blissfully contented within the monotony of paradise. In a little silo of isolation, I spend hours re-ordering a sparsely furnished yet mossy and ragged world, a luxury: no dire urgency to procreate.

Naked I came into this lagoon, and naked shall I depart. My body bereft of blood, at death, shall be light as a knot of wilted lilies lying on a dresser. Bare furnishings occupy my lair, neither a wardrobe nor a chifferobe in sight, but as you can see, I'm equipped with a tidy encyclopedia of codes, an organic microlexicon if you will, and love to write using the ink sac under my digestive gland, splashing little scribbles across the walls. This microlexicon is the size and density of a pearl you might wear on your right hand, say, on the index or ring fingers, a verbal pearl of a litterateur's letters. An amateur scrivener, I jot down words on my gratitude list as a tangible way to improve my outlook. Today, I wrote, *octopodean*. It's

not difficult to maintain a rosy attitude in paradise, but this life does risk monotony under halcyon skies. The weather doesn't change much at all, everlastingly sunny with a chance of showers. Instead of focusing on what I do not have, however, I focus on what I do have, a mug half-full, in a manner of speaking. While I'm on the subject, please indulge for me a minute as I expound upon my choice of the plural *octopuses* and less frequently used *octopodes* rather than *octopi*. A citizen may or may not already know that the singular *octopus* derives from the ancient Greek *oktopous,* and *octopus* is a Latinate form of the Greek.

So it follows linguistically in the Greek that *oktopous* would become *octopodes,* not the Latinate *octopi.* However, nobody ever says *octopodes,* although it is a nifty word. To this end, I slightly prefer *octopuses,* even if it's not quite Greek. Why would any lifeform in their right hemisphere, even one decent brain of average intelligence as opposed to nine ganglia-rich brains, reject the pretty-sounding *octopuses* or the equally musical yet enigmatic *octopodes* with its metrical stress on the second syllable, an iamb fused with an anapest? Not much of concern to editors of stardust who're engineering progeny with designer genes, I suppose. Will these playful words ever spawn a utopic future for our generations? Regardless, I favor *octopodes* as a moniker for an isle on the other side of the universe or a lagoon brimming with fresh rain and kelp forests down under like the antipodes, yet *octopodean* in a translingual migration, if you will, with a hint of a lyric afloat therein.

Nobody's flawless, even those rigorously edited by genetic pens.

Despite my wishy-washiness about how boring it is to be quarantined—bioexiled, rather—I've never blamed the stardust editors for inscribing then expelling my blob of protoplasm into this world, and I still don't bear a grudge. How could I blame the editors for tinkering with stardust, the life substance

of the universe? They're only machines, in other words, robots of artificial intelligence in the scriptorium. As for the genetic enterprise itself, the gene generalist at the Genome Omnibus Database dangled an alluring promise before the citizens of the Genzopolis. Dear genetic citizens, you desire a pandemonium-free future for your children. You don't want your progeny to inherit your gene for a congenital heart condition, or your spouse's set of genes for sporting a jelly doughnut around the belly. Even if the gene sequences influencing obesity are muted, you don't wish to transmit them to your spawn. Control gene expression to delay the whirlwind, hormonal onset of adolescence, if you wish, to prolong your spawn's juvenile years.

Thanks to the data repository in the Genome Omnibus Database, we've mapped the genome for every lifeform swimming, creeping, flying, or drooling upon the ancient face of the Genzopolis. With our new-fangled editing pens, we can safely alter the gene expression of your loved ones. Elegantly adapted from octopodean enzymes, we've safely engineered these tools for domestic use by common citizens. Our new genetic pen is light as a modified feather quill and safe enough to edit your children while they're zygotes. Every pen is capped with a genetic eraser so you can wipe out undesirable sequences in their genomes. Now you and your spawn can be speedily edited to migrate from this besieged planet of flood and fire to settle a new colony among the stars, your physiology modified to survive our beloved yet blighted Genzopolis. You can live out your dreams as space pirates swashbuckling from biome to biome like warriors of light, if you wish. Yes, ladies and gentle genes, this is how we spell love in our generation. Secure your peace of mind by ensuring a flawless future for your progeny.

As an octopus, I wonder, how do we spell out a language of love in an age of unregulated gene-editing? When the sequences of one flesh are spliced into another, is love operationalized in a molecular alphabet of life? What about an

Emily on the other side of the universe; whom has she loved in secret? How do we seek our soul mates in a sensory universe of genetically modified pheromones, those molecular chemistries of attraction? How about the dream of a future generation of adorable, anti-viral spawn with eidetic memory recall, immune to chicken pox, influenza, mumps, and measles; a future without hereditary disorders like hemophilia, cystic fibrosis, or phenylketonuria? Optical chlorophyll harnessing light through the eyes, green energy calibrated to bloom with changing seasons, and optimized for star system migration? A generation equipped with the facility to slow the rate of metabolism during interstellar migration to another star system? With the advent of genetic pens and molecular scissors, allegedly safe for home use, who wouldn't want to design their own progeny? Of course, no tool is absolutely perfect, and lifeforms don't always turn out as desired.

The edited genes might go rogue, for instance.

A substantial proportion of protoplasm exited the flesh factories as rogues of variegated shapes, colors, and gumminess. My lifeform blob of cells multiplied into a gummy capsule of tissue about the size of a pomegranate pip, then expanded to the mass of a fava bean. To the automatons of the omnibus, I was unmistakably an accident, if you'll excuse the oxymoron. My destiny was not to serve out my days as a designer citizen, but rather, a dysmorphic lifeform. A recombined set of lettered sequences, an alphabet of errors. Mayhap an erstwhile Emily blooms in another universe in the lifeform of an aleatory poet, remixing her arcane—if not metaphysical and elliptical—lexicons. The fog bottled up inside her head, swirling in wisps of water vapor, then cleared by a pot of breakfast tea, gives way to a wordsmith's cloud of lexical delight.

It's no accident to wake up as an octopodean Emily.

Accidental, I mean. The error wasn't due to the fact that I never started out as an eight-armed hatchling, a paralarva, or embryo. It wasn't a philosophical inquiry about being-in-time or thingness-of-itself in objectivity. Adverbially, it wasn't a hypothetical why or how or when of my existence, but rather, the whatness under question by the stardust editors of the Genome Omnibus Database. While incredibly exact, genetic editing isn't perfect—molecular scissors might snip the wrong spot in a strand, or a slip of a genetic pen might yield target errors—yet we're the ones hit by the consequences. Were the stardust editors programmed to feel a frisson of terror when viewing images on a radiograph at the flesh factory, an inkling of this indigo-to-jade, kingfisher green, rambutan-to-orchid-to-jonquil melonhead? I doubt it. The wrong body in the right universe, yes. Is this rogue genome refundable? No refunds, rainchecks, exchanges, or consolation prizes. The omnibus whisked me away into one of its snowflake-sized black holes perfumed with an irresistible fragrance of rhododendrons.

In a twinkling of a horizontal pupil, here I am.

Once upon a time, eons ago when the great freshwater lakes in the glacial valleys were not yet inner seas, a strange biomyth circulated in the vintage cities about children who were born with hydrocephalus, spinal fluid in the brain's cavities—and who were dubbed melon heads, a two-word moniker which indicated their status as pariahs, i.e. outcasts. The children were orphans. No one claimed them as their own, and the asylum staff neglected the boys and girls. As the biomyth goes, the orphans burned down the asylum and ran away into the woods where they roamed as feral kids, growing up to bear progeny of their own, ghosts among ghosts.

How did the children find such bravery, or was it the word rage, as in courage?

If a person stood still in the woods up north, one would supposedly hear little feet running. How did the orphans learn to set a fire—a blazing conflagration like adult arsonists? Most likely, the boys and girls used wood-burning stoves and kerosene heaters at the asylum. The biomyth of the melon heads still haunts the citizenry to this day. A melon, a head. In my mind's octoeye, I see the asylum with flames shooting into a night sky of broken casement windows, presaging the rise of flesh factories in a not-so-distant future, then bare feet running on leaves, the lost children with enlarged heads on bird-like shoulders, and their frightened souls, famished and fearful, crying and running with all their might. To where, only the maker of the universe knows. Now, we are either all orphans, or else none of us are orphans.

That's all moot now. A sprinkling of black holes like a field of poppies, shall we?

Other lifeform editions I could've enjoyed—if the scissors and pens had eluded me in one version, or edited me without slippages—might've be one wherein another Emily, in a mid-life existential crisis, seeks refuge from her reputation as a mystical woman-in-white—unmarried, half-cracked, and slightly batty—by swimming to a rocky cape of lighthouses to sip lemonade or rose-hips tea then sherry in a glass, then lapse into a meditative silence by the shore. Her shoulders, still youthful, are slim and supple. More frequently over the years, she's shunned other human lifeforms, refusing to receive guests face-to-face in her family's parlor. This other Emily dons a cotton kimono—not a flared hanbok or satin cheongsam—and a well-worn pair of mustard garden clogs. In a villa on the cape, this brooding Emily tastefully arranges silk orchids with maidenhair ferns and waits for the mail courier to deliver valentines from her sisters and cousins in the late morning, rinses out her unglazed zisha teapot or nibbles on a tea biscuit at eleven o'clock—she bakes an assortment of

shortcakes, chiefly of strawberry butter. Out of the kitchen pantry, a box of stroopwafels: Emily selects one to place carefully over a cup of hot tea, letting the caramel soften inside the waffle cookie before eating it. In the afternoon, to the rolling of sea waves, she writes affectionate letters to her sister-in-law, whom she loves dearly.

The pen, needless to say, is not a genetic pen. It's a quill.

Let's say this designer-gene Emily is one in a genealogical tree of Emilys traceable to the original Emily—an organic first edition, not the code name for an atomic weapon—whose bones are now buried in the sea. On the other side of the universe, this hybrid Emily arranges her bottled spices by color and texture rather than scent, along with other miscellaneous household objects like thimbles, hooks, and buttons; thanks to the original Emily, she has a genetic predisposition to arrange things in order. Humming a lullaby from her girlhood, she composes lists in her journal like me, with one exception; she weaves in memories from a girlhood experienced firsthand, years ago, not fabricated ones. The organic microlexicon in her doughnut-shaped brain—lodged in the left inferior frontal gyrus—is far more comprehensive than mine, which is an abridged version, in my opinion. What's the word for these collections of miscellaneous objects—haberdashery, millinery? Notions, she recalls, and scribbles it in her journal. Notions, notions. Spools of thread, needles, and butterfly clasps lying jumbled as her stray thoughts, the other Emily juggles her various and sundry notions. Notions. With her eyebrows knitted, she circles *notions* in turquoise ink because this color denotes objects in her sewing basket as well as the notion of thoughts, and she loves the dual meanings. Notions and notions, she muses, humming under a breath scented by menthol wintergreen oil, a tincture of a girlhood remedy rubbed on her forehead for fever-free dreams.

With a fine curl of chestnut rather than auburn hair tucked behind an ear, this other Emily—one whom I could've known in another life, or one whom I could've easily been myself, if I were human—presses freshly plucked specimens from her herbarium into the folded pages of her daybook. First a wild fern named maidenhair. Her genes allegedly predispose her to gathering these botanical artifacts as well as their arrangement, a love for order. This Emily touches the silky petal of a streaked tulip, whose coloration is feathered and flamed by a potyvirus called the tulip-breaking virus in the history of virology. The inside of the tulip petal: a rabbit's ear. Her lines divulge fond remembrances as a girlhood lived among trees—walking through apple orchards with her sister and cats; reaching above her brother's head to pluck a blushing apple, sinking her front teeth into its crisp flesh with a satisfying crunch; finishing her lessons in geometry and microscopes. In this Emily's nightly dreams, cotton dresses hover above her head as if pinned to a clothesline, each one winging into a wild swan. We must learn to forgive and to let go, which in turn means, paraphrased, we let go to make room for newness, and so forth.

Yes, with talcum-dusted shoulders and a tulip-shaped mouth, this other Emily harbors a human edition on the other side of the universe. In other words, she's a successful designer-gene Emily, one among a multitude of copies inscribed with new sequences in the scriptorium. Do I envy her girlhood among blackberries in the modified hedges of needleleaf evergreens, now scorched by global warming? And her wicker basket and little cherrywood desk by the window overlooking the flower beds? A summer calico frock in the closet, hemmed by her mother's hands? Octopodean sequences mixed with excised human ones, or human sequences mingled with octopodean ones: aphonia, rectangular pupils like steel rivets, a mute octet of waving arms like rolled flags. To this end, I will

never aspire to common citizenship; my genetic codes and I vanished into a black hole, yet I survived to tell the story: a mystery of the maker's grace. Yes, an act of unmerited favor, I must confess, a miracle. Unlike cats, octopuses don't have nine lives: we live only once, albeit with nine brains.

Nope, you see: I don't merely wish to survive but to sparkle.

On the other hand, a lagoon on the wrong side of the universe isn't a place where fretting will lead to useful solutions, never mind razzle-dazzle and pop. Our streaming forecast, of course, is misty interior monologue with bouts of stream-of-consciousness, especially those novelettes exploring a woman's foggy state of mind after her spouse dies of consumption and his body dismembered, then dragged out to sea, limb by limb; the shadows filtering dappled light—blurred by cigarette smoke—depict her quiet, stately movements through domestic spaces, engaging in quotidian duties like scribbling longhand on a page of her daybook or pressing irises and lilies therein. It's a film noir Emily, or better yet, a femme fatale. In a close-up of her face, she casually sprays her shoulders using an atomizer of perfume with undertones of musk. Yet another Emily, this one in a steampunk edition, rides on a simulation decked out in riding boots, an ostrich plume hat, and epaulettes like dishes of scrambled eggs; abruptly, without warning, here's another Emily in a sci-fi flick, a winsome yet ridiculously cthulhian—yes, cthulhian of the biomythic organism, a cthulhu—a kraken-like female waving her tentacles in the midst of the octopodes.

With apologies, I'd like to retract the awkward label, *tentacles*, but I've already used it. Nobody expects me to learn anything; neither to input data in my noggin, nor ponder metaphysical questions on time and being, to put it baldly, no pun intended, never mind use an alienating term like tentacle, so dehumanizing. It's like the word *mutant*, which I also use sparingly. Goes without saying, honestly, I know no one on

either side of the universe; maybe only I take issue with the offending labels, not anyone else. Who cares about whether my dignity is bruised, or about our liberties in general? Who'll glue together the shards of this microfiction shot through with autobiographical impulses, a biological autofiction of microflash sorts, by analyzing my genetic constitution? A tale engraved on the fleshy tablets of my three octopodean hearts; my raison d'être is reducible to a reusable ink siphon. On a side note, I prefer arms to tentacles, normatively speaking. A tentacle emphasizes my alien nature, neither a common citizen of the Genzopolis nor an octopus of the original wilderness.

Speculatively, what are flesh factories and autofictions but flights of fancy, fragments of magical thinking? Ideaphoria, a portmanteau of whimsical ideas and euphoria whirling on the periphery of the imagination, an unfettered yet impractical realm, especially aroused, for me, by faraway lights or strange odors? My nervous system is slightly overactive, you see, and I am attracted to gathering kaboodles of shells and shiny thingawhoozers for my garden—sand dollars, whelks, rock oysters, coquinas, scallops, mother-of-pearl abalone, and the like.

Or envision the moonlight as a shy courier of lost letters, a slender man carrying a deck of codes in a mail pouch. On this side of the stars, a nocturnal ghost delivers a bundle of lost letters into my eight arms, of which a few will curl around the pouch: a hug unfolding in slow motion. A peony as a pompom of petals and shyness at once: shall I bloom, or shall I close? In this pod of my episodic memory, I'm madly in love with the mailman in the moon, about as mad as an octopus could be, but this isn't a typical case of unrequited love. The taciturn, lunar man doesn't reciprocate, of course, thanks to who I am. An octopus, I mean. And it goes without saying

that the man, after all is said and done, is a fabrication of moonlight.

A jumble of yesterday's odds and ends, if you will.

On the upside of this rogue saga, a rude octopodean awakening helps everything else fall into place, or at minimum, there's more purposefulness in my day-to-day musings rather than idle lollygagging. By no means am I a mindless creature void of sentience or volition, and my burbling stream of ruminations yield a polychromatic pageantry richer than those ghosts reflected in the gilded mirrors of alabastrine palaces, the mansions of yore. Was it the spring rain whispering a ballad in the heart of the night? Over the lighthouses of bluffs on the other side of the universe, in sea light? Was it the ebb and tide of hormones due to the ticking of a biological clock in my glands? Am I hallucinating as I enter the beginning stages of octopodean senescence, in other words, old-fashioned aging?

If I were the other Emily, perhaps I'd dash off a thousand poems plus eight hundred more, a reclusive dynamo of poiesis generating eight poems a day thanks to the equivalent number of ganglia in my arms, each one an autonomous scribe. I can see how this phenomenon could potentially occur in her biosphere of lifeforms as a single woman in her era: forty handbound fascicles of four hundred poems, no less. The skies, which say nothing, mirror a rhythm of domestic interiors, an infinite repetition of genotypical Emilys stashing their literary brilliance in chests of drawers, or scribbling their poems about the fires of agony and ecstasy, bobolinks, and prognostication on the backs of envelopes.

Should I do the laundry now or wait?
No, there is none. No clothes to wash.
Do I ever recall doing the laundry?
No, of course not. Never wore clothes.

Should I line up the jars on this shelf?
Who cares whether jars align or not. No.
Should I move this rock to the right?
Like the jars, it makes no difference.
Should I close the window in case of rain?
If I leave it open, the rain will come in.
Is this a blessing or a bugaboo to be fixed?
Does the snow viburnum look like snow?
Blossoming crazily in late spring, it does.
Everything is right except the season, yes.

A bugaboo of naught—a tit for tat—this dialogue with nobody presents little beyond its routine cadence. As for the mute mailman who materializes out of the lop-eared moonlight of levitating albino hares, is he a ghost? No. Apparition? A projection of the unconscious, a subliminal fantasy about rabbits? My repressed psychological urges, desires, or defenses projected onto objects? Nah. A revenant? Not at all. A lunar rabbit under a cassia tree? Nope. A vestige of a civilization flourishing before the warmed seas flooded the coast, triggering a mass migration of citizens to another star system? No, no. He rides on a moonbeam, a lost sleeve of rays, or rather, the moonlight itself is a genteel suitor in an epoch when vanishings occur, when rogues are forbidden from roaming to and fro as common citizens. Don't blame the automatons for this. The stardust editors of the Genzopolis are programmed to alter the gumdrops of tissue in dishes. If an extinct arthropod like a three-lobed trilobite arises, not early traces of human sentience, who can fault the stardust editors for just doing their jobs, even if an obscure sequence in a trilobite could save the blighted Genzopolis from biological warfare and genetic subterfuge? Truth is, no one cares if it's a polyp, a trilobite, or an octopus: in sum, not a human. Not a citizen of

the Genzopolis selectively bred for the future, thanks to one's designer-gene pedigree.

We can't fathom what we don't know yet, is what I say.

For the time being, on the other side of the universe, the seas rose in the globally forecast great flood of this millennium, the postdiluvian deluge triggered by vanishing glaciers. It rained as never before at the north pole. A cavity two-thirds the size of a borough yawned open in the melting polar ice cap, and the seas reached the low mountain ranges of the evergreen, intralpine valleys. I know this history by the marginalia of moonlight upon my lagoon on this side of the universe: flood on the surf, fire on the turf—famine and flight by sea and by land. The Genzopolis of designer-gene citizens and their photogenic karyotypes of flawless physiology were destroyed by the tides—gallons of denatured genes, drowned micrographs of chromosomes lost to waves of nostalgia—the forbidden city of flesh factories, the biodata cybraries and bioinfusion bonanzas, demolished. Rife with null hypotheses, I assume the Genzopolis vanished. Where did the stardust editors of the omnibus go? Did they succeed in their dream of a star system migration or colonize the moon with their designer-gene bones in disease-free biodomes? The Genzopolis brimmed with brackish water in the outlying shantytowns, murky as its souls. If only I could glean the dust of these missing fragments as I squint, pupils narrowed, into the fog of this autofiction.

This lagoon is sheathed in germinating nanosprouts and modified spores flushed down the gullet of black holes, I assume, those fragrant portals of gravity where my soul plunged—or perchance rose, aloft, to this side of the universe. Here, I find everything my heart desires, as if it were a heavenly blueprint of my private utopia, designed by an invisible maker: paradise without a sea of blue monsters or a legion of marauders, but rather, the loveliest and loudest of dawns

in full color, the lagoon free of the irksome artifices imposed by civilization, and a charming mailman of moonlight. Who made this lagoon for me, its dazzling shores of biodata to delight, in triplicate, the three hearts of an accidental octopus? This place is no mass midden of the millennium, neither a biohazard junkyard extraordinaire. It's my personal stronghold, an undersea retreat tailored to introverts—beware of the octopus— without looky-loos, where I serve out my curious life sentence as a rogue soul.

I CHERISH THIS MOTLEY FOLIAGE OF ODDBALL genes detectable only to a molecular botanist's eye: dotting the sandy beach, modified bougainvillea double as fly traps; phytoplankton blooms devour oil spills; genes spliced from rabbits generate air purifiers out of houseplants; disease-resistant algae in the kelp forest; brittle starfish with flexing, light-sensing pores; ylang ylang with canary yellow petals the length of my uncoiled arms, a fusion of beauty and utility in its aphrodisiac, anti-depressant, antibiotic, and antihistamine uses. This lagoon begs a terrarium of botanical pleasures and breathable air, thanks to spikemosses and selaginella, maidenhair ferns, zoysia grass, aerial tillandsia, and the orchids: the freckled zygos, the ruffled cattleya of lavender petals, moth orchids and lady slippers, plus elegantly ribboned brassia. I'd love to see a puffy cabbage rose, puffy as a sea-sponge loofah, and how would rose hips manifest in bone as plant cellulose? Would a bony pelvis widen a rose, swaying in the hips? I'm not adequately equipped to ambulate far enough from my abode to test this hypothesis, regardless.

Shapeshifter of hurricane lamps, glass jars, and bleached coral alike, the latter fringed by dulse or kelp forests, and dexterously skilled in camouflage, I'm a chimera of Emily and the octopodean: Who in all of paradise, however, gives a jumping gene

about my phenotype? Will my genetic predisposition towards shyness reveal a hidden talent to become the most belletristic of octopuses, an inkhorn of letters? The stardust editors of the omnibus inserted sequences in short, palindromic repeats: neither copying nor transcription, rather, direct inscription by genetic pens. In fact, they used snipping primarily as a verb, not snip as the acronym, S.N.I.P., for single-nucleotide polymorphism. When old-fashioned gene therapy altered viruses to function like syringes, the designer genes in viral capsids would enter a nucleus and drift quietly as copies. Parenthetically speaking, I prefer to classify them as spies. As an aside, I must add, the very notion of viruses acting like blood-sucking mosquitoes gives me the willies. Not to say I'm ungrateful for the benefits of gene therapy in banishing single-gene disorders like sickle cell anemia and cystic fibrosis, which is marvelous; rather, maybe I've an inkling of conspiratorial ilk, or am just outright paranoid. I've a hunch it was a mistake to modify the octopodean enzymes for gene inscription. The cephalopod enzyme, at a biomolecular level, is more sophisticated than human analogues, not the reverse. In this way, the stardust editors botched the slicing and splicing of my gene sequences. In a sad turn of fate, I came out looking like an octopus as well as feeling plangent and literally blue as one.

How many others exist like me, on this wrong side of the universe?

I envision how every other Emily of the diaspora, of soft arms and lithe bodies, undulate in their dresses of under-a -thousand thread count woven of cambric, rayon, cotton.


ON THE RIGHT SIDE OF THE UNIVERSE, I imagine the original Emily coughs, if she is there.

Do I exist, and does she? Where is this primogeniture Emily? No one gives a jumping gene. I shouldn't complain. In my bioexiled status, I've survived in a tolerably pleasant

habitat, albeit a rather monotonous venue where I live in a quarantined state. No roads, no signs, and no names. It isn't quite the vortex of extraterrestrial drama one might expect after falling headlong into a black hole, a fragrant portal of mad honey wherein spacetime expands, then slows down before collapsing. Poof! On the contrary, I land in a lagoon without an inkling of other sages of sentience in the vicinity, never mind octopuses or even a vampire squid. Nobody discloses the risks of an overloaded data repository in the Genome Omnibus Database. No one is worried about what might happen if it implodes, or if the hermaphrodite trilobites return, i.e. trilobites ranging from the size of a pumpkinseed to hammerhead sharks. No one eats grilled octopus braised in sage, thyme, pink lemonade, and roasted elephant garlic, and nothing much else occurs with regard to mindless violence, my dear sea stars. No blinking editors, no heat-seeking drones of artificial intelligence in sight. Honestly speaking, I've nothing much else to do with this gift of leisure time, other than washing, arranging, and displaying my pet peeves and sulkiness as I please.

On the right side of the universe, the original Emily whose genes spawned the rest of us doesn't wonder how many copies of Emily genotypes exist in the world, a diaspora of Emilys. I surmise, Emily has no idea there's one whose phenotype is a mutant octopus, namely, me. This first edition Emily is dead, long ago passed. In my mind's octoeye, the original Emily meditatively launders her dresses, bangs her spices in the kitchen, and pens poems about affliction, agony, perfidy, ecstasy, and God: indeed, with everlasting poiesis, I believe. Prickled by a surge of dysphagic envy, my skin changes from eggplant to bilious green. Why didn't the original Emily, a prophetess and futurologist ahead of her time, foresee what was coming? Why should other clones named Emily enjoy the privileges of the Genzopolis such as a consanguine family

of inherited genes, while I must dwell in isolation and see nobody at all? How much Emily must an Emily demonstrate to be enough of an Emily? A duchess of reclusion, if the original Emily once considered herself a nobody, then who am I? It's not as if I carry salmonellosis or vaccine-resistant bat rabies. The original Emily of yore, the aforesaid blessed one whose fingerprint generated a platoon of other Emilys in subsequent generations, was exposed to a lot of germs in her day like tuberculosis, bacterial pneumonia, typhoid, and scarlet fever. She succumbed to a chronic kidney disease, or more likely hypertension; the tools of gene editing, which would've taken care of these organic dysfunctions prior to birth, wasn't available in her time.

A pickle in a jar, this original Emily is a true first edition.

Zoonosis no longer means viruses jump from one species to another like animals to humans, thanks to biotechnological tools. Risking the temptation of ingratitude, I'm ranting and raving in a vortex of boredom, I suppose, not sheer exhaustion or heat fatigue. In my mind's octoeye, I visualize the other side of the universe where modified dromedary caravans—amphibious, equipped for surf and turf—solemnly trek across deluged dolomite ranges in the dead of night, arrested by automated scribes of the omnibus who relentlessly scour the Genzopolis for rogues in caves, dens, and other remote places. As the dromedary caravans travel slowly, the rogues tuck their flexing suction cups, hydrostatic curlicues, and horizontal pupils out of sight. An octopus can't hide for long, however; the omnibus will stake you out, and an irresistible vortex of ambrosial fragrance will yawn open, attracting you with an odor of mad honey. You're siphoned into a cosmic vortex of overpowering aroma, the ineluctable perfume wafting in the dark spaces so intimate yet crazily byzantine among the stars. The stardust editors have it down to an art, designing black

holes the size of snowflakes to fling you into the universe with the flash of an octoeye.

Perhaps not long ago, the engineered citizens would toss genotoxic cocktails at gap region guerillas armed with infectious agents like altered fungi, bacteria, and viruses; now it's small black holes where anyone can fit like a genetically modified angel on the head of a pin, one I could've used in another galaxy for hemming any Emily's summer dresses. Fragrant black holes, I daresay, yawning with a mystical redolence of modified mad honey, gorgeously maddening in the molecular sense of the aromatic, a whiff of divine ambrosia. Heaven is supposed to exude an irresistable fragrance, the way saints do. A delicious flavor, I may add, those drops of auburn honey spiked with grayanotoxin extracted by honey-hunters who rappelled on braided jute ropes down sheer cliffs. The cosmic perfume evokes the spikenard costing a year's wages, spilling out of an alabaster box in the slender hands of a woman, full of earthy roots and spices. It's where humming clouds of bees made their hives before the seas rose out of their ancient beds. Yes, the honey-hunters sought out the modified rhododendrons on the edges of black holes. The ambrosial perfume might drive you mad if you take a whiff. Yes, the mad honey oozing in quantum pathways to this side of paradise might make you mad if you quaff it. Be forewarned, my friend. This is a dreamland, so don't be surprised by intoxicating elixirs. Does the maker grace each cell, spore, and blossom with a mystical potion; the drifting clouds of fairy shrimp, mindless phytoplankton, and gelatinous miasma of transparencies bobbing in the blue yonder? Do biodegradable microgels last beyond their expiration dates along with rogues which didn't come out as designed, like those goldfish with oversized swim bladders or dorsal fins clamped shut like paper fans, iguanas without dewlaps, or hyperactive cockatoos who shriek out of sheer tedium?

My genetically altered belly, of course—by way of apology, I diligently avoid using negative labels like freakish or alien—this voided gut, if you will, the gastronomical bag by which I mean the sum of a digestive gland and minor appendages, grumbles for no apparent reason. Am I hungry again, ravenous? Did I eat anything this morning after the rainshower? Can my nine brains recall what it was I ate, if anything—will my brains reach a consensus in aggregating their sensory recollections for the organoleptic delights of shrimp or lobster? What time is it, elevenses yet, a spot of tea? No, not yet. The bubbling indigestion I endured after I woke—in more ways than one—has subsided, giving way to hunger pangs. An upset tummy wasn't due to eating too many sea snails after all, but rather, those amorphous inklings called emotions. Once again, ideaphoria has obscured the physiological origins of my feelings, even hunger pangs. If a prefrontal cortex and opposable thumbs could solve global crises like war, poverty, and famine on the other side of the universe, then sadly, the citizens of the Genzopolis have yet to devise solutions. This overthinking involves a lot of mental calisthenics for an octopus bouncing up and down on a cognitive trampoline. Yes, I bounce, conceptually. Now I need a snack, preferably a spoonful of anchovy tapenade, maybe a bit of uni sushi, raw sea urchin. Is it eleven o'clock? The height of the sun over the banana grove, on the contrary, indicates it's not quite elevenses.

Outside my octagonal lair, the overnight spring rain has raised the level of freshwater pools on the limestone cliffs where lumps of microbialites and cyanobacteria thrive, leaving carbonate deposits in the shapes of rocky turrets and chateaux and other monoliths like undersea castles. In the low tide, the sooty deposits warm as ashes in a hearth while fireplace cinders fly haphazardly upward. To an unschooled octoeye, the microbialites look like moth-eaten velvet or an otter's fur

until you touch it, rough as a scorched crust of rye bread forgotten in an oven. What shall I enjoy as a morsel of paradise? Mossy oysters on the half-shell? No, I'm angling, once again, for a vegetarian diet, although a cephalopod has every right to consume an oyster. Fig and gorgonzola crackers instead of a mollusk, alive or dead? With a ladle of saffron bouillabaisse, of course, and a jar of olives. It's too bad that I don't like bananas; they're overabundant on this island. If I liked bananas, I could make rum-laced bananas foster, bran and wheat germ banana muffins, and mashed bananas sprinkled with chia seeds on avocado toast. Most of these ingredients aren't in my pantry, though, even if this is paradise. In fact, I only see anchovies on the shelves.

Forget about the bananas, my dear fishy ones.

On second thought, if we share more than half our genome with bananas, wouldn't we be committing an act of cannibalism of sorts if we ate bananas? I shudder at the mere inkling of such an act of atrocity. If we eat bananas, we eat ourselves—or at least, half ourselves.

Then I realize, I am not human. My stars, I'm an octopus, if not a banana.

In a dream of a tribe untampered by gene-editing, everybody is an original edition. Emily opens the door to her father's cellar, where black spice cake waits like a treasure trove of jewels in an octopus garden, soaking in brandy and loaded with raisins and currants. This original Emily, who is a poet, is oblivious to the micropoetry of genes and chromosomes. In her world, microscopes—not a new invention then, like the steam engine—are already known to magnify the cells of onion skin and cork and protozoa, but yet to see a mitotic spindle pulling apart duplicate chromosomes like docile puppets in a dance of life. Her domestic concerns focus on tasks at hand: Why not hazelnut liquor or sherry? Amaretto or cognac? Future possibilities, she muses with pleasure: this black

spice cake will be marvelous, and she nods with satisfaction, pulling up her sleeve as she leans over to brush the cake with brandy syrup, oblivious to teeming microorganisms like the streptococcus germ or the harmless lactobacillus.

In sum, this is the atypical story of a rogue mollusk named Emily dreaming of an octopus garden, not one under the sea, but rather, a milieu with a hypnagogic journey into alterity. Yes, I'm a fish out of water, so to speak, if you'll allow me to extrapolate from the hackneyed expression; octopuses are not fish, after all. As invertebrates, we lack true bones, as I mentioned, and proper cartilaginous fins. We are cephalopods like squid and cuttlefish. The castanets inside my melonhead, the stylets, don't count as bones. Or consider this tableau vivant as a grotto of lovers in a space opera, one wherein the leading lady, by all appearances a flashy octopus camouflaged as a prima donna, awaits a mail courier who arrives at night with a bag of lost letters from the sea, delivered in sheaves of light brushed by ant hairs, by caterpillar fur. The letters do not harbor the sentiments of kindred souls writing to one another; on the contrary, they harbor the lost codes of genes sequenced down to base pairs: A for adenine, T for thymine, G for guanine, C for cytosine.

Ladies and gentle genes, note the whisper of chromosome fragments like bundles of long-stemmed roses passing over ballroom staircases in the moonlight. On the other side of the universe, the other Emily brushes a black spice cake with an elixir of brandy, then speaks to her sister or brother at the door. Incidentally, her flaming brother is a bit of a rogue—he's indulging in an affair with a friend's wife, not a fling—yet not rogue in the genetic sense we mean today. In another life, one which might've transpired in a parallel universe, this Emily could be one of many obscure women in a biomythopoeia: not an agoraphobic poet, rather, she's a prima donna who sang coloratura in underwater operas decked out in macramé

butterfly knots, trimmed with streamers of maroon satin. Another genotype variant of Emily is a retired film actress who waits all day for a courier to show up with raffia-tied bags of fan mail in the shade of a banana grove, no solitary octopuses in sight.

Or else this other life is one I'm already living, nonetheless, one in infinite variations of Emily, mostly human, I presume, except for me. Imagine nine miniature hearts to break, each one named Emily, hypothetically speaking. It's the terrible hand you're dealt in this life. Deal with it, I say, pun intended. Fortunately, my melonhead brain—the one shaped like a doughnut—will gladly subdue the eight other brains into obedience if there's any whit of cognitive dissonance. It's not an aquatic opera, no mezzo-soprano diva singing underwater, nobody crooning to hydrophones with bubbles cruising up their foreheads, napes bedecked in pearls and brooches. Frankly told, it's an unlikely tale about a rogue octopus—who lives in seclusion on an isle of octopodes, similar to the antipodes in the sense of polar opposites, an upside-down place at the bottom of the world, and who falls in love with a mail courier, an obsession typical of a maddeningly petalous, fragrant black hole, a room of slaughtered stars, dark as a reverse snowflake—light darkness on light—in an epoch when it's commonplace for rogues to vanish, or in this case, a sort of antipodean paradox. And it's moonlight, figuratively speaking, so why wouldn't this biochronicle pivot on the axis of unrequited hearts?

In other words, the smaller a place, the potentially larger the universe.

The antipodes, I mean. It's backwards logic. Rogues are not refunded, and no exchanges permitted. If our windows to the soul turn albino gray or pink instead of one eye ice-frost blue and the other green or hazel—an attractive heterochromia of the irises—or eight arms wave at the stardust editors

instead of two, then you vanish if this is not what was ordered; this is the law of supply and demand in obeisance to rapacious appetites. I could always run away to a flying circus or hop on a migrant caravan. Ladies and gentle genes, the gene-edited flying octopus, the first and last of its kind, was rescued from the bowels of the flesh factories; she soars like a sky pod without wings, ladies and gentle genes, without antiquated nuclear energy or mechanical aerial wires. I kid myself: surely, I am not wholly unique, yet where else would my genetic kindred exist? In a fish stew of hothouse tomatoes, roasted cloves of elephant garlic, and chardonnay with octopus, calamari rings, and mussels? Or a saffron bouillabaisse with scallops, halibut, sea bass, pufferfish, monkfish, or skate? Or a chowder of chopped quahogs and cherrystone clams?

On either side of the universe, who is truly one-of-a-kind?

In other words, could the real Emily please stand up? Not only uniqueness but usefulness and ubiquity are overvalued; these traits work in contradistinction with each other, besides. If a gene is a unique modification, it can't also be ubiquitous. None of the above matters if we'll vanish in the wink of an octoeye, worthless as a bonfire attracting glorious insects to its flames, than a gloomy bog of drowned dictionaries and abandoned lexicons; a sea of ghost fishing, a tureen of bitter goulash, a breezy asylum of sand dunes, and a lagoon in an inscrutable world within a world. No one knows exactly how far away this venue is; no one has documented its geolocation or topography, or which sky pod to ride in order to visit—not the northeast express, nor the southwest skyway. The migrant caravans lose their way in the outer darkness with weeping and gnashing of teeth, as ancient scriptures once forewarned.

Emily, who are you? Are you near to my trio of hearts?

Or more accurately, I should ask, how many are you, Emily, in this universe?

No one can visit this lagoon without a quantum pass-
port—or a fragrant black hole without aisle lights or yard
torches—but nobody knows how to obtain one. What's the
currency in use, besides? No economic, climatic, topograph-
ic, or other maps are sold for cold cash. You're attracted to
the black hole, its puffs of intoxicating perfume, the negative
radiance and alluring pull of intense gravity. What shape or
lifeform of grace or divine love exists on the other side? Is
there anyone who prays for us, an intercessor who offers peti-
tions on our behalf? This is beyond a cartographer's pen and a
surveyor's compass. You're the only Emily on this side of the
universe. There's no starlight to illuminate the way for you, no
guide to take you by the hand, nobody to show you a window
or aisle seat with complimentary stroopwafels of flour, butter,
and spice.

You must figure this out on your own in the rainy dark of
the universe, awake.

## 2 | A Jar of Hours on the Other Side of the Universe

Our octopus heroine crawls into a glass jar. A meditation on her solitary existence as an Emily variant on the wrong side of the universe, dialoguing in riddles with the moonlight. The sea of lost letters.

# A JAR OF HOURS ON THE
## OTHER SIDE OF THE UNIVERSE

After nibbling on olives with gorgonzola crackers and figs, I crawl into the jar, a place smaller than this lair where I find joy in one retreat, namely, hiding in a jar. If you'll please forgive me, the next few hours will consist wholly of an octopus pushing herself into a jar, suction cups pressed like cherry blossoms or gourd vines in a botanical monograph as I withdraw my mantle into a space with one opening, my melonhead pushed all the way inside like a planet giving birth to a galaxy, or vice versa. My nickname isn't Emily for naught. I believe Emily is an ancient expression for diligent, striving, or industrious. And yes, in a quixotic manner, I ruminate about strawberries although they're rare on this side of the universe. Jammed in this manner, a pair of bony stylets pressed together inside my head—my fingerling castanets, I call them—clap to the rhythm of my coppery blue pulse, not unlike the pip-pop of spring rain. The balloon of my body, mouths pursing under my arms, and the wriggling of my bare, untangled arms: everything tucked inside this world within a world. The opening of the jar is the size of a large plum, and this balloon goes in first, then my head, arms, and mouths. Nope, let me adjust the order of my members.

My head and balloon are fused together in a melonhead, so it's a straightforward feat; no sophisticated choreography required. Serendipitously, I'm more of an aquatic contortionist, an awkward convulsionnaire than a ballet dancer, no room for a *pas de deux* with me.

An oddity occurs when I hide inside a jar, navel-gazing without a belly button as my spot of origin, if you will. A sense of calm settles over me, lowering my blood pressure, a triptych of hearts slowing their hidden blue butterflies in synchrony. It's the effect that chamomile tea or other herbal sedatives might have upon the citizens on the other side of the universe. The nine brains, with little tingles, quell their adrenal noise in response to stimuli. The sides of the jar, cool and smooth without nicks, hold the totality of my soul and body with a strong reassurance. I could stay in here forever, mouthing my moniker silently: yes, Emily as in Emily D. Yes. I feel as if I'm an octopus confined to a meta-cage of history, a room from which I'm perpetually escaping to create my own mythopoeia.

It's not a bad rap, a trio of hearts like a chapbook of blue asters and cornflowers, my jewels in a copper vault of viscera, a drop of ocean dissolved therein. On the other side of the universe, the forget-me-nots are also known as blue birds, but in name only. The flowers never morphed into birds, at least, not to my understanding. Poiesis operates as a form of genesis in poems, not literally in terms of lifeforms. I am a ship named Emily with three sails, or a volcano touched by a fleecy trio of clouds, or the kissing spots of loaves made while touching each other in an oven, each one called a baisure. The hearts, three daughters of my soul, pulse with the ebb and tide of the sea. If you chop out one of my hearts, I'll still have two left. Emily major plus dual Emily minors. Please don't try it at home, regardless of what I say. A warning: I'll bleed to pale

blue death before your eyes, all of my mouths arching open in soundless agony to the snapping beak of my orifice.

With one jellied octoeye pressed against the glass wall of the jar and the other inside an arm, my purple body coiled softly like a sweet roll in its own papillated flesh, I tighten my musculature to cause the jar to roll side to side, rocking a bit. My puffy flesh is a pillow for itself. In this fashion, I tumble across the room, under a rolltop desk where my extra abalone shells are stored and where my fruit basket awaits friendly donations of tea biscuits, muffins, crumpets, or spice cakes which never appear. I don't bake much, although black spice cake beckons with a brandy-soaked loaf of magnificence delivered from the other side of the universe. The world is an oyster within a universe inside this jar, and I'm content to go inside this space for hours at a time. The temptation to retreat into this world forever is powerful; I roll back across the room, in no hurry to come out. Sadly for my belly, hunger pangs eventually arise, so I must emerge from this little space after a few hours.

Yes, I love doing this yet can't fully explain why. It's not that I feel clever while tucking myself into a jar the size of a plum, nor that I feel wholly safe while hiding inside this tiny igloo. An underwater ziggurat of privacy in a lagoon, this shore-hugging zone of fiddler crabs and starfish at low tide? I derive a measure of satisfaction from shrinking the volume of space I occupy. Is it delight in knowing I can hide at will, despite the fact that I'm one of the vanished? To be genuinely invisible is to vanish while already unseen. Of all the small places, this one takes the longest to occupy, and it's my favorite, hands down, so to speak. I carefully tucked myself into an abandoned conch shell once, but the ridges snagged on my skin.

I'm inordinately fond of this jar, yet I ban certain bodily activities while I'm hiding in it. For instance, I can't pee. I can't

get the hiccups. Woe unto me if I get the hiccups while hiding inside this jar—with each hiccup, my body jerks against the glass. It's not a chamber pot, and not an air sickness bag. I guess this is what plum preserves must feel like on a daily basis: wrinkled, hermetical. And I can't eat olives while I'm jarred. Already ate olives today, besides. This jar held the olives I ate. I love olives, but I can't have any while I'm tucked inside this world. Hungry for more olives? Forget about it. I'm not supposed to eat much sodium, but that's moot right now. No olives while I'm in the jar, and no more after I come out. It's unknown whether the other Emily, the original one on the right side of the universe, loved olives or not; she loved bees, hyacinth and violets and fringed gentian, words like *cochineal* and *flambeaux* and *mazarin,* but does she ever mention pickled olives in her thousand or so poems, including the fragments she scribbled on the backs of envelopes?

Why do I love olives so? Did the original Emily adore grove-variety olives? Olives don't give me indigestion, for one. Fig and gorgonzola crackers larded with olive tapenade, especially the tasty hexagonal wafers crumbled onto a salt broth, are a favorite. The only drawback is hypertension, which would put me at the risk of a stroke. However, I don't believe the risk is severe. So, I eat as many olives as I want, and nobody shames or blames me for indulging my appetites. I've survived a black hole, after all; why not enjoy my days in a paradise of gastronomic abundance, if there exists a world so agreeable where the quantity of olives is adequate for a lifetime's supply. Wishing more rogue olives were bioexiled to paradise for the sake of my appetite, I could've worked as an advocate for the welfare of genetically modified olive groves.

What's odd is nothing's apparently wrong with the olives. No detectable chemical odors, no discolorations, no obvious flaws in their skin, texture, or taste, braised in a garlicky parsley sauce or a mock bourguignonne with a quarter cup of

dry burgundy, on toast or served in a chafing dish, pits rolled inside the flesh, their bodies tucked away like little tongues. I wonder, what stories of the designer-gene citizens and the flesh factories would they tell, if they could, of gastronomic gastropods grazing on blades of grass? Did the original Emily take notice of the dew-snail's route in her garden, carrying her own haven, the size of an olive? Or in another life, would I have preferred to eat the snails as a delicacy known as escargot? And lest I am guilty of cannibalism—for the gastropods are distant mollusk cousins to inkfish cephalopods—let me just say that on this side of the universe, I am happy to devour a jar of olives instead of snails.

And what a bountiful variety of olives: Brine-cured and lye-soaked, dunked in freshwater first, then dehydrated in the direct sun and salted, or marinated in a range of flavorful vinegars—balsamic, red wine, and apple with strokes of fermenting bacteria suspended in translucent scarves—pitted or not, halved or whole. Buttery and robust in the mouth, glowing like oil lamps. What's not to love about an olive? The stardust editors chucked them down a black hole, and poof, they ended up in my small place on this lagoon.

Let's say, hypothetically, a batch of genetically modified snails triggered a panic among the citizens. The editors of stardust made them vanish prior to their expiration dates. However, this tale would not explain so many jars of olives appearing over the duration of my stay, populating my pantry at the same rate I consume them, never dwindling to zero. Haven't ruled out the possibility that I'm an experimental subject in a quantum universe of oddball thingamajiggies made of, thingamaboppers to serve as humble plectrums for the legendary music of the spheres: string theory, I surmise, holds us together in this cosmic space opera of love and courtship.

One thing I do know for certain: Negatively described, I do not live in an aquarium where other creatures of sentience

named Emily are apparent to the naked eye. With zig-zag jolts of heightened awareness, I also know I'm an atypical octopus. Otherwise, I wouldn't need these jars of hyaluronic acid mixed with aloe hydrogel, rows upon rows of pear-colored jars near and dear to my three hearts. Not an aquarium octopus, I don't have to deal with feeders or keepers, and no looky-loos who press their nosy rhinoplasties and lidded blepharoplasties and greasy fingerpads against the glass, or grope for my body inside the tank to see if I'll touch them back. I can't stand being touched without permission, and I can't imagine what I would do if I were imprisoned in an aquarium. The upside, I suppose, would be the provisions of nourishment, but I'd probably have to give up the olives, daikon, ginger, and papaya unless the feeders and keepers figure out that I like them.

Dew-snails aren't on their epicurean radar for octopuses like me.

Far away from the fires and floods and fury in the Genzopolis, bottles of sparkling hydrogen dioxide and prosecco show up on the shelves of my pantry alongside the jars of olives from time to time, but I don't like the fizziness of those beverages, and I don't like altered mind states, including tipsiness. When poured, champagne looks prettily crystalline in a flute glass with columns of microbubbles, but don't be fooled. This drink will knock me out in a nanosecond if I take more than a sip. Bubbly carbonation tastes like a pint of bitter, anyhow, copper to gold in hue as a coin. One might say, what does an octopus know about malt or hops? What do I know about quinine, the distinctive ingredient in a tonic, and old-fashioned cure for knocking out malaria? Yet I tell you the truth, I prefer ginger root beer and gooseberry tangerine pop and sarsaparilla flavors over fizzy tonics, and no one cares if quinine can fight malaria because the editors of stardust, long ago, altered our gene expression to do the trick.

Please leave a drop of sherry in the glass for Emily, ladies and gentle genes.

On a tangential note, I am curious to know how sparkling water sweetened with tangerine syrup and a ginger infusion or an orangeade squeeze might compliment an olive. I'm talking about gingerale chilled on the rocks or a foaming sarsparilla float with a scoop of vanilla ice cream, which might be a good medium between a bubbly glass of champagne with a dark chocolate-dipped banana on one hand or a gin and tonic on the other, but none has shown up here. Besides, I'm trying to adhere to a low-glycemic, vegetarian diet to reduce food-induced inflammation, and my guess is that I could be lactose intolerant, too. Moreover, I have no one to share a drink with at night, although I love the way the agave moonlight comes to me in the form of a vintage mail courier, an old-fashioned mailman from the days of yore, when the moonlight was personified as an ossan, a male companion. A nightcap, I believe it's called. The drink, I mean, not the ossan.

You're my nightcap.
Just the night, he'd say.
What do you mean?
A nightcap is a hot drink, ma'am.
Isn't it a night and a cap?
No, ma'am.
Isn't it a cap worn at night?
Not a night with a cap, either.
You only appear in the moonlight.
Doesn't make me a nightcap.
Let's start this again.
Yes, ma'am.
What type of drink is it?
Brandy with milk.
Served warm in a shot glass?

Yes, ma'am.
Bourbon, a flash of moonlight.
Maybe the world is on fire, ma'am.
What?
Yes, ma'am?
Did you say *mutant?*
No, ma'am.
What did you say?
Nothing, a menagerie.

On the other side of the universe, I believe that male phe-nomena and masculine paraphernalia—accidental rogues or not—are very rare birds, in a manner of speaking. Not actual birds with trills and plumage, I mean, just rare. One male for every four hundred seventy women was the ratio at the last demographic census, conducted not long ago, I believe. Or maybe it was a confabulation of the future, I don't know for certain. Let's say, in the genitive singular, once upon a time, on the other side of the universe, males were very scarce, and women rented clones as *ossans*, a moniker for middle-aged men, short for *ojisans*, the word for uncles in Japanese, a holdover term from the economic recession—followed by a rebound after the fiscal cliff—at the turn of the millennium. Alone at a bistro, and no one present to enjoy bread dipped in avocado oil with a tangy side of guava chutney or apple jicama slaw? Hire an ossan clone for an hour, one who'll eat at a leisurely pace and ask if you'd like to order a scoop of lychee sherbet or a dish of black grass jelly for dessert. Or a serving of coconut flan and crème brûlée? Beaujolais nouveau with glazed pear and marionberry cake, garnished by a sprig of mint leaf grown hydroponically in a rice cooker? A spoonful of breadfruit marmalade on a heaping mound of modified jackfruit pudding, made in a bamboo steamer?

Or let's say it's just spring, when a feathery wind named the chinook blows softly over your cheekbones, if you have cheeks and bones in your face. Does the chinook only blow down mountains and across prairies, or does it blow on the sea coast, too? In paradise, the chinook could be a southerly wind, for all I know, scented like honeysuckle and night-blooming jasmines. Perhaps the ossan will say yes. Pesky wrens or sparrows nesting in your eaves? Dial an ossan who specializes in bird nest removal, summon him out of the troposphere, and remind him to bring a two-story ladder. Ask him first to make sure he has insurance before he climbs the ladder holding a gutter cleaning attachment in one hand, his hat in the other.

Make sure he has a roof permit that hasn't expired.

Are you riding an aerial sky pod at night after a gallery opening or a string quartet performance, feeling hesitant about the lateness of the hour and uncertain about star navigation? An ossan is *en route* to the station right now to escort you safely home. This mail courier, a clone—or a wingless angel lying on a moonbeam, a butler of the wee hours—is impeccably versed in etiquette with a host of small courtesies from a bygone era, a so-called knight in shining armor, all crock and nonsense on the other side of the universe. For what purpose, I wonder. Imagine, for instance, how a proverbial knight in shining armor would respond to the vagaries of an accidental octopus? Would the chivalrous man say, may I open this portal to a black hole for you, ma'am? Are you allergic to the cosmic fragrance of rhododendrons? Is mad honey more intoxicating than its antithesis, chamomile-and-lavender infused honey, calming and sedating, not maddening? Instead, may I offer you a box of truffles glowing with flecks of radioactive stardust for your interstellar flight?

IN MOONLIGHT THE COLOR OF MAGNESIUM HYDROXIDE and goat's milk, or magnolias genetically adapted for beetle polli-

nation before the rise of bees on the face of the Genzopolis, I'd ask the mailman: Is our mysterious co-existence but a sheaf of messages loaned to us by the maker, the one who tinkers with our inklings of eternity beyond the great blue yonder? Or let's call this tale of an off-grid lifestyle in this world, of uncertainty about who you are or where you are going. Who knows how these drowned chromosomes end up in this sea of lost letters, where gene sequences are never retrieved for transcription? Do you know the answers to my questions, sir? How would you impart—or would you, ever—the cherished secrets in your sunken archive of genotypes, an inkhorn treasury of heterozygous traits? Please forgive the ridiculous off-rhyme, but do you also know the world is on fire? When you soar on the unpinned wings of a moonbeam, when luminous shafts touch cabochons of lunar opals on the waves, can you read what is written on this silver band of absence? Is the ocean blind to its weathered fables of yesteryear, its drowned indices and codons, its pelagic frontispiece and aphotic back matter, or its saline indices of despair and triumph? If I served as an archivist for the sea of lost letters, what would I put into my index? With my ink siphon, I jot this down.

> Nocturnes of water, microlexicons at midnight.
> A ballad for the sea of lost letters, of course—
> The ultimate hydrotherapy spa in paradise.

If I were a human Emily variant on the other side of the universe, not a rogue octopoid variant, I'd go to visit an egg woman as often as I could afford to do so on my meager salary as an amanuensis for a fleet of imaginary muses—a poet, I mean, which could indicate that I'd visit the egg woman only once in a blue moon, in a manner of speaking. I'd learn to sing hymns and memorize the accidentals for each key signature on a series of scores; the accidentals related to pitch, not genetic accidents. I'd be free of stigma in this regard. With insomnia

as my perpetual muse, I'd rise from my bed at midnight to gaze at the waxing moon, em-dashes unscrolling across the retina of my inner eye. At this wee hour, I'd read the dictionary aloud to myself in a room furnished with a cherrywood desk. In the summer, I'd wear hand-stitched dresses of cotton and bake little patty cakes with a pound of sugar, half a pound of butter, half a pound of flour, and a cup of grated coconut, spelled c-o-c-o-a-n-u-t, cocoa nut. I would've written out the recipe in my loopy, arcaded script.

Or garlanded rather than arcaded, on hindsight.

Yes, I'd wear sleeveless frocks with buttons undone in midsummer heat, sitting with my bare legs crossed at the knees, not the ankles, so unladylike. In this other universe, I might order dress patterns on tissue paper, which would arrive folded in chapbook envelopes, deceptively thin. How could a whole pattern for a nightgown fit in this slender envelope? I'd wonder. Yet it would. I'd cut along the lines dotted with lavender ink, then pin the sheer, fluttering shapes to unrolled bolts of fabric I stored by a sewing machine. I'd draped the leftover fabric on an ironing board while I hemmed a cotton frock dyed the red color of azaleas in my garden, putting my foot on the pedal of the machine, running it with focused attention. Red frocks dyed in vats of beet juice, what colorful dresses of convenience for the monthlies, if I may. As an octopus, I don't need a wardrobe. Don't wear any clothes, only my skin tender as a marionberry named Marianne or Emily, I mean: the skin apart from a soul. You see, I'm an octopus, not a clothes horse. I can eat figs and their shade-giving leaves for nourishment, but the proverbial fig leaf is not a special privilege of mine. By the way, I favor black mission figs over chopped petite green figs, although I tolerate the latter dunked in curry.

As an octopus, I can't wear dresses, yet I honestly don't give a rip. Would I like to expound upon my sartorial style? Who cares? I have none, besides. What do I wear, instead?

Shame, of course. As an accidental octopus, shame and deni-al are chronic ghosts, bleeding like chokecherries out of my emotions like the monthlies of a human female. Do I want to bleed every month? Not if I don't have to bleed, no. Do I wish to wear dresses? If I don't have to, why bother? It's no fault of mine that I look this way, and who cares. There's no audience. I'm wooing no one. No suitors. No botox injections and no henna dyes, and never use electrolysis or revitalizing creams infused with radish blood. I exude lots of slime, thanks to my rogue designer genes. Just can't stay out in the sun too long. I love the iridescent way the chromatophores in my skin change from gradations of blue, emerald, beige, and pthalo to dusty rose, then cremello in response to my moods or the weath-er, or both. My iridophores are marvelous, too, shimmering while I press my body against a rock in the garden, or coyly slide glistening slices of papaya up my shyest arm into one of my puckered mouths, then pickled olives, one after another, while my skin goes pomegranate, the ruddiness of grenadine.

In my other life as an Emily whose body mirrors her internal design as a soul, my ossan could double easily as a mailman, it's true. He'd deliver the daily mail, then go to the fruit-seller market with me. There'd be no romance, court-ship, or fling; he's just a man I'm employing by the hour, so to speak, to make small talk, hold an umbrella over my head when it rains, and ensure that I get home safely. He could palm me a pack of mentholated cigarettes once in a while, and I'd decline them. I don't smoke. They're bad for you, I'd say. Besides, where did you get these? The omnibus outlawed cig-arettes years ago because they're genotoxic, and the nicotine is addicting and nastily yellow-staining, besides. You're right, the ossan agrees; the coal tar messes up your genetic material, and your lungs will melt in the molasses-colored sludge of mutagenesis.

Yes to a clove cigarette?
I shrug. No cloves.
Okay, he says.
Both are carcinogenic.
Is it the tar or the nicotine?
Doesn't matter.
Try this stick of mint gum.
It won't trigger a mutation?
I doubt it, he replies.

Back at home, resting my elbows on my kitchen table after the ossan bids me farewell with a kiss on the cheek—good night, Emily—I'd use a butter knife to slit open letters addressed to me and read about my sister-in-law's new joys in planting narcissus bulbs; the herbarium she and her husband envisioned in the form of a botanical monograph of pressed flowers; the pleasure of baking corncakes one afternoon to stave off the dreary cold of the winter doldrums, followed by a superbloom equinox, when they slept on the floor with fans spinning through the night, and left the windows open to the aromatic wildflowers. This would be my life as an Emily on the other side of the universe, an Emily variant who imparts love to her kindred and to strangers alike, and who receives love from them in kind, as well. This is a reciprocity that I find extraordinarily romantic, in a way, not unlike cupping the face of a stranger who has your mother's chin or your father's shock of hair at the temples. Why does the maternal chin look so familiar, and the paternal shock of hair so recognizable?

In a word, genes. Our maps show we're more similar to each other—even a human in the Genzopolis, an octopus, a dewsnail, and a banana—than dissimilar. Families, by comparison, are facsimiles of its members, recombined copies of copies.

The river of moonlight delivers a raft of glowing nucleotides, the base pairs nearly illegible in this archive of the cosmos, I imagine, the largest dead letter office in all creation. How old are

these genes? Once upon a double helix, how far did fragments of chromosomes fly to this small place? Over a starry creek of time, a thousand million alleles were discarded while others were not. To further complicate matters, faded postmarks of time became more obscure to decipher in the sea of lost letters. In a sense, I'm imagining the letters as blank signifiers, placeholders of absence set adrift in an abecedarian space opera of floating signs. Is A for Anticodon or for Adenine? Is C for Chromosome or for Cytosine? Only the moonlight in the octopodes, this small place of solitary cephalopods, explores the sea of lost letters, the pulp of discarded genetic material digested in the bellies of numerous hungry yet faceless organisms, drowned.

Night after night, the mailman returns, so we resume our dialogue in riddles.

The moonlight, he says.
What about it, sir?
Aglow, a stick of mint gum.
Glow-in-the-dark gum?
It glows in your mouth, yes.
Where is it? I ask, not knowing.
This stick of gum in my hand.
Where did it come from…?
The other side of the universe.
Is it radioactive or genotoxic?
No, why would it be?
Did a citizen not want it?
I believe so. A woman.
Did she chew it already?
No, don't be silly.
Was it edited?
It's gene-free.
I'll try it.

With a thin stick of nongenotoxic, chemiluminescent mint gum in this episode of my space opera, I muse. In the long-boned hand of moonlight, it blushes like mushrooms in a bog, or the bellies of squid and bioluminescent plankton in the nocturnal tide. Hovering at the edge of a black hole, there's an octopus floating in a sky pod, or better yet, just an octopus. No pod. No glow. No light-emitting, glow-in-the-dark chemicals. Can it seal the edges of a black hole to the universe? Hiding in your mouth, does it rival the little starry fires in the twilight? The flying octopus spreads out her arms, opening like a massive sunflower in outer space, the exosphere where no sunflowers could grow outside a biodome. In my dreams of other Emilys in the universe, outer space burns with the pungency of hot irons a thousand times over, or singed hair caught in a wood-burning stove. How could this possibly be a thousand, even a million times over, if there's no air in space, not even for the colonies of space pirates? Yet space is always on fire, sky pods and supernovae rotating without air, a grandiloquent bonfire of stardust blasted without galactic wind, no methane gas. No ether in outer space, sorry. No atmosphere, only nuclear fusion and other givers of light like spelunking glow worms in caves.

Miraculously, a flying octopus named Emily glows with a halo.

The halo flashes like a siren. Is it radioactive like the clock dials of yore? Did the octopus swallow a lightbulb? Is she a saint or martyr or other sanctified being? Is this a superluminal cephalopod zooming faster than the speed of light, than the music of the heavenly spheres? Can she levitate masses the size of paperclips and pitted prunes in a gravitational field? None of the above. Yet here's another thought experiment with a twist. As one Emily travels near the aromatic horizon of supermassive gravity, time dilates as she's pulled into a black hole, one irresistibly oozing with mad honey, thicker and richer than pleasure itself. Curiously enough, the original Emily won't age as fast as a monozygotic twin might in the Genzopolis.

Spacetime expands as the first Emily zooms through the event horizon and enters the singularity, an airless zone wherein to lay Emily's head, no garden of mosses and ferns. It's a one-dimensional point of infinite density where a continuum of Emilys is compressed into a single Emily. Or perhaps this is either zero Emily or else a totality of Emilys. Now I must stop because I've reached the extent of my paltry knowledge of quantum physics, the realm of thingamajiggies—in a universe of even zanier thingamaboppers beyond fixed objects like a stroopwafel perched on a cup of tea—where nothing yet everything exists at once, not to mention black and green olives, the latter shot through with chili pimientos. The moonlight explains nothing to me, no verbal elaboration on the nature of time dilation, no derivations of formulas using c as the constant for the speed of light, and no poetry of the universe, no music of the spheres, to harmonize the metaphysics.

You see, I get a lot of thinking done while I'm inside a glass jar.

If I were a woman, I wouldn't hide in a glass jar, or would I, my hips and belly curved like a snail or the anatomy of a paper nautilus? As an octopus named Emily on this side of the universe, I don't have a lot of real-world problems to solve, thank goodness. Ruminations and brainstorming are what the omnibus would categorize as useless ideaphoria, a torrent of highfaluting ideas—pies in the sky, if you will—without practical applications, dangerous to the Genzopolis due to their ambiguity in an empirical world. For instance, even with omnivorous data analytics to predict the future—even what we'll do before we even do it—no surefire formula for prophesying the end of time for certain, and whether it will end by fire, flood, or a big bang. I ponder these questions inside my watery melonhead, turning them around and around in my doughnut-shaped brain. Didn't the postdiluvian poets and prophets say fire, or was it flood? I say *post* after the flood of the ancient days, and diluvian because the lifeforms survived the great flood of the millennium, due to the melted polar ice caps. After the flood, yet before the flood, too. Thank goodness for the scientific expansion and contraction of the

empirical universe, yes. With regard to the flight of souls out of the world and future floods, I'm uncertain. The transition might occur in the flash of a flickering octoeye, for all I know; then what would be the next act of this opera in outer space?

If an end of time exists, an octopus certainly wouldn't predict it, even a flying octopus who's journeyed to the outer reaches of bioexile. In a singularity, time curves infinitely; I don't wholly understand what this means. Where's a universal blackboard where I can plug and chug formulas and work out derivations regarding this question? How do I sequence myself into genotypic normativity? Who will decipher the intricate codes of the maker for me? Will anyone tutor an octopus named Emily in the fundamentals of quantum physics, never mind the nuances of the wave-particle nature of light? The maker of the cosmos, who dwells outside time, says boo to methodological atheism while I seek love on this side of the universe. Love is not the lagoon, not a skinny banana berry in a banana suit, not a moonbeam, and not an olive. Not in the wicker basket that I'll never lower into a garden overflowing with hydrangea, blueberry and other bushes, violets, and phlox and because I live in a one-story lair at sea level. A cloistered octopus, I patiently await a soul companion, hoping the moonlight might cleave open this mystery, or at minimum, deliver a gazette I can read, the newsprint spread-eagled in my nook by the window. At best, I'll vaguely resemble another Emily who awaits a shower of valentines shooting out of a starry wilderness on the other side of the universe.

Of course, I receive nothing except the moonlight itself.

## 3 | NOON PROMENADE WITH PROTOPLASM

In search of her misplaced sun hat, a kelp leaf. The octopus ventures ashore to visit a banana grove. A tour of her undersea rock garden. A biomythopoiea of octopuses in folklore. Musings on the Emily variants of the Emily diaspora.

## Noon Promenade with Protoplasm

WHERE, IN THIS GENETICALLY ALTERED PARADISE, is my dulse beanie, my favorite sun hat? The sun filters overhead at noon in the kelp forest, flashing east to west like a hooked fishing spear. An afterthought occurs to me: the fishing spear shines by reflecting the sun and isn't the sun itself. Is a moonbeam the same as moon, after all? I don't use spears, in any case—I fling rocks and shells in annoyance, not spears. My wayward, hydrostatic arms wrestle one another with zany ganglia of their own, a miasma of nervous reflexes more agile than any tools I could wield, and I use all the objects I need in my lair, including blades of kelp to serve as fashionable caps for my melonhead, a natural camouflage. I use halved coconut shells for this purpose, too, although the coconuts double as personal protective equipment. In paradise, however, I have no need for armor. Although my skin is photosensitive, I don't carry a paper umbrella wherever I go. Parasols would limit my mobility on the go, regardless. Of course, I'd also prefer not to strut around bareheaded. Instead, I sport a floppy leaf on my melonhead as

72

I venture ashore, wearing a green hat without a jot of rain in sight. The sky has cleared up quickly, thanks to the agreeable weather in the octopodes on this side of the universe: sunny yet slightly cloudy with a chance of nocturnal showers, partly cloudy and mostly sunny, and so forth.

If only olives, figs, or even pears…

On a side note, a kelp forest in paradise means at least one genetic accident on the other side of the universe. This isn't a biomythopoeia wherein the stars in the night sky align in a one-to-one correspondence to the unborn, each one a twinkle in the maker's eye. As I crawl onto the slippery tide pool rocks, one of the first things I always notice is the banana grove on the beach. One tree, nourished by sunlight and rain, propagates additional banana trees until there's a grove. Anything wrong or peculiar about this bumper crop of bananas? Too green, too starchy, too plump, too short? Too easily bruised? Too firm, too mushy, too bland, too tart? Is there such a thing as too much immunity to soil-borne fungus? Too bad I'm not fond of bananas, whether the petite variant called lady fingers, the dwarf yellows, or squarish burros more like thumbs than donkeys; they're plentiful on this island, and to my octoeye, there's nothing obviously wrong with the bananas sewn into banana suits, masquerading as none other than bananas. A mashed banana in a mug of breakfast grits, or a banana pudding with a meringue topping of a dozen egg whites beaten into stiff peaks wouldn't be noxious if a person liked bananas. Mushiness, a masticated sweetness—isn't suited for my algal palate and taste buds; the mere thought is enough to give me the hiccups for hours. And isn't there anything slightly nefarious about their lasting yellow color, the way the sun never gets snuffed out?

Can't ruminate much with a plague of bananas on the brain.

Ere long last, after slouching and sliding around my underwater lair in search of my hat, I find the kelp cap sitting in the reading nook, so I put it on my head and go for a stroll. There's nothing about this leaf that would suggest it's an accident except the sultry leaf never withers. Yes, it's suspicious, in a way. Why wouldn't a kelp leaf wither with exposure to sand's abrasive caress, detached from its source of nourishment, a tree? What's natural in this environment, anyway, I muse. I inherit whatever the stardust editors reject, such as a kelp forest whose leaves are perennially and suspiciously robust, or a banana grove of the unruly sort that could mutiny by signaling with other plant hormones in a grove, a fast-growing invasive species with ultra-lush shade and suspiciously bruise-proof fruit: are you real, immaculate bananas? You don't undergo senescence in a sidereal frame of time, say, days rather than months. I'll bet your bottommost melons that the bananas were edited for a much longer shelf life. If only I could extract oils from the bananas or figure out how to bio-engineer more durable plant leather from their fruit. Edibles galore as banana purses and fanny packs, banana lotions and emollients, banana bikinis, banana soles and clogs and zoris. Yellow is a fashionable color for the girlish, slender Emilys on the other side of the universe, where citizens obsess about the pedigree of their designer genes and call the sun a big yellow ball in the sky. At minimum, I could fling banana peels over my shoulder to aggravate the back-fence gossips, but no such prattlers loiter on this lagoon.

All this to say, the banana tree is not a tree, and a banana is not what one might think but rather, a berry. The banana is a berry, I assure you. The tree is an herb of overlapping leaves, not the usual trunk as one might expect. The banana tree is a giant herb, yes. A berry bush, one might say. It's not the niche bananas are typically assumed to occupy. In other

words, bananas grow on herbs, not at all trees, and they're berries. The banana isn't the size of a berry: it is a berry, a funny notion.

Banana berries with a dose of ketones and esters, an extra blushing fragrance? Maybe we'll all change into banana gooseberries: a quarter goose, a quarter banana, quarter berry, and a quarter gooseberry, a cousin to cloudberries the size of thimbles on our thumbs, if we sprout fingers and thumbs. We'll all wake up one day as altered berries the size of thimbles, sugared and ready to go into a fruit tart or cakes dubbed thimbleberries. What hour is it, we say to each other now. Hour of this-or-such a berry, will be a reply in the near future. I mean, the hour of gooseberries, or the hour of blackberries and thimbleberries, for instance, whichever berry is the star o'clock. Though I never met her myself, I'm positive the original Emily loved berries of all shapes and flavors in her season of life. I imagine she might've whispered to a rival, if she ever had one at the female seminary: Your fate is doomed as a berry sentient enough to grasp its destiny in a pie. What? The rival would say. What did you mean by sentient, Emily? Indeed, I wonder what Emily would've thought of genetically modified, rust-colored heirloom berries tasting like rib-eye steak, fortifying the blood with organic iron, namely, heme, spelled like crème yet rhyming with meme, squeezing out their juicy jingles of genetic promise? Cloudberries, salmonberries, black hybrid raspberries, and waxberries or snowberries? Don't get me started on which one of these will get chucked into a black hole.

This original Emily, blissfully ignorant of the vicissitudes of gene drift and flow in an ecosystem, goes on banging spices in her lawyer father's kitchen without a jot of worry about the future of genetic engineering: nutmeg from seed, mace from the shell, and cloves from dry flower buds while violets, cabbage roses, viburnum, and lilies in her garden sow

their gametes into one another, an act of cross-pollination. Nutmeg is nutmeg, mace is mace, and cloves are cloves. How will these flowers gradually change when humans transcribe and inscribe their genes into other species including humans? This is not even on Emily's radar as she pounds the spices for gingerbread which calls for molasses, whipping cream, a quart of flour, and of course, a spoonful of ginger.

What is molasses, anyway? She wonders. Darkest syrup of the night skies, flowing out of a celestial honeycomb laced with blackstrap nectar and sugar beets? How do you start with sugar beets and end with black treacle, the gravity of sweetness and centrifugation, producing a night darker than blackberries under a new moon?

For now, as I sashay across the tide pools to the beach in broad daylight without fear of kith or kin, my skin moistened by gummy seaweed gelatin, and the balmy wind huffing, I must abide by learning the secret of contentment in every banana. For instance, a banana leaf might suffice as a rainproof hat with a pleasing floppiness, almost like a soothing blade of kelp, supple to the touch. On a side note, I've often wondered, yet cannot prove, whether the mistakes of gene-editing each get quarantined in its own small place, or if I am one of the rare rogues to survive the editorial rite of passage through a black hole. What in the world went wrong with this shrimp flickering in a tide pool, for example, or this prickly sea urchin? What genes went haywire in this tide pool and this grove of bananas? By my left octoeye and its horizontal pupil, I can't tell you. My right octoeye is myopic, so all I see is a garish cloud like a green ball gown with scalloped edges—curves, not mollusks. Don't wear spectacles, but I could use a contact lens to focus the vision in my right octoeye. No matter, there isn't much I rely on in terms of my sight these days. When nine brains process sensory data at once, I'm definitely not

lacking any information, so I can easily compensate for myopia.

With six arms splayed like dice on the floor and two in the air for kicks, and my body flattened to the buffed limestone—yes, the floor of my octagonal lair is tiled with limestone, cool to the touch in more ways than one, and even the shyest arms love caressing it—I perambulate slowly towards the garden. Introverting, nine brains seek refuge as if I'm lost in a throng of people. A throng of lifeforms, I mean. You see, I'm already introverted, and now I sense my personality retreating even farther into the recesses of my mind. For instance, I have no way of knowing whether other singularities exist like mine, and if so, if permutations of octopuses or other folks hobnob in one singularity as opposed to another. Do mirrored lairs exist within mirrors in one-dimensional time? Is a mirror an apt visual metaphor for a singularity? My uneducated guess is, probably not. Mirrors reflect light, and there's no light in a singularity, I imagine, just spacetime curving infinitely with jagged edges, whatever zigs and zags shape the jigsaw puzzle. While inching across the buffed floor, I toss up a couple of my arms, shrugging. The shyest arms do absolutely nothing, dangling as if in diffidence or indifference.

Fortunately, I'm an octopus named Emily, not a phenomenologist or astrophysicist.

I envision how one Emily, on the other side of the universe, imagines her brain, a mass of gray matter, rolling along like a plum pudding. A body-brain divide: I wonder if my tingling corpus of nerves, laden with gustatory and tactile sensitivity, constitutes a soul like this other Emily? Is my meek parcel of consciousness more than a summation of nerves? It's like asking whether the fragrance of a cabbage rose is the soul or a spirit, or if the plums and the pudding comprise the whole smorgasbord of body, mind, and soul. In this world, my body is also a brain—or brains, nine total—and vice versa

for my body, but what is a soul? This sum of nine includes one in each limb, flowering with a surfeit of sensory data about my whereabouts in the moonlight. If I spend time arranging jars in my rolltop desk or looking for snacks in my pantry, then my firing ganglia tell me where I am or what I want, and maybe who I am at a given moment, but not necessarily why I am.

> First brain: Push the jar to the left so it catches the light.
> Second brain: No, leave it as is.
> Third brain: There's no reason to move any jars.
> Fourth brain: I like the arrangement.
> Fifth brain: Let's see whether olives are available.
> Sixth brain: I found one under the shelf.
> Seventh brain: Is it still good?
> Eighth brain: Never mind, a pebble.
> Ninth brain: All of you, I'd like to take a nap.

Now I've popped my fantasy bubble about ostensible personhood at this point. If it weren't for the nagging awareness that I'm an octopus, not a woman named Emily, this small place could be a tropical resort with its lagoon tricked out in banana groves and rambling coastal shrubs with bell-shaped flowers that reek of rhubarb kiwi popsicles and which, kissing the dewy air with their stamens and pistils, explode into blossom after a rainstorm. Who cares whether or not it's a stardust paradise for editorial rejections, i.e. if your ears protrude too much or your skin is maroon like mine at this very moment? The rainwater tastes just like agua fresca made of watermelon meat and lemon zinger. Why not a spa? I am not kidding. And it's wonderful for introverts like me, utterly private, so I can recharge my energy reserves at will. No photomicrographers, no pundits or paparazzi, no fawning hoteliers and concierges: No one to ask whether you wish to buy an exotic gene sequence on the shores of the octopodes.

On the flip side, for those who prefer the glittering Genzopolis and its cosmopolitan allure, there's much going on with floating points operations or network traffic on this side of the universe. However, there's no rush hour. No projects. No moving walkways. No blockchains. No graffiti. No gondolas. No mountain bikes. No search engines. No byways. No traffic. No marquees. No ticker tapes. No organ thieves. No gene infusions. No gas galas. No data analytics. No pivot tables. No depositories. Nothing. On my noon stroll around this abode, objects might provide clues to an observer about my inner life in this place, a topographical autobiography of things, yet I don't own many possessions. I don't own a boat, for one. No scuba-diving equipment, no water wings or aqua lungs, no fitness trampolines or volley nets. No yacht, no catamaran, not even a kayak or water ski or paddleboard. My home isn't a renovated sand castle or an ivy-adorned, pilloried mansion of many rooms; I don't desire to own either. My humble abode is round as a hill for a troll, or a grass dugout raised on one side of a creek and lower in front, if that makes sense. The rock garden lies aslant on a berm, a knoll by a ridge.

There's a sandbank, then a hillock, and a stone's throw away, a patch with smooth pebbles, a suitable place for a picnic with sea cucumber sandwiches and a pitcher of cloudberry lemonade, but there's no one there. Imagine you vanish into a black hole and surface in a paradise of oddities like this one. Did you remember to take the wicker basket of mint sea cucumber dip with pickled anchovies and a thermos of lemon zinger tea? What about a slice of seaweed cake with sliced figs topped by a dollop of foam, wholly vegan? What about the jars of strained yogurt thickened by spoonfuls of genetically modified acidophilus, bioengineered to nourish the colon with bacterial clouds? A row of crystallized violets on a rum-soaked plum pudding? Certainly hope so, except for one

problem. In order to reach your own rock garden, you have to drop your whole body on the floor, then slither on eight arms across the floor, haul your melonhead across the threshold and out the front door of your octagonal lair into the blasting unknown where an agoraphobic octopus imagines attacks by gulls, angry bumblebees, or squadrons of fire ants, or outright stepped on. Auspiciously, there's no one in paradise with predatory tendencies, at least, whom you've ever encountered, unless it's you. Oh my sea stars, the monsters lurking murkily within us, even in those of us harmlessly named Emily, taunt us with the crazy idea that we have nothing to fear but our shades.

The other Emily, who confesses a mounting sense of dread, has no idea how anxiety will cloud the mental landscape of future generations; her state of mind will be more typical than atypical. Fortunately, I do harbor a no-nonsense, practical streak, which anchors my sanity. That's why my yard is mostly hardscape, in contrast to the other Emily on the right side of the universe. Flower beds are notoriously fickle, while I can rely on the static, if not outright stoical nature of stones. By characterizing my beloved rock garden as undersea and therefore drought-resistant, I'll spare you the catalogue of details elaborating on their geology, lithography, and topography. Rocks in their rockiness, after all, are inherently resistant to drought; otherwise, they wouldn't be what they are. If rocks are your hobby, first and foremost, don't expect to receive undying adoration as a reward. Rocks are rocks; if I named each one Emily or emerald, not one would notice the confusion: Esmeralda ensues, not the Esmeralda mine of emeralds, the beautiful cyclosilicate beryl. Tending to my delightful rock garden, if it's even considered work rather than a hobby, requires not only discipline and stamina but long hours of patiently shifting the obdurate masses.

Before I venture a length to wax rhapsodic, however, it is time to return to the sea. The wind over the lagoon carries a mild fragrance vaguely reminiscent of rosewater, coconut, limonene, and a hint of linalool, the latter which reminds me of rose petals rushing into a copper vat for distilling perfume. The other Emily, I imagine, would appreciate this comparison, although I don't know whether she was partial to fragrance beyond her spices and flower beds. Despite my photosensitivity and hydrophilia, I've forgotten to apply the seaweed balm before, yet never gotten sunburned. As I've said previously, my skin might be genetically edited to serve as an organic ultraviolet shield. Wearing the leafy hat for its robust shade, however, can't do much harm, and one could say it's a sort of look, a fashionista's style, as far as octopuses go. Admittedly, I'm not much of a fashion-influencer on this lagoon, with not a shred of linsey-woolsey in sight.

The fengshui dynamic and aesthetics of a rock garden—like bonsai cultivation or floral ikebana—is no less than an art. There, I've said it at last. An extension of the quizzical art of being an octopus. My three hearts jump in unison when I mouth the words, rocks and bonsai, in the same breath, one of the unfussy diversions in life. The key is to resist a compulsion to push the rocks into tidy rows like peas in a pod. Of shapes, angles, and texture in an aesthetically pleasing rock arrangement, the ruggedness of unbuffed igneous and unhewn shale, I ask, do you like river pebbles or rough sandstone? If flecked granite is on hand for a raised garden bed, would you still use flagstones? Or slabs of marble with dark streaks like rain gliding on the horizon? Buffed alabaster instead? What about lava, and how about porphyry, or flint and rose quartz?

Please note, in the remote chance of doubt: I do aim to grow absolutely nothing, if I may present a disclaimer. I've a brown thumb. Bald truth be told, I have no thumbs, green or brown. The sage and chaparral in my yard are barren sticks,

jagged as boxes of pencils after an earthquake has shattered the edges of time. I don't have a green thumb. Yes, I echo, I have no thumbs. Come to think of it, I prefer to feature the rocks in their pristine, stoical quality, and therefore only rocks in their adamantine state. Rocks exist for their own sake, not intentionally as fire pits, catapults, or walkways. I don't use mortar, and I stay away from epoxy glue. Adhesive liquid is a nefarious trap, and after it hardens, I won't be able to peel it off without removing patches of my skin. I exude a lot of slime but not enough, mingling it with hyaluronic acid to keep my epidermis pliant and plump as a ripe plum, and do not like adhesive substances like aloe fillet sap or other goo like carrageenan.

I adore rocks in their obdurate, geologic durability. To say the least, hiding under a rock could save your life in a pinch, no trivial matter. And I should add that I love rocks with flinty minerals in them like chalky marl or quartz. If you feel the urge to be rambunctious, juggle a few rocks, drop them, be a buffoon. No one's watching my conduct in this small place, anyway. Although bioexiled, I'm not on parole from life. Hug a rock and call it happiness. Call it beautiful, call it bizarre, call it occupational rock therapy. Don't be a curmudgeon or a nit-picking doryphore. This is the sheer elegance of rockery without an audience, the nonverbal yet eloquent wilderness which generated those black pearls of moonlight I love, and the equally nacreous manner of things which shines with an inner light, even the moon without a glow of its own origin, or the cute yet ravenous potato beetle of gold and black tiger stripes on its forewings.

Beetles and tigers, why not in this world of hybrid phyla?

Octopuses also love the hillocks to the cairns and hummocky moraine. I imagine the other Emily on the right side of the universe never encountered an octopus in her lifetime, but like me, rambled on small hills and rocky terrain on a

weathering coastline where she looked out to frigates at a distance and envisioned mermaids in the basement of the sea. Em-dashes hover like dragonflies in the air over this other Emily's head. She opens a jar of fireflies—not unlike my olives jars—and captures the sinuous lines, reeling them in like fishing twine onto a spool inside the jar. The spool has a tiny handle in the shape of an L, two straight lines intersecting at ninety degrees. No joke, it's an ingenious way to catch inspiration whenever it strikes. The jar is large enough to contain the long word, floccinaucinihilipilification, which sounds like the name of a disease, but actually means the act of deeming worthlessness. Is it big enough to house the psychological condition, hippopotomonstrosesquippedaliophobia, a fear of long words? Yes, but never fear, my friend. The fireflies escape from the jar into the midsummer light while Emily screws on the lid. Inside the jar, a new poem starts to hum. How I envy the reclusive artist and her exquisite creation: Emily's poem is a humming cloud of phosphorescence.

In her grotto of solitude, this other Emily has no idea that a doppelgänger, a spoof of her charming, belle existence—exists on the wrong side of the universe. At minimum, I'm an affable though lonely octopus, not one of the fabled monsters of yore. In my biomythopoiea, for instance, the akkorokamui is half cephalopod, half human, and hurls boulders at fishermen. It's angry because nobody accepts it as a person, and none of the cephalopods welcome it, either. Upholding one's sanity and positivity are some of the challenges of this chimera. For instance, the akkorokamui can pop off its eight arms and regenerate each one, similar to an octopus in the wilderness. As a mutant who can do this, however, it's grotesque in every sense of the word, downright frightening, to boot. However, it also harbors a useful trove of ancient seafaring wisdom. With mystical grace, it harmonizes with maritime winds to guide fishermen and safeguard their boats. Don't sail to the

southeast; storm winds will arise soon. Beware of the whirl-pool to the west. I assume this means the akkorokamui has a tongue to speak, unlike an octopus of the wilderness who has a multitude of soft mouths yet no tongues. On hindsight, please allow me to refashion this biomyth with a confession, having shamelessly fabricated the part where the akkorokamui is a wise friend. In fact, it is a notorious destroyer and champion rock-hurler who started out as a gargantuan red spider—in a higher altitude than sea level near a fishing village—who terrorized its inhabitants by going on rampages. Before the advent of gene editing, he morphed spontaneously into an octopus thanks to superpowers and lived out the rest of his days in the ocean without a chance to ask for clemency or pardon, serving his bioexile as a monster of the deep.

Fortuitously, I have no aspirations in this regard, thank you.

The akkorokamui's cousin, the koromodako, is small enough to hold in your pocket. Translations of this tale say either it's cloth or paper, like a chapbook or folio. In other words, it's an octopus of cloth, yet it doesn't wear clothes. If offended, the koromodako swiftly expands into an enormous tablecloth bigger than a ship—several acres wide, in fact, swallowing phytoplankton, lifeforms, and fishing boats alike, thanks to its polymorphism. The old adage goes, don't make either one angry, neither the akkorokamui nor the koromodako. With pomegranate skin and a tangle of string-like arms rising out of the water, the akkorokamui changes the sky and sea to red, and you'll vanish in its maw in a minute. The koromodako will open like a giant tablecloth and swallow everything it touches. To the koromodako's defense, however, the cloth octopus only attacks if provoked.

Most of the time, it's happy to swim about as a harmless argonaut, minding its own molluskan business in a spiral paper shell. The akkorokamui, on the other hand, goes into a

rage if it's hungry. With any species of yokai octopus, whether he is an akkorokamui or koromodako, however, you can't win single-handed. We aren't talking about adorable, wide-eyed cephalopods at the aquarium who press their blushing melon-heads against the glass. You cannot make the yokai monsters love you or calm down when they're annoyed, no more than you can tame the open sea or hold a typhoon in the palm of your hand. The moonlight, however, has wisely pointed out how real monsters aren't the ones at sea; of course, the true behemoths of the deep lurk within us.

What's a yokai? The other Emily believes she must be dreaming.

Emily stirs in her sleep as visions of sea monsters loom in her mind's eye—the buzzing neural activity of rapid eye movement, to be exact. In fact, what occurs on this side of the universe has a ripple effect on events in Emily's world. The atuikakura is a sea cucumber who arose when a woman's lost undergarment washed downstream into a bay, centuries ago. Was the woman kneeling at a creek, washing the laundry on a heap of stones, when the undergarment floated like a koi fish into sight, then out? Is she a victim of a sartorial malfunction? A survivor of a violent assault? Missing the backstory, I read between the lines and embellish a little, or else circumvent it entirely; I don't know what elapsed. As the story goes, the undergarment settled at the bottom of the aforesaid bay and morphed into a giant sea cucumber, one who attaches its mouth to fragments of driftwood and more often, the mer-chant ships crossing its path.

I've pondered, why a sea cucumber and not a beluga whale or black pearl oyster? The koromodako drags them under the waves, right to the watery graves of seafaring bones with no return. Thanks to the atuikakura, genetic citizens of the Genzopolis no longer eat sea cucumbers for supper with stir-fried vegetables. On their dishes, in lieu of an innocuous

sea cucumber of the wild, a giant atuikakura balloons before their eyes and attaches its orifice to a leg of a dining room table: an upcycled panel of distressed birch, a plank of varnished maple, or a refurbished door of acacia. Instead, they're plagued by one giant sea cucumber after another, including the atuikakura who seals itself to a table leg and belches out its guts over the carpet so no one can dine in peace. Its grabby mouth attaches to the wood with such force that it can't be pulled it off with a detachable vacuum hose.

Is there a koromodako named Emily on the other side of the universe?

This is a long-winded way of explaining how a cucumber on one side of the universe might fuse to a table leg on the other, for whatever it's worth. The mythical sea monsters don't exist outside our heads; as we're alive to recount these tales, they're real in a sense. For the rest of us, not one of the stardust editors of the omnibus successfully knocked out genetically programmed cell death. I mean, who has the authority to mute death? Show me an abundance of pearls on this side of the universe by virtue of midnight quiet, and I'll show you when moonlight drops opals onto the water; the coolness of these slippery gems is about as close to a lifeless state as I'd ever been, the mineralized rigor of death. In a parallel universe, in one of the permutations of Emily, I'd wear a double-strand of cultured pearls around my neck, a rope of near-roundness like the night of a gibbous moon, beads shaped like extracted milk teeth dancing under a pillow.

In the body of this other Emily, I'd soak in a tub wearing only these lovely pearls, twirling them around my index finger while I stare into space. I'd adore my cypress tub for its honey-colored wood, organically repellent to decay and wood-boring insects. My two legs, with calves solid as radishes from daily runs on the beach, would stretch to the length of the tub while I breathe calmly in and out. Thanks to the

brains of this Emily, I'd daydream about my girlhood years before greenhouse gases wreaked havoc and genetic engineering
caused mayhem, warming the seas to the extent that genetically modified sharks were more ubiquitous, less unique. I'd
remember the long winters when my mother would open the
front door of our house and a foot of snow would reach to the
height of my knees, deposited by a blizzard the night before. I
was only a little girl named Emily then, and I'd reach out with
a bare hand to touch the snow; it burned my fingertips, so I'd
put them in my mouth.

If I were equipped with a photomicrograph of this other
Emily's girlhood memories on the right side of the universe,
I'd fondly recall my first crush. Puppy love, the elders of my
generation called it, between a boy and a girl. Our mothers
would speak to one another about our friendship—how adorable, promising—and one mother would pick us up at school,
then chauffeur us to one of our houses, where we'd eat green
apples with wedges of sharp cheese and sip wax-lined paper
cups of juice set out for us on a screened porch facing the
backyard into the woods. What was it I adored most about
him, at this juvenile age? That he'd sit behind me in math class
and try to copy my solutions to problem sets, when his scores
in math were as good as mine? When he'd read the rhymed
poem I'd composed for an assignment and say, I know the
teacher will love this? What was love to us then, so young yet
under the illusion, in our innocence, we were wise beyond our
years, surpassing the bickering of adults and their day-to-day
anxieties?

In a voice gentle as milkweed, this other Emily would say
to the boy whose breath was sweetened with apples and fox
grapes, do you believe in the orphans who set fire to the asylum? Do you ever hear their bare feet running in the woods?
And he'd solemnly reply, with eyes wide as springtime mud
pies and a hand whose soiled knuckles closed over mine, of

course I do. That's what grown-ups do to children who don't fit. Then he'd close his eyes and nod with pursed lips as if he, too, had drunk the bitter elixir of adulthood even at his youthful age. He'd open his eyes again, and we'd look at each other's faces with sober judgment while crickets stridulated in lazy greenery, the waist-high grasses brushing a screen door in the woods where we dared not venture without our vigilant mothers, the progenitors of our maternal mitochondria, without whom we wouldn't exist.

This other Emily, the one of black pearls in the Emily diaspora, had no inkling that an infinitude of Emily genotypes existed in parallel universes: Emily of the cherry blossoms, Emily of the bougainvillea, Emily of the azaleas, Emily of the troposphere, Emily of the exosphere, Emily of the space operas, Emily of the rock operas, Emily of the dogwoods, Emily of the little dogs, Emily of the bonanzas, Emily of the fashionistas, Emily of the biomythopoiea, Emily of the circuses, Emily of the mandolins, Emily of the sea waves, Emily of the fields, Emily of the doves, Emily of the night sky, Emily of the gypsies, Emily of the mustangs, Emily of the red ponies, Emily of the tantrums, Emily of the rafters, Emily of the mezzanines, Emily of the credenzas, Emily of the mermaids, Emily of the oil lamps, Emily of the cliffs, Emily of the creeks, Emily of the strawberries, Emily of the spiders, Emily of the red pears, Emily of the ferns, Emily of the daybooks, Emily of the star gazers, Emily of the herbariums.

Emily of the quills, Emily of the heather, Emily of the calla lilies, Emily of the dandelions, Emily of the black peppercorns, Emily of the upright pianos, Emily of the ophthalmologists, Emily of the iriditis, Emily of the myopic, Emily of the marshes, Emily of the reeds, Emily of the brains, Emily of the grasses, Emily of the beaches, Emily of the seashells, Emily of the sundresses, Emily of the spindles, Emily of the creek pebbles, Emily of the bright hearths, Emily of the armadillos,

Emily of the garden snails, Emily of the aardvarks, Emily of the orangutans, Emily of the forests, Emily of the dogtooth violets, Emily of the evergreens, Emily of the homestead, Emily of the zoologists, Emily of the angiosperms, Emily of the gymnosperms, Emily of the quarries, Emily of the peacocks, Emily of the ostrich eggs, Emily of the baleen whales, Emily of the behemoths, Emily of the frigates, Emily of the pearls, Emily of the rain, Emily of the echoes, and Emily of the everlasting.

The original Emily, whose ancient bones were buried in a necropolis long submerged by the rising seas, has no idea that she has unwittingly spawned more than a thousand clones dispersed as biomolecular stardust across time, with a branching geneaology of names: my moniker, Emily Dystopia, for one; then the following variations of other Emilys in other parts of the universe, for example, Emily D for Dyschronology.

D for Dominant.
D for Discordant.
D for Double Helix.
D for Duplication.
D for Deoxyribonucleic Acid.
D for Denaturation.
D for Dermatoglyphics.
D for Differentiation.
D for Diploid.
D for Dizygote.
D for Disruption.
D for De Novo Mutation.

Who knew what dystopic future of designer genes dimmed like a dying bonfire ahead of us, this boy and I? Our fates diverged. We'd eventually spend our latter years apart, he as an apprentice to the kinase kingpins up the ladder to the advanced level of gene editing, and I, as far as possible from denaturing or cloning

double-stranded molecules. Those were days of snipping the octo-podean genome using molecular scissors, and the gene pen wasn't in its research and development phase. The polymerase chain reaction, to be honest, was considered a dinosaur in molecular genetics; scientists understood the processes of transcription but had yet to devise the technology for inscription at the level of base pairs. As for me, I'm a poet, not a pluripotent cell, I'd protest to family and friends. I'd rave about how much I loved the unedited wilderness, my girlhood of samaras spinning down from maple trees, of mossy brooks swarming with minnows before the climate shifted. Reverse engineer the molecular scissors and genetic pens from our human enzymes, not the octopodean ones to ours, I'd rant in the booming manner of a naturalist whose genetic tinkering was limited to cross-pollination and ingrafted branches: basic gardening, in my humble opinion. What if we turn into octopuses, I'd add, looking directly into their questioning eyes.

After a while, I'd withdraw into my cozy world of routine: cleaning my hairbrushes, washing the house clothes, and leisurely contemplation. After bathing in a cypress tub, I'd put on a cotton kimono, roll up my sleeves, and push rocks around in my garden. Using hearthstone bricks, I'd construct an outdoor oven for my cast-iron skillet, which I'd use for baking. I'd haul a long bread table of buffed pinewood outside, hiring an ossan for the afternoon to assist me in carving a bench, then I'd bake a tray of tea biscuits for our elevenses. With a pastry blender, I'd briskly cut the shortening into flour and baking soda, then add the buttermilk. The ossan would offer morsels of dialogue, nothing intrusive. For instance, the weather today, isn't it gorgeous? The ocean is exceptionally blue today, isn't it. I think I see a sailboat out there, or a historic ship with four to seven sails.

My kimono sleeve would hover by the moist, crumbly dough. I'd ask the ossan to roll it a few inches up my arm. Right arm, then the left. Instead of eight, I'd only deal with two. Doing one thing at a time is not always the best way to manage a recipe, I'd remark, and

the ossan, perched solicitously on a stool, dressed in an ironed shirt and khaki trousers, not denim jeans or shorts, would agree, you don't have eight arms, only two. Can I help you with something? Of course, I'd politely decline, and the ossan would await my next line of dialogue; he doesn't speak unless addressed, as a proper ossan shouldn't. Don't mind a little small talk, though, initiated by an ossan, if he understands his role as a man of artificial intelligence. On the other hand, I don't necessarily prefer light bantering over silent lapses between associates, especially if an octopus wishes to imagine herself as a woman on the other side of the universe.

To THE DOUGH, I ADD A HEAPING SPOONFUL OF cashew butter if I'm baking nut butter biscuits, or a handful of highbush blueberries and crushed hazelnuts if they're blueberry hazelnut biscuits. A tablespoon of honey. Honey of the wilderness, I mean, whose flowers budded lavishly in fields when I was a girl, before the maker's original honeybees died out from widespread colony collapse, and their genetic clones populated the world with newly minted wings. The wild, unedited clover would draw honeybees alongside sundry other insects—gnats, beetles, mayflies—in the open field; dew would wet the clover at night with the poignancy of the chins of lambs. The honeybees, having sucked their nectar and caked their bellies with gold crumbs of pollen, would return to their hives, mapping a choreography of sweetness, their invisible routes to abundance. The bees, the bees, the bees. How I would miss the humming of those original bees before mass extinction, their tragic demise due to global colony collapse. With their colors fading soon after late spring, the copies aren't as bright and quick-witted as prototypes in the wilderness.

The ossan watches me as I prepare the biscuit dough, rolling it out with a pin. I sprinkle turbinado sugar on top. Other recipe variations include chopped cinnamon apples with cranberries soaked in orange juice, molasses and glazed pecans, or lemon zest and coconut. I'd tell the ossan how I learned how to bake the tea biscuits as a girl,

and he'd listen to me describe my favorite types. I'd pantomime how to bake them on hearthstone bricks. You pat the dough this way, one inch thick. Then you roll it out like that. He'd watch my gestures. I'd explain the making of citrus peel simmered in water, then soaked in brandy and dipped in sugar. Yes, he'd listen to me pontificate on these subjects, and agree with my questions about the weather. That's what he's expected to do.

> Why is the tide so high, I say.
> I think it's the moon, my dear.
> Is that a rain cloud out there?
> If you can't tell, I certainly won't.
> What would you like for supper?
> Your braised sea stars.
> Don't have sea stars today.
> One of your fruit tarts, then.
> No fruit tarts. No tarts, in fact.
> What do you have, then?
> Only pickled olives, sir.
> Aren't you the one with tarts?
> Must be a woman in another universe.

As fate would have it, I'm just an octopus. To this end, my conversation with an ossan might occur in a moonlit lair overlooking the lagoon, instead of a bougainvillea-garlanded terrace with an evening sea wind blowing in our faces if I were fully human, the night carrying with it a fragrance of night-blooming jasmines tipped with salt: free swathes of water-cut jasmines, jessamines, yazmins. We'd have to carry out this dialogue in gestures or sign language because I lack vocal cords and lips, only a beak snapping open and shut the way a mouth naturally ought to where a woman's privates would be. As an octopus, this beak is all I have, an orifice at the point of all beginnings where my eight arms meet under my head with a puckered mini-mouth under each arm. In some ways, I'm more of a multifoliate flower than fauna, I think. A flower with

mouths, I mean. This lifeform, however, is a woman who speaks to the ossan in fluent vocalizations, and does so without confusing her privates for a beak. An octopus, on the other hand, has no such advantage, even if she had a voice: she's still a cephalopod, not a human lifeform. Let's say, hypothetically, she engages the ossan by remarking upon the fugues of moonlight.

Isn't the sea especially bright?
What do you mean, hey?
Bright as a silver tureen, sir.
What do you know about tureens?
I use a tureen for my bouillabaisse.
How does an octopus know about broth?
It goes with my oyster crackers.
Oysters? Well, that finally makes sense.
Oyster crackers. Not oysters.
You octopuses eat oysters, right?
I said crackers, not oysters.
You're an octopus.
You're denying my personhood.
You're accusing me of what?
Please leave. Right now.

And so forth, sadly, I could've held this same conversation and substituted the word, octopus, with wildebeest or fungus beetle, and still arrived nowhere. As an octopus on the wrong side of the universe, I find no gentlemen available with the exception of the ghostly ossan who appears out of the moonlight. He carries bundles of genes like wilted calla lilies from a funeral, the reams of lost sequences. The night, our backdrop, is a black field of irises. Am I truly so grotesque, or is this a matter of chance? How do I participate in this perplexing dance of love, a choreography of mixed genetic arts? Why can't the stardust editors on the other side of the universe toss an ossan or two down the chute to keep me company in paradise? Are they concerned that I might eat them? Are none of them wild? I mean, who are the ossans?

Are they edited like me, or holograms, or waterproof machines of artificial intelligence, those annotated modules of prefabricated thought informed by algorithms, those lineated vectors and flow-boxes of mechanized thought?

Are ossans made of slippery patches of moonlight, nothing more than the moon's reflection of the sun as it sails soundlessly in space over ninety million miles away? Is the moon no more than a mirror? How much should I expect of a man whose artificial intelligence confines his sentience to the realm of algorithms? Or wherever I am, I should add, on this lagoon. The original Emily on the other side of the universe had her mysterious loves, a man who moved out to the west coast, or a man who was a good friend of her father's, or maybe not a man at all but a woman who lived next door; I have no one on this lagoon. No one has told me anything, and I don't have any instructions. Every night, the world folds up like a hidden bookshelf with the sun setting over the sea, and the inkling grit of stardust over windswept sand pours loneliness on the lagoon without murmurs from the living or the dead. I put on my kelp hat and stroll back to my lair on eight arms radiating around my body like the guiding rays of a windrose. If only I had an intuitive sense of my place in time. On the contrary, I have no instincts in this regard; I have no idea whether I am in the past, present-future, future-perfect, the outer fringe of the exosphere, or time itself. The sea of lost letters, awash in lovely translucencies, rarely surrenders its secrets, lucid yet recondite. Once, written in the sand, these beautiful lines appeared with ellipses.

. . .

*You have come to the shore. There are no instructions.*

. . .

*Both art and faith are ventures into the imagination; both are ventures into the unknown.*

. . .

*I'm not very good at praying, but what I experience when I'm writing a poem is close to prayer.*

. . .

Whose fingers wrote these lines in the sand? Was it the eidolon of the original Emily or one of the other Emilys, or maybe an Edna, a Marianne, an Elizabeth, a Hilda, or a Denise? Surely the ocean didn't randomly assemble these syllables into words. What would be the probability of shuffling the ciphers into intelligible phrases, similar to the likelihood of apes or opossums in a room typing out the works of an ancient bard? As I gazed at the lines, wondering whose invisible hand wrote them, a tongue of foam rushed ashore and erased the inscription, pilfering grains of sand out to sea. *You have come to the shore. There are no instructions.* The glorious presence of the maker stirred within me, the one who instills a sense of awe under a starry night. *There are no instructions,* I echoed. Was this a prayer? If so, of what? Adoration, praise, supplication? If so, by whom? Was this a biochronicle of unrequited love from the octopodes? If so, whom do I love? Was this a blessing of footless mollusks like me? A gift to the humble denizens of the deep sea? My nine brains ached with the neural exertion of metaphysical invention while my three hearts pounded asynchronously, cruising on different sets of roller skates.

One heart skates towards the future, yet gazes steadily
    at yesterday.
The second races wherever my wishes go, wistful or unbridled.
The third is the crazy one in the roller-skating rink,
    the one I watch.

Yes, this third heart is the one who knows the universe is always on fire, and knows the maker of the original wilderness is omnipresent, even in apparent silence. How could the editors of stardust carry on with their work and not know all this, even with the invention of portable black holes? Fires are

burning everywhere in the universe like nascent poems, and an octopodean paradise might exist only a singularity away. As a line in the sand says, authored by an invisible hand, *You have come to the shore.*

*There are no instructions.* What I do harbor is a body on this lagoon, and in this body, I engage the absence and presence of my rogue genotype at once. I have no legs—no human legs, I mean—yet many legs. The legs serve as arms, too. I lack a human countenance—I cannot smile—yet I grin through my multitudinous mouths. No head, rather, a melonhead. No spine, an invertebrate, while a figurative backbone—or what I like to call the grit of stardust—kicks in with my guts. Do I love this existence as a rogue? It's the Genzopolis who abandoned me, not the other way around, thanks to the whims of the omnibus. No family, no soul mate, yet I am not without a soul—a flame, the spirit of life, the essence of genesis, yields more light. Cautiously, I slide back across the tide pools, out of the direct sunlight, back into the shallows and shadows with a little sigh.

## 4 | Ballad for the Sea of Lost Letters

The octopus indulges in a seawater bath. A hodgepodge of colors in a technicolor dream. An abecedary of alternate names other than Emily like Ayesha and Lois and Phoebe and Xiaomei. The paradox of bioexile. A migrant Emily of the Emily variants. The flawless, designer-gene boroughs of the Genzopolis in ruins. Poetry is paradise on fire.

## Ballad for the Sea of Lost Letters

ITH A HYDRATED BODY LOUNGING LIKE a raincape or a slab of silken tofu on my waterbed, I sense this hour of the afternoon warrants a siesta. In other words, I'm drowsy. Do octopuses dream? Yes, I'm an atypical octopus, yet I certainly do, vividly so. Although octopuses in the wilderness are colorblind—graced with optical rods, not cones—I dream in orthochromatic pixels, thanks to edited dream genes influencing my muscarinic acetylcholine receptors. Yes, I am genetically predisposed to oneiromancy. In other words, I sleep with a parasympathetic response, the heart rates slowed while triggering glandular activity. After a stroll in my rock garden, I usually like to take a siesta on my waterbed. First, I bathe myself in a tub of seawater warmed by the kettleful on my stove, then slather my body, head, and arms with hyaluronic acid infused with aloe vera, the gelid inner fillet only, unadulterated and unfiltered. My shy arm, the fourth one, is a little slow in responding to stimuli today, ignoring sunlight and sea snails, so I prod it with my other

suction cups, which open and shed their skin-colored petals like cherry blossoms, a flock of pink-tinged cream.

The multifarious, spindly-armed, flour-dusted Emilys of the universe also blossom in their disparate existences as the flamboyant spawn of a feckless kind, the poets whose madcap blood simmers underneath their cool, blue-veined skin. Backyard rose gardens beckon them out of their inner rooms to explore a brambled existence as hybrid tea, floribunda, grandiflora, and damask. The other Emilys, variants of the original one, flutter around my bath like imaginary wasps and dragonflies, the angelic lifeforms of an ancient epoch when arthropods covered the world. Shall I take out a butterfly net to capture these lovely beings as keepsakes from a dream? Or shall I put aside these imaginations and bake yolk-gold loaves of cake, instead? Tea loaves, gingerbread, caraway seed cake, and black spice cake doused in bourbon or brandy? Clip the snow viburnum for a vase in the living room, or shall it be a bouquet of daisies, instead? The original wilderness, unedited by the profusion of transcriptions and inscriptions, were established under the maker's invisible hand: the first gardener.

I get out of the hydrotherapy bath, squeeze two of my arms in a pretzel, then inch across the floor to my seaweed-fiber mat, where I dry myself, then apply several jars of hyaluronic acid to my skin. I crawl onto my waterbed, breathing evenly with the window open to the sea, and drift into the land of reverie. I dream about a tribe of space pirates engineered to govern the universe wisely and with dignity, and how the stardust editors failed to splice the correct sequences to design this species of fly-by-night wisdom warriors effectively. Instead of fighting, they soar like refulgent angels and haloed seraphim of the ancient days, harbingers of peace. In fact, they are no less than fireflies in human shapes. The modified warriors of light populate the world as rogues, recombining their glow-in-the-dark genes with those of other species to bear progeny

with bioluminescent skin. The lights are visible by satellite all over the globe at night, and their luminous children sprout wings. To what end, I don't know, other than the usual, i.e. to forage for sustenance, to find a mate, or warn friends about danger; the lights, as signals, imparted wisdom about navigating the darkness. The children shed their wings in adulthood.

What danger, I wonder, and why darkness in the world if there's light.

In a hodgepodge of colors, in the defamiliarized hues of negative exposure, I dream of the rise of colossal, glittering insects of the most exquisite morphology, like flaming warriors and seraphs messaging a dystopian world with warnings on their wings patterned in code, or like dazzling, postdiluvian insects buzzing past your eardrum with the great flood of the inexorably warming millennium: a cyclical rise of cicadas, dragonflies big as angels, griffinflies and fig beetles. Moondrops of honeydew deposited by fat aphids shine in globes of syrup on leaves. I squint at the blazing sun which hovers close to the Genzopolis, burning the crops like rice, cotton, and bamboo edited to boost immunity to fungal and viral infections, although vulnerable to the harsh weather. It's a polychromatic dream awash in color dyes, however, so the shapes of angels and mold spores appear in negative, one dark as gargoyles, the other, ellipses sleeping under a star-brindled night.

Other lifeforms named Emily float solo like polyps, each one sealed in a bubble of her own: every somber Emily is brown-eyed and chestnut-haired in her watery sphere of immunological restoration with biological aging reversed by epigenetic clocks altered to regenerate the thymus gland—which ordinarily vanishes in adulthood. In chronological age, a gene-edited Emily might be centuries old, but in bioengineered age, only sixteen or seventeen as she appears in a daguerreotype, an everlastingly youthful provocateur whose

T-cell stimulating thymus spreads its left and right lobes like butterfly wings behind her sternum, radiant and pulsing in the warm, posh darkness nestled between her lungs.

I witness the expansion of a fluffy cloud in the stratosphere, a nimbus the shape of a granodiorite translation cloud among rainclouds. Silver-mane pappus like a humble dandelion puff, it grows to the size of a dozen zeppelins and translates languages in the tongues of angels, light as spun sugar floss. It beams rare languages in parallel translations with melodious recordings by young women named Emily all over the universe: Emily of tongues spoken in distant star systems, Emily of dialects rhymed in mossy treetops, Emily of diphthongs on our fields and savannahs, Emily of intonations under ammonia skies, Emily of yodeling on intralpine valleys, Emily of finger whistling and playing the bones, Emily of signers and interpreters in a sky pod with other migrants, Emily of pictographs and hieroglyphs, or Emily clicking her teeth in a jubilee of noise. The phyla and families of languages, mapped in outer space in an interstellar tree of families, flow together in a confluence of biological and digital routes through the Milky Way: nebulous clouds of the galaxy, faraway radio satellites, the flowering veins of a lung or a leaf, and the inklings of a genetically altered octopus, this humble omnivore.

AN IMAGINARY, MIGRANT EMILY VARIANT OF SPINDLY ARMS wonders, spinning her thoughts like a cotton gin while she zooms through interstellar space in a pod: Did I ever live as a girl on the right side of the universe, in a deleted act of this space opera, careening from planet to planet? Is there truly a flying octopus on the other side of the cosmos, a creature who loves free verse? If so, who or what is the purpose of her existence? Is the shape of the totality of biodata in the

universe an octopus, metaphorically speaking, an omnivore of information? Or is the universe a lotus-shaped pod of rotund universes tucked inside a larger pod? Not for those with an aversion to the sight of little holes, a symptom of trypophobia, I tell you. Or of the little dark holes inside a lotus itself, one whose flower dropped eons ago? And who is the mysterious maker of all these things?

How has the onslaught of biodata in the Genome Omnibus Database deluged the systems of the Genzopolis? While there's an abundance of data available on the pod about navigating the stars or lowering the rate of metabolism, there's not much information about why or how she should live. The migrant Emily sighs as she gazes out the window into deep space, then shivers a bit as her metabolism slows in response to her gauge for homeostasis, a modified thyroid remotely controlled by the Genome Omnibus Database.

Drifting to sleep, this migrant Emily imagines there's an octopus flying at lightspeed near a black hole, motion sick from zooming so fast at the event horizon. Vertigo in proximity to the vortex: A zillion nanoseconds worse than hurtling across the galaxy in a pod. The octopus, alas, carries no gingermint lozenges or acupressure bands to mitigate the waves of nausea. On the shores of the Genzopolis, the modified kelp forests give off an aroma like roses and gasoline, breeding microorganisms who clean up biohazards. Due to greenhouse gases and thinning ozone, brushfires also rage in the world, regardless of the rising sea levels; beloved horses—the stallions, mustangs, and thoroughbreds—are freed from their stables and pastures before the fires reach this side of the foothills. Emily's shire-bred horses at midnight, restless with fear, whinny as the brushfires destroy houses, jump creeks, and even freeways. The terrified horses run, wild-eyed and quaking with fright, into canyons and arroyos where no one will ever see them again. In the indigo heart of the night, the

whinnying horses run with wolves and coyotes, three species forgetting they were once foes in the wilderness as they flee a common adversary, the fire and famine.

Does this migrant Emily know how the first edition loved horses?

The wildest midnights, not horses, she recalls vaguely as her organic microlexicon kicks in for a split second, flashing across her brain like magnified images of words illuminated on film. Emily lowers her chin as her metabolism decreases to a point beyond sleep, but rather, hibernation for distant space flights. As she drifts into the netherworld, she faintly recalls the horses, the wild horses, the sleek, reckless horses. Bathed in a subtle fragrance of rhododendrons, descending a forest of hydrogen molecules, escaping the scissors of stardust editors, the maker's fingerprints shine softly, holding the universe together with a hum. The horses sprout wings, fly over the sea of lost letters; with hooves reflecting direct sunlight, the horses circle back to the breathless horizon and run unfettered with the wolves and coyotes, merging with the dawn: horse, wolf, coyote as kindred. In a lagoon, a glowing fog of words glides inside a flying octopus, a microlexicon she cannot utter aloud because she is mute. In meditative silence, she recites words in reverse alphabetical order to calm herself: zeppelin, yo-yo, key, door, applewood. The orchards of blushing apples, and the light flung through the trees like her young sister's laughter. Why say applewood and not apple? What is biologically special about applewood, anyhow? Is it applewood smoked gouda, applewood cheddar, applewood bacon, or applewood smoke itself, none which attracts me? Does it matter that anagrams for applewood include dapple woo, awe pod lop, and paw poodle? Emily's thoughts, caught up in an echo chamber of syllables, cannot stop in mid-flight, like a flying octopus.

Where did the flying octopus go? Shuttled into those black holes the size of lotus seeds cradled inside lotus pods?

Once inside a black hole, the octopus never comes back out again, at least, not to a typical citizen's eye on this side of the universe.

Or is shuttle too gentle a verb? Shunted, rather.

On the other side of the universe, migrant caravans arrive in the night to transport the genetic refugees inland, high up into the mountains, where they're afflicted with vertigo from ozone. With hypothetical parentheses enclosing my aerated zone of ideaphoria, I muse, if it isn't vertigo from traveling at the speed of light, then it's dizziness from altitude. This millennium is not distinguished by existential nausea, however, as vertigo characterized aspects of modernism, as well. With a stench of rotting effluvia, ruined coastal cities lie underwater with tides driven up more than usual, even for a full moon. The citizens wonder, how can they mitigate the damaging effects of the fires and the flood? Will we see more of these aberrant tides? In other words, will these floods no longer be abnormal, out of range? After doffing their felt hats and mackinaws to don inflatable tubes, the citizens swim in the squares where doves used to flock, now driven away by gulls. The flesh factories are flooded to their garrets while incubators, hoods, centrifuges, and orange fishermen's polymer waders bob in the marshy water.

In the Genzopolis, at the luxury underwater spas of ancient hydrotherapy galore, those centuries-old aquarium ballrooms of faux splendor, doubly kitsch, sadly flooded, short-circuited, inoperable. The water alarms, sounding off all day long, had to be disabled; the marquees and gondolas of data, ruined by the leaking water tunnels. Seawater drowned the genetic baptistery, mingling the marina animals with mineral drops of designer-gene creatures, thanks to our lady of the starfish of the sea. The ocean's rough saline caress gradually dissolved the calcium carbonate in weathered marble baths, the flexible reed footbridges from one hydropod to another for

sleep, the polyvinyl water piazza and its plexiglass clock tower, everything deluged like a city of glass submarines. Bell-shaped jellyfish with altered gullets—pouches enlarged to hold more fish, more food—circled hungrily, dissolving the glittery sardines at the foundation of the basilica. In due course of time, the underwater basilica of ballrooms will cease standing. For now, it is a dimming thread of diode light among millions of lights.

A monster wave, the tsunami, draws up its towering curl, a frothing veil of fish and squid mud, exposing the wriggling transparencies of the sea. It recedes far beyond the reach of the horizon, than the gray shapes of islands in the distance. In a moment, it rushes back with a force of freight trains in the night, a torrent of water shoving rubbish and uprooted trees and the refuse of the world far inland where no one can flee the tsunami fast enough. Who's in control of this, the maker's hand in the unedited wilderness? The long-armed cephalopods exchanging thin envelopes of genetic resources in their mating rituals? The paper nautilus who morphs into the koromodako unfolding its enormous cloth to swallow maritime vessels and their helpless passengers? The tectonic shifts of continental plates under the Genzopolis with the energy of atomic bombs detonating, fathoms deep? The buzzing editors on the omnibus are baffled by the failure to predict and pinpoint catastrophes by their seismographs, whose baseline microseisms never budged. Not every tsunami is triggered by tectonics, texts one of the stardust editors to the seahorse-eyed gene generalist who runs the omnibus. Undersea avalanches might cause them, too, or dangerous cliffs sloughing into offshore waters.

The citizens of the Genzopolis mobilize their domestic resources inland to the mountains and intralpine valleys, past the watery grave of swollen seas. Those who dwell in pods on the impoverished coastline cannot summon the resources to

move: no sky rails, no migrant caravans, no camels modified with bovine genes for enriched milk and cheetah sequences for speed. On the steppes of a high-altitude desert, my skin barely moistened by the marine fog of rising oceans, I dream of visiting an apothecary of eons ago, a portable shop of fragrances dispensing aromatic *materia medica,* remedies from the old history of pharmacy, to those citizens afflicted with ailments without a diagnosable cause like nausea, insomnia, or generalized anxiety. Those who choose not to opt for gene therapy use other options from the apothecary's delicious essences and soothing herbs, an archive of tinctures, extracts, and healing balms like pine salve or eucalyptus wax. I hover deftly in a room of iodine-hued bottles with glycerin-wet eyedroppers and hand-blown flasks of amber oil giving off the aroma of clary sage and chamomile flowers, tea roses and saffron, with cilantro for vertigo, foxglove for palsy and heart palpitations, and camphor salve to zap a post-nasal sinus drip for a good night's sleep.

Parenthetical sinuses, I mean, since I have neither para-nasal nor maxillary, ethmoid, sphenoid, or frontal sinuses; no nostrils, naris, or nasal polyps, either. The original Emily on the right side of the universe suffered consumptive symptoms for two years, I assume sinus issues, for which her physician administered a remedy dissolved in a glycerine solvent. Arsenic, I muse, or maybe opium. I guess this cure was designed before germs were fully understood, before the isolation of penicillin and other antibiotics. Most likely, the subsequent Emilys were genetically modified to resist active and latent forms of tuberculosis, so they encountered no life-threatening illnesses caused by microbes. This old nasty pathogen, ironically, was eradicated by bioengineered viruses targeting aerobic myobacteria.

This is how leprosy was wiped out, too, according to my microlexicon.

# LOVE CHRONICLES OF THE OCTOPODES

If I were an Emily of the diaspora, one who earned a salary adequate enough to spend at an apothecary of diverse fragrances, I'd especially love to buy almond oil as a base for tea tree extract mingled with wintergreen for the bottoms of the feet to stave off rhinoviruses—no idea what the soles of feet have to do with the common cold, but this remedy works wonders, allegedly—alongside coconut oil blended with bergamot and cassia bark for the thighs, attar of roses with sandalwood and geranium on the calves. Alas, I don't have feet; I offer a messy profusion of purple arms with chemoreceptors for tasting. What's an octopus to do in a far-flung sensorium of fragrance but twirl her body, a protean gown of bliss thanks to a thousand vials of aroma, of tear-shaped coriander seeds and cardamom pods, of reddish mad honey sealed in biodegradable straws the length of any Emily's index finger, of camphor and beeswax, not to mention the joy of pots with fitted lids, and bowls with spouts? I savor every dimension of flavor and texture with relish, siphoning essential oils mingled with squid ink.

While tasting the apothecary's psychoactive delights, in my mind's octoeye, juvenile octopuses bloom in fringed bells as paralarvae, the delicate baby octopuses drifting at the vaporous mercies of the imagination. In this dream, I'm an aquamarine mermaid named Emily who ventures from the apothecary into the sea and doesn't fall in love. Instead, it's the fairy tale of a little mermaid told in reverse, in other words, an upside-down world on the wrong side of the universe. This unyielding Emily, a tough bachelorette mermaid, refuses to dance on knifing legs in exchange for attention from a human; she sees unrequited love at the end of the tunnel. Truth be told, on a side note, the original mermaid tale has always irritated me. Frankly, I harbor no ill will against mermaids; rather, I'm annoyed the little mermaid fell in love with a human prince in the first place, obviously an accident. A princely irrelevance,

I correct myself, which isn't quite the same as an accident; he isn't known to harbor rogue genes, only royal-blue blood in the sense of aristocracy. As a mermaid named Emily, I'd find this intolerably deficient in the manner of the laws of inheritance: social prestige aside, aristocracy is a sign of inbreeding.

Here's the familiar saga with an octopodean twist for Emily's good measure.

Once upon a time, on the other side of the universe, a mermaid better known as a wise octopus never falls in love with a prince, never drinks a potion or grows two slender legs like shallots; in this revision of the tale, she refuses to dance on knives, or even to dance, period. Dancing on knifing legs, how horridly human. I already have legs, besides, she muses. Why would a little mermaid dance on sharpened knives to attract a man who cares not a whit for her and who erroneously believes another woman saved him from drowning? The original fairy tale doesn't give the mermaid a fair shake, so to speak. There's another woman, maybe a human copy waiting in the wings, or an android who did nothing but allow her mistaken identity as a human in disguise. Fortunately, Emily the mermaid is actually an octopus who's smarter than any mermaid who wishes to acquire human legs, or who falls in love without getting to know a man in the first place.

The wise octopus knows the end of the tale, so when she sees the leggy man drowning, she swiftly drags her tailfin underwater and swims away with all the might of her hydrostatic muscles and nine brains. Flee, flee. A sophist in matters of the heart, far away from princely princedoms, the octopus bathes contentedly in the sea, a type of hydrotherapy she uses to calm the neural storms in her nine brains, and floats with jellyfish who tease her for having an imaginary friend like a mermaid. The octopus protests, she's real, and her name is Emily. Don't you see her lovely tailfin? A vampire squid darts away as if the octopus is crazy, ejecting a smoky cloud of ink toward

her melonhead. Unlike mermaids, the cephalopods don't have any luxuriant hair to cut in exchange for a knife to backstab the human prince; they don't yearn for romantic love. As mollusks, they're bald as cantaloupes yet beautiful in their own cephalopod way of phenotypic expression, and wouldn't give the skin off their backs for a human.

For this modified version of the tale, there's no man who jilted the mermaid. None of the iridescent scales on her tailfin morph into squamous cells for skin; she never throws away a knife or flings herself into the waves. No knife, no blade. The mermaid won't change into sea foam, and the prince, who is ultimately in love with himself, will never know what he missed. The egotistical prince is a human jerk, so he'll marry a human waiting in the wings, not a mermaid with an octopus sidekick, certainly not an accidental one. Biogenetic ignorance is bliss on all counts. A denizen of the deep, the jilted octopus bathes among seahorses, turtles, and undersea anenome in the most palatial turquoise room in the world, far from the allure of fairy tales that make girls desire illusory happy endings and honeymoons and all such nonsense. The octopus is content to roll into a ball with her papillae poking up in pips all over her mantle, mimicking an innocuous rock on the seabed.

This is the art of being an octopus named Emily.

In a luxurious octopus garden, albeit one missing abalone staircases and dangling chandeliers, without inlaid mother-of-pearl bathtubs and goblets of moondrop and sapphire grapes, using siphon-powered water propulsion to jet through the largest turquoise room in the world, the octopus doesn't wonder what it'd be like to marry a prince, but rather, if she had a dazzling voice and could sing coloratura like an opera diva, with the full tonal range and qualities of a human voice. Bel canto? Mezzo-soprano? The artfully executed nonchalance of a sprezzatura? Whistle register past the range of our hearing? A pop star diva with highlighted, finger-waved hair? The

soprano whose voice cuts through orchestral strings? The one with bouquets of star-gazer lilies and cabbage roses overflowing from alabaster vases in her dressing room, who insists on ordering rose-petal drop scones glazed with mad honey, then cups of ginger-flavored turmeric tea for gargling? Why doesn't she ask for a cherry cola, or fizzy champagne in fluted glasses, or bottles of sparkling wine? Why does she insist on possessing so many hearts at once, slaughtered with shellfish knives on a tray of tea cups; who is she, an octopus or a malevolent queen of hearts, each one shot through by poison-tipped barbs like the stinging nematocysts of polyps?

In this turquoise room, the octopus drifts to a portal left ajar, draped with ruffled seaweed, and pushes it open with her melonhead. At first glance, she sees nothing but oceanic, pelagic darkness, the delicious rain of organic matter like a bath of undersea bouillabaisse. As her rectangular pupils adjust to the gloom, the octopus extends a quartet of arms to explore the walls. Inching slowly along the wainscoting at the bottom of the hall, she discovers herself in a basement vault burgeoning with chromosome fragments and lost gene sequences like rosaries of genetic ephemera, a dead letter office of yesteryear overshadowed by the murkiness of a way station for migrants and refugees in days of yore, those bony catacombs which flooded with rising seas in the designer-gene boroughs of the Genzopolis. Sprinkled by undersea rain, the vault of nucleotides overflows with chains of thymine double-bonded to adenine, and guanine triple-bonded to cytosine spilling out of disintegrating genetic material.

In this basement vault of the sea, biomolecules sway in twisted, ropy tresses the way sumptuous dry-cured sausages or onions might adorn a delicatessen window. In another universe, pluripotent cells and polymerase chain reactions once yielded designer-gene fauna and flora: oneiromantic to a degree, the octopus named Emily dreams within a dream of

lost letters spanning the ages. The unraveled chromosomes go back through the years, never finding their way to the recipients; misplaced base pairs were stored by the invisible hands of time behind this secret door: homozygous or heterozygous alleles, genes for green or hazel or brown eyes, dominant or recessive phenotypic expression, the molecular alphabet of our biogenetics spelled out in base pairs. What else could be found there, wonders the octopus without a question mark, only a dangling participle swinging open like a hatch.

Whom do I ask for instructions?

The letters in this nocturnal dreamscape of gene sequences glitter inside the room, a jambalaya of biomolecular information: in sum, a lush garden wholly of discarded nucleotides, a biogenetic compost of chromosome fragments, the lost letters of recombined legacies of inheritance inscribed in base pairs. Gingerly, the octopus probes and suctions to taste the genetic material with her arms while her beak nibbles the sea-marinated flavor of rogue sequences mingled with metallic specks of ancient stardust. She savors the bloody tang of iron oxide rust, the briny solution of iodized salt, and the smoky sepia not unlike her own ink fringed by the benthos of the deep. The other Emily, on the right side of the universe, dips her aching feet in steaming bath of mineral salts imported from a saline spring overseas, then lowers her knees into the tub, sighing with contentment. Emily doesn't realize a lock of her hair, tucked like a softer edition of a chestnut burr in a folded letter, could yield scores upon scores of biogenetic copies populating the universe with her likeness in diverse permutations of shyness and candor, of rebellion and reclusiveness, the polar opposites yoked together in a recombined splendor of paradox and beauty.

As an octopus without an arsenal of wordsmiths at my disposal, I don't mind using Emily as a loaned nickname. I often wonder, though, what if I inherited a real name instead

of a moniker, a unique and proper family surname, not a ninety-digit alphanumeric serial code? Say, a pretty name like variolation although it means small pox inoculation, or a poetic name like phosphorescence, even if it reminds me of algal tides. Or how about a given name like Ayesha because it sounds lovely and means life or alive, and Beatrix for voyager or blessedness, Candor for the sake of honesty, Dora as a moniker for Theodora, Elaine after a neighbor who lived down the street whose daughter was a comedian, Frieda after a psychoanalyst, Gertie as a nickname for Gertrude, Hilda after the one whose last name was Doolittle but went by her initials, Indigo after the vivid color in the fields, Jasmine for night-blooming jessamines, Karen for the crazed and feckless one named Karen, Lois for someone's cousin twice removed, Mei-mei for the daughter of a female mathematician who became a poet, Naomi for the mother of Ruth, Odile for the black swan in a ballet, Phoebe for the chirp of a little bird, Queen for the last name of a woman as her first name so she is styled doubly royal as Queen-Queen, Ruth for the aforesaid daughter-in-law of Naomi, Sakiya for the loveliest cherry blossoms, Trayi for the intellect, Udaya for a beautiful sunrise, Vanita for gracefulness or Vanna for golden, Wafaa for loyalty and faithfulness, Xiaomei for a little sister, Yasmin as a variant of Jasmine or vice versa in otherwise unrelated languages, and Zhenzhen for jewel alongside Zhu for bamboo.

A for adenine, C for cytosine, G for guanine, T for thymine, the nucleobases of nucleic acid whose base pairs rotate like crystal steps on a winding molecular staircase, illuminating names recalled from the sea of lost letters: Azucena for a lily, then Aadhya, Adrienne, Allison, Anhwei, Anna, Annemarie, Amelia, Amity, Augusta, Ava, Azalea. Appearing on the pages of songs without words: Yazmin, Yuliana, Yesenia, Ysabel, Yusra, Yvette. The brightness of a moonbeam doesn't render the text legibly to an unaided eye, and nothing of their

muted concerns surfaces in the night. Zaalia, Zabella, Zadie, Zoey, and Zuri. Who are we, and where do we come from? The octopus swims upward for a gulp of air, crying without weeping or vice versa for the lost letters because she doesn't have tear ducts; while crying without a voice, her mantle's vascular muscles morph into the shoulders of a woman who drops the letters, her long hair flowering around her head in a hybrid of seaweed and hanging wisteria fragrant by the ocean in a summer dusk.

I wake. This was not a dream, was it? Who is this elusive Emily?

Let's face it. I'm still an octopus marooned on a lagoon. Base-pair letters of inheritance blow gently through the window with a fragrance of lilacs, those lost codes which can't be revised further unless stardust editors on the other side of the universe tinker with their nucleic alphabets—or else irraddiate them with ultraviolet light, and then, only if fluorescent markers are used for tagging. Murky dominant and recessive traits, mislaid molecular letters of unchronicled love, the maker's vestigial fingerprints reside in the codes, even the altered ones: As for the missing valentines of the unrequited, those letters of disinheritance and inheritance, only the maker can read the archives of heartache, of those whose damaged molecular alchemy exists in limbo. The maker inscribed these genetic codes as love letters of the creator to the created. The maker loves the accidentals, yes and yes, the disenfranchised and downtrodden, perhaps more so than the designer-gene citizens of their own vanity fair. Yet I turn bilious green with a hint of chartreuse and pistachio not so much with sadness but with envy; I suspect myself of exhibiting a choleric humour although I lack a gallbladder. I shall never aspire to perfection.

As a perpetual octopus, why am I so petty? This life is not so bad, after all. Penning an octopodean chronicle of the unrequited with the midnight inkings of a siphon means

weaving colorful fabulae with variations in modes of storytelling; though bioexiled, I am a miniature maker in the universal maker's hand. Those lost letters in the sea are maps of nostalgia telling us, even in their errors, what might have surpassed in a designer-gene world without the rueful and the restless, those who thought they had oodles of time to live out their wishes and dreams without regrets. This ocean of phosphorescence and toxic algal blooms—of damaged chromosomes and deleted phenotypes with other genetic artifacts which nobody has rounded up in ghost fishing nets to jettison into the exosphere as space garbage—this sea of lost letters is a room of base pairs frozen in time, an immoveable feast without verbs. With slipshod drippings, I pen these lines with my siphon.

> This ocean of high tides and toxic algal blooms,
> of rusting typewriters and dictographs and telegrams
> and other vintage artifacts, this sea of lost letters
> is a turquoise room, an immovable feast without verbs.
> In sum, is this a biochronicle of octopodean love,
> or is it a testament to the unrequited?

As a modified octopus, I don't harbor any bitter regrets about missing out on bioinfusion bonanzas, bimonthly infusions of biomolecules, or even bionic boyfriends. I don't remember a childhood because I didn't have one. I was edited directly in the bowels of a flesh factory under the surveillance of the chief generalist of the genome omnibus. Maybe I don't need an education; perhaps the wisdom and knowledge of the universe were inscribed directly into my genes. Never ate cake dolloped with berries and cream as a girl named Emily, never lost a tooth nor received tooth-fairy cash under my pillow, never had tonsils removed surgically, nor felt the sedative effects of chamomile tea in my nervous system. I had no adolescence as a teenager named Emily, and I don't mind. Those are pipe dreams, trifling wishes for what could've been. In other

words, the asteroid turf is always greener on the other side of the universe. My rude awakening was recognizing, in a stark moment of self-reckoning, I was an octopus. I am, I mean: I am what I am, an octopus in a curious palindrome where supotco is octopus spelled backwards and means nothing at all, a sup of the octopodean in an odd portmanteau with the prefix, otco, the obscure acronym of an octopus transmigration cooperative.

From the aforesaid jolt of awakening onward, I've never forgotten. I could nibble on a fig biscuit and sip rooibos tea from a jar, yet I'd never cease to be cognizant of how the stardust editors on the other side of the universe dealt with my fate when they tagged me as a rogue. Am I the better for this moment of reckoning? Do I wax sappy and romantic or call it an epiphany? Or a lightbulb, so to speak? Of course the truth is preferable to a lie, but it's froth and bubbles on sea foam, moot for an octopus. No one cares whether I carry a moral compass, no one expects me to carry one at all times, and no one is curious to know whether a sparkling, molecular language of love is coded as base pairs in my genome.

Do I sound ungrateful? Believe me, I do practice gratitude.

On the other side of the universe is a woman named Emily whose life I could've lived. Let's say, in a new variation of the tale, this Emily is a noir poet whose nape is adorned by an opera-length necklace of shining black pearls, a doubled rope of grace and sophistication. It's longer than a collar, a matinee, a princess, or a choker necklace. The black pearls make a stunning effect with her lustrous, dark eyes, more like poured cola than sherry in a glass, as the original Emily once wrote. As aforesaid, she prefers to take baths in her cypress tub with the pearls on. Why black pearls, I ask, more of a declaration than a question. A noir poet who doesn't need to

provide responses to frivolous questions, this Emily doesn't answer immediately.

Black pearls to wear just so, she whispers, in a noir tone for an Emily who writes darkling poems in the wee hours of the night by the flame of a candle. Later, she adds in lowered tones, I wear them because the freshwater black pearls are irradiated by gamma rays in order to attain their hue, reminding me of the black rain which fell after the tsunami. Beauty in shadows, she continues, triumphs over death. Freshwater black pearls aren't organically black—dyed, rather—yet they're beautiful and elegant, all the same. Saltwater black pearls arise organically in the wilderness, original and unedited as rambling strawberry vines or kelp forests.

I've compiled a list of questions for this Emily on the other side of the universe.

Why are the pearls black?
Irradiated or dyed, she says.
No, the ones in the sea.
The maker said yes for those.
Do you believe in the maker?
I do. A wilderness once existed.
An unbounded wilderness?
No, an unedited wilderness.
Wilderness is no longer wild.
Do you mean due to editing?
Yes, no longer a wilderness.
Why live on the other side?
The editors bioexiled me.
How is it? Are you cold?
No, it's paradise out here.

Poetry is paradise on fire, I'd add, while the noir Emily would pause before replying, yes, with a barely audible sigh. You're a poet, I'd repeat in a small voice inside my head like

a petulant child. A kookaburra bird chuckling. A flaming phoenix of cinnamyl aldehyde. It burns like a bubbling lava lake. Don't you know the world is on fire with poetry? If not, why? In spite of everything, our drowned basilicas and flooded factories, don't you know outer space is hotter than a zillion hearths, than a spray of ash from a brushfire, or the flaming glory-hole of a furnace? More piquant and spicy than licorice notes of a pink lemon, than yellow-skinned dwarf suns? How about the pulp sloughed then daubed with honey bathed in pink quartz marmalade, wherein the licorice notes mingle with the tartness of pink pulp, the marmalade afire with citrus and spice at once? Waves of mad honey aflame, sweet clouds of smoke wafting in and out of the fragrant nostrils of the universe, puffing molecules of celestial perfume?

FINALLY, WITH A SIGH, THE NOIR EMILY RESPONDS BY tucking a strand of her dark hair behind an ear, her crooked arm—sleeved in black charmeuse—casting a V in the wavering shadows. The exosphere of the Genzopolis, outer space, is very cold, she proffers in a low, intimate voice, her fingers angled as if balancing an invisible cigarette holder. Everybody knows it. It's colder than the ice caps at the bottom of the world, than frigid atoms of liquid hydrogen. Due to global warming, icebergs the size of financial districts are melting, and nobody can stop the swollen seas from rising. Despite the greenhouse gases on this planet, however, this is a localized phenomenon, as the universe still remains the coldest place of all. Nobody can survive out there in a birthday suit with a bouquet of lilies. Outer space is colder than the liquid nitrogen used for cryogenics, which freezes flowers, skin warts, and the skin itself.

You're a poet, I'd say again.
Silence.
Don't you know the universe is on fire?
Silence.

Forgive me for questioning this noir Emily in a dogged manner, but I didn't ask to materialize on the other side of the universe, and I'm bubbling with curiosity. Through the fragrance of the black holes, I believe, the warp and weft of our fabricated genes find an elusive home in the very act of vanishing. It's the paradox of a bioexile. Popping pomegranate pips and succotash balderdash hash are my favorite expletives. I speculate about life as any garden-variety Emily on the other side of the universe, lifeforms of designer genes or not. Why was this ink sac designed if I don't have enemies to stupefy or stun with smoky clouds of ink? Paradise is stink-proof and antagonist-free, so I don't have any foes. Out of the notes piled on my reading nook is a fragment of my ballad, a longish octopodean siesta, an afternoon nap not to be confused with a sestina, a poem of six stanzas with six lines each plus a three-line envoy. The first line says, paraphrased, welcome to a sea of lost letters in a room of nucleotides, their glowing monomers like black pearls and sapphires wound in double helixes. The second line says, let's see if we can decipher the aromatic fragments of the universe through the chemoreceptors on our supersensory arms. However, I've never composed a ballad before, and I don't write in closed forms. I get stuck. The limitations of meter, rhyme, and one-word repetitions befuddle me. I write in free verse instead. Even in free verse, however, I'm dazzled by the negative space of line breaks whose parallel horizons look, in sum, like a flickering reel of little fires.

If black holes are the size of pins where angels dance,
portals in motion like revolving doors or elevators,
imagine how stanzas might illumine the halls of time—

a starry night of words in a flock of carbonized dots
versed in bright alphabets of eternity. Why does poetry
endure in seasons of love and loss, promising forms
of feathered plumes and flames? Love is blind, after all.
We say the opposite of what we mean, yet in spaces
between the words, our hearts grasp what is true.
Even the octopus in a lair feels the world chime,
ringing in the ganglia of nine marvelous brains—
This lyric isn't a ballad, yet it dances and sings.

## 5 | Takotsubo or Broken-Heart Syndrome

In which we learn about octopus jar syndrome, a consequence of heartbreak. The magistrate of genes and his oppressive regime. A scriptorium. On autologophagy or eating one's own words. On wordsmiths and worker bees.

## TAKOTSUBO OR BROKEN-HEART SYNDROME

O f course, I don't wish to appear impish or rude, but I do wonder, from time to time, what life could've been like if I weren't chucked into a black hole, and if I'd stayed on the right side of the universe instead of vanishing. There's no ombudsman for the omnibus, and I don't have an advocate or a union, either. What would I do for a living as an atypical octopus in a Genzopolis? How would I navigate the bizarre codes of the latter days? Would I serve as a genetic apprentice on the omnibus, a coveted entry-level position for the upwardly mobile? Would I train as a sous chef in a bistro by an airborne bed-and-breakfast, slinging oyster shots and raw sea urchins, the latter whose spines jab the air like knitting needles? I'm not talking about a hypothetical life as a woman named Emily on the right side of the universe, but rather, as a self-cognizant octopus with hypercritical, overthinking proficiencies, and yes, enamored by olives.

On the right side of the universe, what if I obtained pod-schooling to earn my credentials in gene-editing, then took a battery of assessments in this field? Speaking of this matter, what's a suitable vocation for a rogue octopus, anyhow,

whose atypical lifestyle defies conventional pathways? I'm versatile, multilinear, a zig-zag fractal of forked lightning in the sky. Not wild, I'm just rogue. If revision is left up to robots wielding molecular scissors, and the proofing of their handiwork to apprentices, then is juggling spools and yo-yos in the shapes of chromosome histones any more rewarding? Shall I join a vaudeville show or hitch a ride with the circus? In other words, come see Emily the Dystopian Octopus slide across the dais! See the octopus juggle figs and clams and a box of stroopwafels! See the octopus shrink her pupils into rectangles! The octopus will now squish her melonhead into a glass jar, a true contortionist! Ladies and gentle genes, the one and only Emily who's an octopus on this side of the universe.

Ridiculous, is what I say. Who gives a jumping gene about the circus when the world has gone beserk?

Maybe I should train as a reiki stress reducer using hot, smooth stones pulled out of the desert where rivers once ran through, or learn to manage an art glass and stamp studio in a warehouse, specializing in hand-blown and fused glass techniques using eight arms. As a bioexiled rogue, I harbor no illusions that I might also end up afflicted by takotsubo, the broken-heart ailment better known as the octopus jar syndrome. This isn't to say retreating into a jar is a signpost for heartbreak; rather, navigating the rest of my days as a rogue octopus on the right side of the universe could lead, sooner if not later, to ostracism, excommunication, a shorter life span, a chronic broken heart syndrome, execution by firing squad, and maybe all of the above. Figuratively speaking, you crawl into a clay jar known as a takotsubo, tilted on its side, and disappear. This jar is analogous to a black hole of sorts, really. In this opening about the size of an avocado, a happy clam, or even a fist, you vanish into the jar's mouth, never to emerge again unless a human hand tips the jar, and you slide out. You sit on your eight arms in the darkness, waiting to see what

your fate will be. Will you be forgotten? Will you be set free if the other octopus jars trapped enough victims overnight? Will you be poured out of the jar to meet your tenderized fate as a delicacy? It's an old-fashioned octopus trap which the ancient fishermen would use in the bay to trap cephalopods.

Wriggling while you're waiting in darkness, you bite the flesh of your arms with anxiety. The fishermen reach into the jar and lift you out, taking you to meet a fate worse than bioexile. On the pier or at a seafood bistro, you'd be sliced into segments while alive and tenderized by a steel mallet or trussed up on strings to dry in the sun, a delicacy for the citizens to enjoy with gusto. This clay octopus jar, with its mouth on its side, the whole vessel shaped on a slant, lends its name, takotsubo or octopus jar, to the broken-heart syndrome afflicting women during life-threatening stress like the death of loved ones swept away by a tsunami. Engulfed by stress hormones like adrenalin, one of the ventricles develops a balloon in the shape of an octopus head. Yes, my noggin. That's what it looks like, a melonhead ballooning sideways on an autoradiograph. It's odd to see the name of this syndrome in association with my noggin. Has my thought experiment run crazily away in the cockles of the heart, an allegorical manifestation of cardiomyopathy that's all in my head? Once inside the smooth borosilicate bowels of an octopus jar, who can sashay back into the limelight alone?

Come see an octopus named Emily mull over a broken heart.

Emily, the octopus of dystopia, is unable to cry because mollusks lack tear ducts, so she crawls into a jar and tries to disappear until she meets a grisly fate. On a cheerier note, let's say I land a coveted job on the omnibus after rocking the vocational assessment with terrific scores, which cross-maps my hypercritical thinking skills across multiple genetic industries: good bread and butter jobs for an octopus named

Emily, including a professional trajectory as an apprentice on the omnibus. However, the humming stardust editors insist that I type up the minutes while they meet and talk. For one, I'm a mute octopus so I can't literally speak or take credit for my own work, even if I perform the heavy lifting behind the scenes and tidy up the stained karyotype kitchens or vacuum up the vectors on this omnibus; two, they say, flippantly, you're a scribe with a knack for verbatim accuracy and velocity. Plus you've got an ink sac in one of your body cavities—or is it tucked in the fleshy bubble you call a melonhead?

Of course, no matter what the stardust editors say, the tone of the editors is obnoxious. I pen a telepathic memo in the air explaining how I wasn't designed with vocal cords but I can ride language like a freight train, and the stardust editors reply in a buzzing chorus, you're inking and scribbling on the walls of the omnibus all night aren't you, doodling on the misty windows of the scriptorium in the wee hours, markering the digital whiteboards and chalking up the liquid crystal blackboards with sticks composed of the spines of diatoms, even defacing the magnetic green ones mounted on a galvanized steel base. Say, why don't you put your melanin-rich juices—your hyperpigmented ink-spatters the color of briquette smoke—to communal use in service of the Genzopolis? Why do you only wish to serve on giant, extraterrestrial projects like the star system migration? Why don't you speak up, you silly cephalopod?

You've got a bit of an ego for an octopus, don't you?

Dismissively, without explanation, the stardust editors in the scriptorium also insist I hush my voice although I haven't said a thing. What they say is partly true; I telepathically communicate my rambunctious thoughts and wishes by non-verbal means, in other words, other than using my multifarious mouths. A mischievous rogue of gesture and genes, a noiseless choreography of unvoiced yet willful volition: a mime of the

mutants. Meanwhile, for a cadre of robots, the stardust editors harbor a grandiose sense of entitlement and far more agency than one would expect of a posse of mannequins possessed by artificial intelligence, demanding this or that from lifeforms like me. Apparently, I'm too raucous for a cephalopod named Emily, or an organism by any other name. The hum of editors switches the topic to my workspace, indicating I occupy too many cubits in proportion to my body size. You occupy too much space on this omnibus for an octopus. Move over here, move over there, hop into the booths across from the organic latrines, the biohazard waste flushed into the gullets of the omnibus all day long, flowing out to the sewage-devouring bacteria festering in the bowels of the Genzopolis. What does this all mean, I wonder. Aren't assignments contingent upon rank in the hierarchical omnibus: the magistrate of genes and his bevy of stardust editors, then apprentices like me, and finally the smiths and bees?

The bees, the bees, the bees...

On the other side of the universe, the original Emily lowers her nose to sniff the petals of a half-budded rose, selectively cut by her sister for its spicy, chocolate perfume—sort of like black chai. Emily has no inkling that varieties of this cut flower were crossed to enlarge the colorful assortment of ornamental cultivars: wine burgundy roses bred with pansies, transgenic roses with genes inserted for rare lilac phenotypes, and so forth. In fact, the blushing roses in the family garden are genetically modified with engineering techniques like cross-pollination and bud-eye rootstock grafting which predated gene cloning, splicing, or insertion, methods in turn preceding gene editing by molecular scissors and direct inscription by genetic pens. Other than their desirableness over ruderal weeds like thistles or dandelions, Emily does not perceive these roses, genetically modified in an antique sense,

in any different light than the little roses rambling in the wilderness.

I do not take up more space than warranted although I'm the smallest in size of all the apprentices and do not work at a station or in an office, but rather, roam in higgledy-piggledy fashion from ultraviolet octagons to fluorescent octagons among the grisly pods of flesh on the omnibus. Finally, the stardust editors wrinkle their olfactory foreheads—attuned to biomolecular changes in stress hormones, i.e. cortisol and adrenaline—and carp mercilessly on me for allegedly exuding gallons of malodorous slime by the minute. This is unfair and hyperbolic; in fact, my slime doesn't give off odors any more offensive than human flatulence. I also carry around a rag to mop up excess ooze in the halls, and bathe daily to minimize body odor. One advantage of my octopodean epidermis is a dearth of sweat pores, those follicular pinpoints in human skin which make perspiring flesh intolerably fetid in sweltering weather.

Any jot of admiration for skills in recombination, transcription, and replication is quashed by my distaste for those stardust editors who work incessantly without, dare I say it, love. To regulate my emotions, I indulge in nibbling roasted seaweed snacks on the sly while roaming around the octagonal labs of the omnibus. Browsing the virtual archives of artists whose works were drowned in the flood, I acquire skills in asemic writing instead, an artful form of script without writing—it's visual and calligraphic in style, not semantic, and not arsenic—and blithely ink the octagonal walls with oodles of non-alphabetic scribble. Oh my calligraphic stars, what ecstasy. The letter o is not an o, the garlands and arcades and loop-the-loops are not anything more than fine traces of sienna dye. I love doodling in this elaborate, baroque manner, inking squiggles and flourishes of a handwritten script from an era when folks had leisure time as well as aesthetic wherewithal

to design for pleasure without inquiring whether or how the products would generate radically improved genes for the good of the species, and ultimately, the Genzopolis. I don't care a whit about designer genes. When the stardust editors ask what in the world you're doing, it's obvious they haven't any notion of what asemic writing is and assume it's graffiti, or the visible symptoms of adolescent impulses erupting with hormone surges, or indicative of aspirations to change vocations from editorial apprentice to a tattoo artist. In fact, the stardust editors don't comprehend the word, asemic, and see *arsenic*, instead.

Asemic, rhyming with arsenic, wasn't programmed into their microlexicons.

Arsenic, the carcinogenic metalloid which damages vital organs and lingers in seafood like me, isn't at all what I'm spelling out. The stardust editors buzz and murmur, chelation therapy only draws out a fraction of the toxic metals in your blood. A. Are you trying to poison us with arsenic? B. By the way, don't you know we're robots, and we don't respond to ingested poisons? C. Consequently, we're designed without living tissue; we're invincible to organ failure, paralysis of the nervous system, and internal bleeding. I ignore their noxious tones by turning my back and facing the wall, where my asemic doodling covers the space with loop-de-loops, garlands, and curlicues of water-based ink, but do not suffice as minutes. This is unacceptable, I know, and passive aggressive, besides. What's a flabbergasted, atypical octopus to do?

The stardust editors in the scriptorium can't decipher any of my scripts, holding each code up to the light-emitting diodes of the omnibus and squinting carefully. What they should declare, but never do, is congratulations, dear octopus, we're promoting you because you're the only one on this omnibus who understands how to replicate esoteric scripts which nobody else can transcribe, and nobody wants to deal with

you, besides. Your blend of orneriness, egotism, and annoying happy-go-luckiness, as well as your warehouse of arcane knowledge has made you an indispensable stakeholder on this omnibus. In your dual roles as a wordsmith and a worker bee, you ought to be grateful we haven't shipped you off to shotgun sequencing.

A wordsmith and worker bee, a smithing bee?

Shotgun sequencing of DNA began with an infectious copy of the cauliflower mosaic virus. It was a precursor technique to full genome mapping. As an octopus, I reject the labels of smith and bee, most definitely any association with infectious copies, never mind cauliflower viruses. I regard myself not as a bag of bioengineered mistakes, but as an artist with volition who emerged out of adverse circumstances, more so than a wordsmith or a worker bee, who are merely cogs in the Genome Omnibus Database, widgets distinct from lifeforms like me. Without an audible voice and only a salvo of telepathic memos at my disposal, I say nothing to the editors, who decide it's not worth the effort to fire me, in any case.

Yes, even now, I wish to care for those biomolecular robots—stardust anchored to a soft substrate of altered protoplasm—who serve out monotonous days performing tedious, mechanical tasks like the classic polymerase chain reaction to copy DNA segments, or else base-pair incision and revision. The seahorse-eyed magistrate of genes reads my neural oscillations and admonishes me, whispering like a vintage steam engine under his breath, the smiths and bees are not your pets or your flowers, and this omnibus is not your garden. In fact, the omnibus is less effective than it could be due to absenteeism. Yes, the black holes served as our scapegoats. Take, for instance, the molecular wordsmith who claimed to fall through a microscopic hole in the floor of the omnibus and couldn't come to work for the rest of the year. I asked,

how did you survive the supermassive forces near a singularity? How did you survive the intense gravitational field? Did you document your spacetime travel on the company's dime using a quantum punchcard? Are you a quark of the hadrons? If so, what flavor are you?

The magistrate of genes persists in his line of questioning, conjecturing aloud while drawing invisible fractals in the air with his fingers. Next, did you capture any satellite images of your unexpected field excursion, and if not, how in the world were you able to send me a meticulously wordsmithed memorandum about your mishap on a distant satellite moon which smothered your naris with rocket-fuel aerosols so corrosive, you nearly asphyxiated? Is this a hologram, too? Am I so gullible as to believe these lies? Have you outgassed the Genzopolis, my darling android?

Magistrate of genes, wheezes the molecular wordsmith, in a tone of voice like a wind-up toy winding down. I mean, yes sir. Yes, if I may say so, grand magistrate of genes, thanks to our blighted Genzopolis, I've endured toxic mutagenesis which triggers flashes of light and hallucinations of flying octopuses. Obviously, the sequences inserted to mitigate this condition went haywire, or maybe their expression was muted due to the activity of my hereditary genes. My tooth enamel is soft as a fish scale, by the way. Can we design a treatment to remedy this, even if we must resort to old-fashioned gene therapy? I'm prone to dental caries, and I can't afford the bioglass veneers. Our gene-editing technology is still experimental, isn't it? Would you consider it a fuzzy or a hard science? Are you one of those molecular free radicals who choose to use the word, innovative, instead of experimental? Do you believe experimentation implies a potential for failure or inferiority, as opposed to innovation?

At gene-and-gas galas—sponsored by the omnibus to save our Genzopolis from imploding with clouds of greenhouse

methane—designer-gene guests who circulate at the bioinfusion balls and bonzanzas routinely ask, why don't you like
hors d'oeuvres, our modified amuse-bouche? Why not snap
up these bamboo skewers of genetically altered squid kebobs?
You're an octopus, after all. Be a cephalopod. Let's see you
engage in autophagy, why don't you. Repulsed, I try not to
eat any sentient lifeform, although I admittedly snack on garlicky olives and less frequently papaya as a rare treat, seared
papaya on black jasmine rice drizzled with ponzu sauce and
garnished with scallions, or chopped papaya topped by sliced
kohlrabi and radish, or slabs of glistening papaya with the
translucency of rose quartz. In the wilderness, my kindred are
known to commit cannibalism, devouring each other dead
or alive, but I'm more apt to commit autologophagy—eating
one's own words—than autophagy, eating oneself. I'm asked
repeatedly by the ladies and gentle genes, aren't you prone
to cannibalism? I continue, no, quite the opposite, no more
than a chin-high flower like a seaside daisy bite into a stalk
of celery. Would a blooming beach aster of the coastal bluffs
commit such an atrocity? Now I suppose we're getting into
transgenic territory if we're comparing ourselves to flowers,
aren't we, if hummingbird sage and stalks of longwood blue
are the focus of our metaphorical impulses?

While the ignoramus windbags flap their jaws at the
gala, down the hall, I calmly lift my siphon and remove the
air in the walk-in coat closet attached to the grand ballroom as
if it were a bell jar, designing a near-vacuum, and lurk in the
gloaming. To my annoyance, the windbags survive the vacuum anyhow, sauntering in with eyes open and mouths agape,
then exiting unscathed with coats over the arm. Pea coats,
polyester dress coats, blazers and sports coats in motley colors.

Watching the windbags enter and exit the technicolor closet of dream coats, I don't know whether it's due to deep-diving or some other survival skill like circular breathing through the nose, using the mouth and cheeks as bellows. I can hold my breath for a duration of time, enough for me enter and exit a coat closet, due to my phenotypic expression as an octopus. However, as an altered cephalopod of slightly above-average intelligence, I'm still vulnerable to subliminal suggestion and will need to come out for air, regardless, at which point the head of the one of the windbags suddenly explodes—pish!—in a splatter of brains while his body walks nonchalantly down the hall to the latrine, as if to protest, we are not a flesh factory. We are an omnibus, so don't treat your stakeholders like cogs in a widget machine. Fine with me, I conclude in a huff. You can believe whatever you want, but I won't clean up the gray matter sticking to the walls. Instead, I sashay across the hall to crash another gala, one hosted by the stardust editors to celebrate the star system migration for which I designed a blueprint.

The magistrate of genes intones, before the winter solstice, we plan to migrate designer-gene citizens from one star system—namely, this one—to another, thereby ensuring the sustainability of the Genzopolis in light of the dire forecasts about global warming and overpopulation. We shall reduce our population by incentivizing the star system migration for citizens who'll enjoy free and unlimited access to gene-editing for the rest of their lives, unregulated. It's not a zoo. It's a prefabricated strategic plan where gene variants of the original Emily, even an octopus like me, would readily discover their ideal audience for poetry, to say the least, never mind supportive editors.

As I sashay into the cube, the stardust editors at the omnibus party look up like click beetles with mock eyes—not glass keratoprostheses, rather, titanium plates whirling like

old-fashioned wheel rims. Ah, it's you, the errant octopus, says the gray-eyed magistrate, looking down his nose while holding a tumbler of genetically modified berry lemonade; the berries, I should explain, self-ferment to produce etha-nol. The magistrate, also known as the attorney generalist of genes, is the only one who isn't an automaton or machine. His grayish eyes are the color of dead seahorses. You've sashayed into our party in a nick of time, he hisses; you've got a knack for showing up right when we need a scribe. Here's a genetic code with a raft of errata in need of fixing. The base pairs in the last batch of gene sequences are mixed up. They need to be deleted, then repaired with the correct nucleotides, specif-ically, the four nitrogenous bases: adenine, guanine, cytosine, and thymine. We'll need those base pairs fixed no later than midnight, he adds.

If I were an auburn-haired woman named Emily, I'd shrug and turn back to my poems. My fountain pen of sepia ink awaits the blooded rush of my fingers, and the oak tree planted by my father, veiled in winter snow, dreams of emerald soon to come with spring; likewise for the cherry, apple, pear, and plum in the starry navels of blossom-end fruit. I'd love the way each orbed fruit has two ends which will never meet: stem-end, attached to the tree, and blossom-end. This Emily of orchards focuses her poem-mak-ing attention upon the mist clouding the window pane, which reminds her of the word, *oxygen*. It's as close as Emily will ever be to the hypoxia of her genetic copies in the diaspora, variants who'll move up to higher altitudes to escape the rising seas.

An octopus reeling with colors from jackfruit and ruby red grenadine, I feel a rush of mixed emotions about his request. My body is a canvas: a transparent one. I turn red, I turn green, and they know exactly what I'm feeling. While I do enjoy this work, I hate it when the magistrate talks down to me as if I'm ranked with one of the robots. My sentience isn't artificial or two-dimensional. I'm a rogue soul, not a smithing bee. Frankly, I'm both sentient

and self-cognizant, for crying out loud. Don't the editorial robots merit a shred of dignity, regardless of their omnibus status, besides? Please don't get me wrong; it's a pleasure and privilege to edit genes, and I consider it an art form. However, it's annoyingly typical of the magistrate to assume my level of genetic expertise is foundational in this field rather than technically advanced. I've known the names of the four nitrogenous bases since my pod-schooling days, for crying out loud; moreover, first and foremost, I'm not a scribe, I protest in the space of my melonhead, while the magistrate whispers: Just like your bioengineered kindred should be, aren't you. A perfectionist, too, aren't you? You're just the octopus we need for this job right now, to work alongside the smiths and bees.

You'd rather duck under the radar than execute this request from your magistrate, wouldn't you? Yes, you're an apprentice, so what I say trumps any of your opinions. Why are you changing colors, my dear octopus? Embarrassed or ashamed of your emotional transparency? Am I making you uncomfortable, dear? Are you mortified, my friend? I shake my melonhead and shrug my arms as if to say, mister, I'm not genetically edited for humility or hysteria, but rather, hilarity. You, mister, are a grotesque, disdainful to an absurd degree. Have you ever wakened on the wrong side of the universe as flora or fauna? Do you understand the profundities of a sacred and holy wilderness? As a kelp forest harnessing light for sustenance, a shred of lichen hugging a rock, shag moss, or little button mushrooms on a tree stump? Do you know what it's like to dwell on this dwindling, flooded Genzopolis as flowering fleabane, an orangutan, or a bee? I dash off telepathic memorandums in my melonhead which neither reach their intended targets nor lower my blood pressure in the long run. I'm a workaholic, that's all, to the ultimate benefit of the omnibus. The magistrate refers to me as a smith and a bee, a mere smithing bee, and all I can do is think to myself, the irises of your eyes are the color of dead seahorses.

Yes, I've indeed come to this shore, and there are no instructions.

As if on cue, the seahorse-eyed magistrate turns around to speak to stardust editors standing ramrod straight behind the citizens on the genetic council. I've noticed the magistrate relishes the word, ramifications. So, in light of the ramifications for this endangered world, let's roll out the blueprint for the star system migration with benchmarks for each stage of the journey: refueling provisions for each food pod, replenishing the oxygenating hybrid plants, nurturing pluripotent cells as organ failure and other ramifications arise, and biometric check-ups as a best practice. A stardust editor inquires: Benchmark the estimated times of delivery against what external sources or comparative references? The magistrate doesn't know; he glances at me. I feel reluctant to help out, like a shy lotus closing up her little shop of enhanced floral fragrance on a lily pad at night, and retreat into a corner of the room, where no one can see me. In my mind's octoeye, I imagine this corner of the room morphs into a vortex, a secret portal to infinity where stars fall out of the night, onto my skin. I use the filtering shadows as a form of quicksand to bury my shame. Why should I provide answers to make them look good in front of the gala guests?

The magistrate reaches under a gas hood to push a button so the oxygen jets push me up and away, jamming me in front of his long nose and chin hairs; he interrogates me about the blueprint which I designed several months ago. Is this the vocation of an octopus? Can you engineer a Genzopolis in another galaxy? Can you plant a blooming violet on the airless moon? Can you draw a labyrinth with one continuous stroke of the architect's virtual pen? And so forth, *ad nauseum*. The magistrate continues, gruffly, why should we believe you did this, et cetera? While a nervous trickle of slime collects on the floor under my eight arms, the magistrate disregards my strategic design for the star system migration, while at the same time implying any hint of miscalculations in the project are my doing. The magistrate dismisses every jot and tittle of my plan, down to the illustrations of chromosomes packed gently like berry drupelets to colonize biodomes in other star systems.

Balderdash, I think airily, in the manner of an Emily with her cotton apron on, wiping the supper dishes in a kitchen overlooking the yard. Alas, on the other side of the universe, this Emily gazes upon a patch of late light on the zoysia lawn without an inkling that a rogue octopus exists in the future, a namesake not yet inscribed in the molecular atlas of Emily's inheritance. After twilight falls, she squints at the stars in the night sky. Does she spy the outline of a giant octopus in the constellations? Is the omnivore of nocturnes flying across the celestial wheel of time?

After a swig of fluoxetine modified to harmonize more seamlessly with calibrating human moods, the magistrate of the omnibus grumbles, how long did it take you to design this, ah, little excursion? I tilt my melonhead with a puzzled look and curl up four of my arms in a shrug as if to say, what excursion, sir—I've designed a highly complex blueprint for a star system migration no one has undertaken in the short history of this fleeting, star-struck planet. We've mastered the art of teleporting to parallel universes but yet to perfect an occupation strategy for ourselves and our spawn among the stars. Every stage of the journey is engineered with precision: maximum number of citizens to transport, the degrees of lowered metabolism including body temperature, the effects on homeostasis as well as on the world's ecosystem due to the mass exodus. The magistrate says, we should run it through the citizens on the genetic council before further discussion.

Frustrated by this filibustering, I send a telepathic memo to the magistrate reminding him this doesn't need vetting by the genetic council because the citizens originated the request, and I consulted with the council at every step of the process, so they're already in the know, so to speak. Back and forth, back and forth, we pat an invisible ball of ectoplasm over an invisible volleyball net where he's always the winner because he's the magistrate of gene transcription, the kingpin of all corrected proofs. Besides, he can't hear me because I have no voice, and he'll probably only read the memo in my neural oscillations the day after tomorrow, at the earliest.

You won't be migrating.
Memo: Silence.
You're not a citizen.
Memo: Silence.
You're an octopus.
Memo: Silence.
A rogue one, besides.
Memo: Silence.
By the way, thanks for the biscuits.
Memo: Silence.
Those biscuits you brought last week.
Memo: No biscuits, sir.
Aren't you the one who makes biscuits?
Memo: No, sir.
You baked cherry biscuits for us.
Memo: I did no such thing, sir.
Raspberry scones?
Silence.
Blackberry? Mulberry? Boysenberry?
Silence.
Was it cloudberry muffins, then?
Silence.
Banana berry?
Memo: No, sir.
Haven't tasted cloudberries since boyhood.

When the magistrate returns to the gala, a flute glass of modified gooseberry blood in hand and his wattles of neck skin loose as an iguana's dewlap, I sashay down the hall to the latrine and put my siphon under the faucet's spigot, swallowing a good liter of tap. After strolling back to the octagonal room, I push open the door—pish!—and unabashedly hose down the whole posse of editors who gaze at me in shock.

On the other side of the universe, an Emily pulls a tray of hummingbird muffins out of the oven: cloudberry, tinned pineapple, and coconut in a mashed banana batter dotted by pecans. I assure you, no hummingbirds were harmed to bake these muffins, she chortles, amused by the whimsical name while reaching for a glass of tap water. This Emily, like the other ones, has no idea that I live a parallel existence where a dollop of lactose-free, galactose-reduced dairy lies outside the realm of paradise. A mashed banana isn't out of reach, however, thanks to the abundance of groves. She has no premonition that one day, on her own side of the universe, the tap water will be distilled from upcycled blue pee from hypercalcemia experiments in the flesh factories. No more artesian springs, no more sedimentary groundwater or drilled well water; no more forest cenotes or lava tubes filled with rain. Sadly, the blighted Genzopolis has lost all its potable hydrogen dioxide.

In sum, did I enjoy this roguish sojourn as an accidental octopus on the right side of the universe? Or an accidental sojourn as a rogue octopus, if I may? The easy answer is, with ellipses, not one nanosecond… this thought experiment was akin to serving as a captive in a hostile territory rife with xenophobia. However, this thought experiment, if you will, did provide a rare opportunity to appreciate the benefits of dwelling in paradise on the wrong side of the tracks, in an anthropocene manner of speaking.

Under the starry heavens of a lagoon in the octopodes, I am my own boss, and I don't have to attend any omnibus parties or the seahorse-eyed magistrate's ridiculous gene-and-gas galas, or pretend I'm wedged in a fabricated octopus get-up when everyone obviously sees my categorical liminality as an octopus. Rogue genes, greenhouse gas, and galas? With nary a whit of tearful regret, I wouldn't dare look back over my shoulder even if I had one like the original Emily. Morphing into a raspberry-colored or sea-foam green koromodako, I could open my gargantuan paper maw and guzzle every jot and tittle of this estranged generation, gulping down a square-rigged galleon of our globally heated soup with

138

it. The whole civilization of designer-gene lifeforms, the kit and kaboodle of gene-edited cannibals and their unbridled autophagy, would vanish into the squiggly recesses of my digestive system. I'll sip fizzy gingerale laced with radioactive plutonium to settle my belly after this orgy of bizarre proportions, in more ways than one, then morph into a ball of hydrogenous plasma, a starry furnace of nuclear fusion. Yet who am I, a rogue octopus, to judge the future as strange?

## 6 | Evening Arrival of the Courier

A fragment of an Emily chromosome. Mitochondrial love. Ice cream as a slice of glaciology. Letters to a non-existent daughter. On watermint and spearmint.

## Evening Arrival of the Courier

Undeniably, I don't recall ever tasting a superfruit berry, lingonberry, cloudberry, thimbleberry, or marionberry in my sojourn as an octopus named Emily. What is a marionberry, anyhow? Is it a fleshiness of drupelets, related to a flaming blackberry, crossed with tender spheres of sturgeon roe, or flying fish eggs colored with squid ink? A mix of thornless blackberry varieties, or a genetic cross between a blackberry and an olallieberry, crossed with a youngberry? What about inkberries? And the wild huckleberry by the legendary rivers and creeks of yore, when rills of fresh water crossed the face of the Genzopolis? As far as my octoeye can see, no blackberries or their hybrids—reddish tayberry, dewberry, or boysenberry—flourish on this lagoon. Is there an Emily berry on the other side of the universe? A berry of black spice cakes doused in brandy? With my arms open to a late afternoon greened by the leafy phosphorescence of banana groves, and while deep shadows lengthen towards a whiff of sea breezes, rhododendrons, and night-blooming jasmine, I detect a foreboding of senescence, an early chill in the solstice, yet it's not the onset of winter.

In anticipation of twilight, my coppery blood flows like a mineral aquifer bubbling under terraces of overhanging wisteria and lilacs, spring on an imaginary garden balcony. On the other side of the universe, I am a shy poet named Emily who brooks no fimble-famble excuses for high fire, flood, or failure, bioengineered or otherwise. In paradise, there's only pervasive acceptance of all living organisms, rogue or not, in their colorful polymorphism. Far beyond the threshold of my lair, the sun drops lower into the empyrean. A sea of lost letters opens its stanzas to diaphanous clouds of radiolaria, the little spines of their mineral bones fine as asterisks, while on the other side of the universe, nocturnal octopuses emerge like eight-limbed gnomes from their underwater dens to play.

At the risk of waxing sentimental, I don't believe I'm as young as I used to be. The muddling brain fog of age doesn't clear as quickly as it once did, as if polyester stuffing plugs up my head. I sense the ebb of blue vitality under my skin, the fading of nerve impulses and flickering reflexes. As a result of aging, I'll soon experience a loss of appetite for the olive I love, along with atrophied musculature and loosened skin folds around my myopic octoeyes. The original Emily had eye problems, too, if I recall correctly, for which she had to visit a physician in the city, a rare journey beyond her father's house in her adult years. How many years do I have left? Do I harbor a special gene for longevity, for the repair of telomeres capping the tips of my chromosomes? Can't imagine a season when I won't have a desire to consume olives, one after another, the way citizens enjoy marzipan chocolates during the festive holidays. I know this day will come when no more snails will be tasted, and the pickled ones no longer considered ambrosia outside the memory of eating them, and my flesh will return to the sea, unceremoniously sloughed with the exfoliation of my skin.

Thanks to the maker, we all carry motes of stardust in our bodies. It's our flesh that anchors my soul to this lagoon and its blue shoulders. I don't harbor any regrets about the manner in which I've lived on the wrong side of the universe; at least I'm not an octopus on the right side, where I'd be discriminated against and devoid of citizenship rights to designer-gene cloning. I only wish that I'd reckoned sooner about my cephalopodian personhood, not languishing under an illusion of authentic, designer-gene humanity. I am, am I not, a person, albeit flawed? Blooming, full-blooded woman-hood of blushing parts, I mean, of lithe arms and lissome legs, two each in sum. I've lived under the shadow of bioexile, yet sense the elusive radiance of the maker in this lagoon. How can this be, if everything in this lagoon is the consequence of a flesh factory? Why was I deported by the editors of the Genzopolis to live out my days in a haven of idyllic seclusion? I was charged with no crime, committed neither fraud nor extortion, nor masqueraded as a designer-gene citizen when I clearly was not. I'm rogue. An accident. From melonhead to mistletoe, so to speak, without genuine toes at all, ganglion to ganglion, I am octopodean. Nobody will provide a genotype refund or editorial exchange for me, and nobody will take me in. I was not adopted as an exotic pet, my dear heavenly stars of this postdiluvian sea.

In short, perchance I was ill-disposed rather than ill-fated.

Mindful of my foreseeable demise, I am fairly disciplined about curbing appetites which rage to a lesser extent within my gut as they might in the wilderness, so I'm not haunted by wantonness or desire, for instance, to devour another's flesh. Sea creatures in the wilderness are known to cannibalize one another, rip apart their own flesh when feeling distressed, and devour their own young, but I've never done this—if the in-stincts exist within me, then none are triggered in this lagoon. Never produced any spawn, anyway. Would an octopus ever

regret not tasting the chemoreceptors or tough armpit beak of another octopus? How repulsive yet enticing, all at once. Would an octopus, on the other hand, ever regret not having tasted a flaky pastry stuffed with roasted pistachios and algae, a plummy apricot jam infused with hybrid orange bergamot oil, or iridescent dates the color of hummingbirds on the right side of the universe? What about those ganache brittle stars overleafed with gold hammered to leafy foil, molded on an unconsecrated wafer? An octopus doesn't know what it doesn't know. How about buffing one's fingernails with sandpaper versus an emery board? Nope. Or what does an octopus know of immortality, the slightest hint of eternity? The papillae on my body tingle and pop into goose bumps while nervousness makes me shiver. Should I entertain thoughts of eating so much sugar? Give me pickled olives, instead, please.

Rather than indulging my appetite, I wait patiently for the lunar mailman, the wry nocturnal angel of dispatches. After the liquid sun has dropped below the horizon and a full moon rests in glimmering shards upon the waves, the taciturn mailman arrives on a slender wing of light with a silvery sheaf of letters, none addressed to me. Not a single one. I offer the mail courier a hug with five of my eight arms for his loyal devotion to visiting me from the sea of lost letters. How does the mail courier respond to a hug from a rogue octopus? This ossan merely shows up on a moonbeam as if astride a palomino horse and deposits the letters in front of my lair. In a soft ray of lunar shine, he looks more like a citizen of heaven than of this world, even a lagoon. I cannot see his lean face, shadowed by his own umbrage with the moon at this back, ramrod straight yet seemingly light as a gull feather.

How many lost genes today, sir?
Silence.
A hundred forty seven? Ninety one? Eleven?

Silence.
How are things on the other side of the universe?
Silence.
May I offer you glass of water?
Silence.
What should I do with this delivery?
Silence.
Would you like to sit for a while?
Silence.
Who else do you visit?
Silence.
Do you visit anyone else?

Moonlight falls in shafts outside my lair, in veils upon my rock garden. It reaches through my window and illuminates the rolltop desk where I keep my collection of abalone shells. One day, I'll design a ventless, first-floor fireplace and embed these iridescent shells in the mortar instead of bricks or stones. I cannot see his face, now turned to the west where the sun vanished. Is the mailman handsome, or is he frightening? Is he featureless, missing a face? It's like asking whether the moonlight has a friendly countenance or a compassionate heart for animals like palomino horses. I honestly don't know the answer. Is the unpopulated moon a barren satellite of this world, attractive in physique, bereft of girdled seas and fertile loam? The moon is gorgeous in the same way that the nocturnes of water are lovely, black sapphires. Blackberries, black pearls. Its glow is a reflection of the sun upon the moon's face, not the moon itself. The vintage mail courier is seen only in this moonlight, long-limbed, sheer, and lean with silvery haloes on the shoulders of his postal uniform, ironed and steam-pressed so the sleeve creases look sharp. His frame is like a marathon runner's physique, the horseless couriers of the ancient days who ran distances with messages of war and peace.

Are you fond of horses, sir?
Silence.
Do you know how the palomino came about?
Silence.
One allele of a dilution gene, the cream gene.
Silence.
This cream gene works on a red or chestnut coat.
Silence.
In a double dose, you get cremello ponies.
Silence.
Cremello, the color of moonlight.
Silence.
Or the color of my skin when I'm calm.

Then he turns in the wind without a word of farewell, one hand resting casually in a pocket of his trousers, and vanishes. I've wondered if he keeps anything in the pocket. Keys to an antiquated, undersea cadaver locker for research? A stick of mint chewing gum? A coin from his boyhood days as a juvenile numismatist, a collector of miscellania from sidewalks? A list of his emergency contacts? A skinny packet of tissue? At a distance, a silhouette of the mail courier appears as if walking on the night sea, the sleeve of his coat fluttering like a leaf. The full moon, about the size of a sand dollar, rises overhead, beaming down with a benevolent façade. I don't know whether this silhouette is a trick of the moonlight or merely a mailman going about his business. If I were renting this professional for an hourly fee, he would be a poor excuse for an ossan, mostly because he doesn't make any small talk. Why should I judge him in this regard, however, when I myself am mute? Our silent exchanges are recondite as the fugues of moonlight in my rock garden, a montage of stills by the sea of lost letters.

# KAREN AN-HWEI LEE

A rather mundane expedition for the ossan, I'd presume, without fireworks or other pyrotechnics to light up this octopus of three hearts, my blue-blooded pumps. I guess it wouldn't matter much if my blood were scarlet with hemoglobin or grenadine like pomegranate pips, not blue like fountain pen ink. I don't have any preferences between copper and iron. No matter, in any case. Somersaulting across the threshold, head over my figurative heels, I examine the sheaf of letters in front of my lair. The genetic codes, soaked in seawater, cannot be unsealed or opened. In the majority of codes, the base pairs are illegible. Once, I thought chromosomes would dry out like blood sausages in blasting light the next day, and maybe one out of twenty-three would be partly readable, which I'd stash under a rock in my garden. The wind would lift the rest out to the open sea from whence they came, whirling like tumbleweed. However, I was wrong, although I kept hoping the genes would survive the night—by morning, inevitably, they'd evaporate with the dew like ancient manna, the bread of heaven.

A fragment of an Emily chromosome, if deciphered, might read something like this following snippet of prose when expressed through the kaleidoscopic life of a single carrier.

Dear lovely daughter: When I visited your mitochondrial grandmother, I left our heirloom genome map on the table, debating with myself whether to transcribe it for you. I did copy the recipe for your aunt's biscuits, which I've enclosed. It calls for a kilogram of genetically modified, grassfed yak butter and a cup of beet sugar, so I must warn you ahead of time; please don't be shocked. Soon the ration coupons will no longer provide for butter, and the tubs of oleomargarine will run out, too. We'll make our own hand soap with lye, lard, and wood-ash from balsam pine for fragrance. By the new moon, we'll use homemade safflower oil and hand soap

of ash and lye as substitutes, brewing rose hips for our tea instead of orange pekoe. For meat, our citizens speared the last of the sharks and squid at the aquarium before releasing the pufferfish and electric eels out to sea. We can afford a few cents for postage, but we're hungry all the time. Our appetites and dispositions are genetically predisposed, inscribed on our heirloom map. For one, I crave a bacon-drippings roast rubbed with garlic cloves and peppercorns, garnished with shallots and pearl onions. And the weather is nightmarish, with rain pounding on top of the roofs along with a rising sea; the blacktop roads by the fishing pier are flooded at high tide. The fish are happy, I suppose, but I hear the waters are not only rising but warming, which will influence our fragile ecosystem in this ailing world. With these designer genes, I pray that you'll be able to live a better life than I did.

If I wrote to cephalopods of a younger generation, it might read like this.

Dear lovely ones: When you hatched as paralarvae, I couldn't be there due to my bioexile by the omnibus. However, please know that I love you, regardless of my absence, and pray for you daily. Often I think of you when I'm arranging rocks in my garden, putting a tea kettle on the stove to boil for elevenses, or fishing pickled olives out of glass jars. Fishing as a gesture, I mean, not for sardines or herring. I've never run out of provisions, which mysteriously repopulate my pantry or rolltop desk when supplies run low. I never go to sleep hungry. I spend my days inking the walls of my room with my siphon. Yes, there's a rolltop desk with a chair and a charming nook I know you'd love, if you ever visit me on this lagoon. My lair is only a stone's throw from the sea, and I take strolls there on a regular basis. The tide pools are loaded with starfish, urchins, and algae. Although I'm outwardly an octopus, I have no true gills and can't remain submerged in water for long, so I dwell on land. Yes, I'm a land-lubbing cephalopod

with eight arms and no legs, thanks to my rogue genes: all this motley molluscan crew and more inscribed within my rogue genotype.

In the solace of maternal wisdom, I love you with all my mitochondria. It's a lagoon where I live, my dears, and we'll have plenty to explore, including a camouflaged army of garden snails. Paper nautiluses wash ashore to hold our attention when we grow tired of the glass jars. The sunsets, too, are absolutely stunning to witness. At the curve of the world, when the sun dips under the horizon, you'll see a green flash caused by hydrogen dioxide molecules scattering the orange, goldenrod, and violet light. This green flash is a good omen, according to our forebears. Tell your mothers, my beloved half-sisters of the world, you should come soon. This lagoon, although modest in size, teems with beauty and abundance, the lush greenery of altered ferns with microspores seeding a supermassive black hole in outer space. I love you even if your birth names are nonexistent, if you hold it against me that I provided rogue genes with dominant octopodean phenotypes rather than Emily-oriented expression, and if your first-degree relative, your father, abandoned my lair long ago in the manner of male octopuses in the wild. Fondly with fern fronds and fiddleheads, your beloved matriarch.

On the other side of the universe, if I were a bona fide woman and not a rogue, I'd befriend the mailman who visits after the sun goes down. He'd whistle in the airy, free-spirited manner that typical postmen are known to do across the world, his head flung back and the crickets making music, and the neighborhood dogs—all manner of beagles, poodles, terriers, chihuahuas, brussels griffons, chow-chows, and mutts—would greet him with echoing barks over lawns of designer-gene turf edited for velvety, perennial green. The mailman would look forward to a slug of cold hydrogen dioxide from my distilled water pump, although it's against

regulations, but he's always thirsty when he reaches my house, and I wouldn't tell, besides. He's younger than I am, a genetic fugitive who escaped the flames of war and fury of natural disasters via migrant caravans in the night.

In his mail bag, illegally, he carries the lost gene for an autosomal recessive disorder already tagged for knockout. It's not the single gene, but the whole person to be knocked out for carrying it because the stardust editors aren't sure how the gene interacts with others. Knocking out, he explains, is a euphemism for killing. The omnibus attempted to stop the migrant caravans by erecting a barricade of sterilized dung around the paradoxical city of refuge, but we dug tunnels and pushed through by night, he'd say. To escape what? We could only run so far inland, ahead of the rising tides, into the mountains where the citizens settled. Because we didn't bear tattoos yet resembled designer-gene humans, no one could tell whether we were actual citizens or rogues. Maybe if you looked carefully at one of us you might see a clue in our phenotypic expression—an aquamarine iris flashing peacock then violet-indigo in the sun, a nanosecond rate of pupil reflexes, or in an ambidextrous use of hands. You wouldn't know for certain whether we carried genes for metabolic disorders, for double-jointed fingers, for resistance to bubonic plague, or for postponing adulthood until the prefrontal cortex was fully developed in its executive functions.

Due to our relaxed friendship over the years—time on the other side of the universe is easy-come, easy-go—the mailman and I would gradually fall in love, the sort of bond shared by older couples on their entwined journeys. We'd meet for bowls of café au lait or tea at garden cafés, ostensibly to trade our new poems for line-by-line feedback, but all honesty, for the intoxication of one another's pheromone fragrances and habitual turns of phrase in conversation—didn't you know, why not ask about it, can't hurt, who was there—then walk

along the longest pier on the coast to watch fishermen cast their lines. We'd converse about the fathomless mysteries of the maker, who dwells outside time itself. How do we experience the presence of the maker? How do we know the maker exists beyond us yet within our lives, the temples of our spirits, unfolding a great design? What is the grand metanarrative about the maker, which the ancients recorded in painstakingly transcribed and translated texts now lost to us, surviving only in fragments? Are supermassive black holes and rhododendrons perfumed? If so, what is their aroma? Jackfruit flowers and sugar apple trees, or the soursop fruit with black seeds? The inflorescence of osage blossoms on a midsummer night? Lavender lilacs and wisteria? The infamous rhododendrons of sweet madness? The hallucinogenic neurotoxin in mad honey gleaned from the nectar of rhododendrons, the intoxicating poison called grayanotoxin?

> This dark roast is burned, I'd say.
> You know I like it that way, he'd reply.
> I'm looking at the raspberry torte.
> I'm not hungry.
> We could share it.
> Yes, I could have a taste.
> Are those mock orange trees?
> He'd squint. I think they're osage.
> How could I confuse the two?
> Both are mock orange, my dear.
> How do you mean, both?
> Osage is fragrant; the other, shaggy green.
> Mock orange alike?
> Their monikers are the same, that's why.

Metaphysics of analog clocks flying at the speed of light—and setting aside the maker's workshop of quantum relativity—we'd buy scoops of modified peppermint sorbet

and sit on a bench by the sea. He might ask whether I believed that octopuses lived in this part of the shoals, and I might think but not say aloud that I could be an octopus on the other side of the universe. I'd make funny, off-beat observations about the weather, climate change, and global warming, with sundry allusions to methane gas. Peppermint sorbet, derived from an old-fashioned hybrid of watermint and spearmint, tastes like an interglacial treat from the quaternary ice age, I'd say. We've got a slice of glaciology in this moment, forever. Why, he'd say, and I'd reply enigmatically, the taste of peppermint forces us to look forward in time, not back. Since I'm a woman on this side of the universe, however, I'd say octopuses are mysterious creatures, and we should visit the zoo aquarium more often to learn about their behaviors: I've heard that the octopuses harbor nine brains in sum, and their skin changes color depending on mood or environment. Fabulous creatures, I'd add, and remarkably intelligent, independent of machine learning.

He would absently yet readily agree. Yes, dear Emily.

On these strolls, the mailman might share an ambition to seek a promotion within the postal service, and what is my opinion of this? Should he pursue advancement? He enjoys this vocation, but he's discouraged by frequent reductions in force, turf wars, toxic managers, and budget battles in his office. What is it all really about under the surface, I ask; are you seeking power, status, or something else? Reticent as usual, he's reluctant to confide in me. I respect his boundaries. Instead, the mailman says that he'd prefer to work as a gene editor and call this postal work quits if the political nonsense doesn't stop. What do I say? If I were a designer-gene female on the other side of the universe, a woman named Emily, I'd say, you must go with your heart and not with your head. If it doesn't feel right, then don't do it. Editing is a shady conspiracy, though, he'd comment. Tampering with our genes

is interfering with the order of the universe and its natural wilderness. Where do those carriers of rogue genes go? How do the flesh factories make them vanish without a trace? Do the supermassive black holes truly begin with seeds the size of the head of a pin?

> What are you thinking right now?
> Did they burn the rogues?
> We'd see evidence of cremation.
> Unless the ashes are tossed at sea.
> I bet they vanish into black holes.
> How would they control those?
> Maybe very small black holes.
> Singularities the size of snowflakes?
> Smaller, maybe. The head of a pin.
> How sad to vanish forever.
> That's the way it is for all of us.
> Programmed death isn't the same.
> Depressing just to talk about it.
> As citizens, we don't have to think.
> About what? The rights of rogues?
> Do you want a spot of tea?

The mailman would persist matter-of-factly, in an amusingly deadpan manner, by stating that the omnibus owns everything under the sun and retains an artificial brain in its programming capacity, but not a heart of compassion. Isn't a literal heart just a muscle with sleek bundles of nerves and oxygenated blood, anyway? What do you mean, Emily, my dear? He rubs his hand on his sleeve thoughtfully. The Genzopolis is an ecosystem of microecosystems, not a factory. When you tell me to go with my heart, are you advising me to go with parasympathetic muscles and nerves? Or do you mean, go with your soul, for which the heart is a figurative cradle? You're actually encouraging me to tinker with all parts of

my brain: prefrontal cortex in tandem with the limbic system, right?

What about the space pirates, I say.
What pirates, my dear?
The pirates in outer space.
There are no pirates out there. It's a biomyth.
I've seen the pirates in my dreams.
Do you think we're trapped in a space opera?
The ecosystem is the ganglia of an octopus, an
    omnivore of data.
Nonsense. Why an octopus?
Why not an octopus?
Why not an orangutan or an opossum?
Octopuses have nine brains, that's why.
What do the octopuses have to do with pirates?
Everything and nothing, sir.
Is it because the octopuses go rogue like pirates?
Maybe, sir.
Octopuses hoard shiny objects and ride around the ocean
    like marauders.
We all have our little roles, whether rogue or not.
You are the most bizarre Emily I've ever met.

On our walk, at last we've reached the front steps of my home. I open the door with my brass house key, half-worried about one percent of elemental lead in the brass which will rub onto my fingers, then possibly make its way into my bloodstream. I'll have to go into the clinic for heavy metal chelation treatments. We live in an age of toxic objects, although the drinking water in our abodes is potable, thanks to microfiltration and distillation technology. After our dialogue of questions without answers, the mailman would take a swig of water from the glass I offer while he wipes his mouth with the back of his hand. I should've

offered him a napkin folded in my purse for occasions like wiping the chin or blowing one's nose. In the kitchen, I've already set out a plate of shortbread biscuits made with bits of candied orange peel soaked in brandy and drizzled with dark chocolate, which he politely declines. With a tilt of his hat and a jaunty salute, a quick whistle with moistened lips and not a kiss, he'd then bid me farewell with a nod, heave a canvas bag over his shoulder, and be on his merry way.

My bundle of mail would consist of bills and circulars, for the most part.

For several minutes, I watch his diminishing figure until it blurs in the gray distance, then I go inside to pull down the shades, put a tea kettle on the stove, and prepare the house for nightfall. I brush out my silky hair of fortified keratin and sit on the edge of a futon mattress with my legs crossed at the ankles, breathing evenly as I reflect on the day's events with fondness, and count my blessings. I finger the double-stranded black pearls on my necklace. Then I rise from the mattress and pour myself a cup of jasmine green tea, drop a spoonful of honey crystals in it, and count myself richly blessed by this sweet contentment of twilight solitude.

A reverie.

In actuality, I am a rogue octopus, not a human woman named Emily, and the ossan says nothing to me in the moonlight. This silence, on the contrary, beckons a heavenly host of angels to look upon the lagoon. Instead of sharing a word of farewell, he bestows a sheaf of lost letters chosen out of the sea of the vanquished; then, wafting like a scrap of rice paper, he vanishes without a sound. Tonight, out of the corner of my eye, the silhouette of the mailman wavers like a watery reflection of a sail. The sea of lost letters gives up none of its double-stranded secrets as the full

moon rises higher in the sky, an eye bereft of amusement or betrayal staring down without a pupil, reflecting a nacreous light with an origin not of its own, a desolate world of basalt meadows and dry seas where nothing dies and nothing grows anew.

## 7 | The Soul of a Rogue

How to avoid the dreadful fate of spaghettification. Thought experiments of an octopus. A space opera. The eidolon, a spirit image.

## The Soul of a Rogue

According to the magistrate's bylaws of the omnibus, we are no more than blobs of protoplasm. Blob, in the bylaws, is qualified as proper usage without quotation marks, in other words, blobs propped up by cartilage, shot through by nerves. Don't know what else to make of all this. The stardust editors, who are automated machines in slick packets of bioengineered jelly, are no more than blobs of biodata at the end of a day, sort of like me, with a few exceptions: editors cannot procreate. However, an accidental, like a singular note played as a sharp or flat not in a key signature—embodies a mistake like an output failure of the flesh factories. That said, on the other hand, I'm also more than a blob—a speck of protoplasm on a huge mound of dirt—because I have a soul.

I honestly believe I have a soul, I mean.

In another world, one where spiritual ephemera like art, beauty, and music coexist as aesthetic sisters, accidentals are exceptions to a key signature; it's why they're accidentals. F sharp, B flat. C sharp, D flat. C flat is B. Wrong notes don't always follow a logical pattern of whole and half steps on a

160

diatonic scale, for instance. Often I've mused, is the genetic wilderness haphazardly rugged and sublime, or ruptured by the disorder of edited sequences? Is random chaos the antithesis of aesthetic value? In other words, what is beauty in an age of designer genes, when a range of pigmentation is wholly feasible in any given phenotype? For accidents with undesirable genotypes like sunburned skin and photosensitivity, vanishing removes any chance our rogue genes would disrupt anybody else's genome. We'd never become accidentally fruitful, thereby multiplying our genes for hereditary diseases or other undesirable traits. No consideration is given to the question of whether or not an eidolon, a spirit-image—what the ancients called a soul—appears like an overexposed angel in a photograph negative on the other side of the universe. No one knows what occurs after we're dispatched to our fates in black holes smaller than snowflakes, tinier than the caraway seeds in the original Emily's cake, in a singularity.

Confession. I overthink my thought experiments, questions to which no obvious answers surface, endlessly looping inside a labyrinth of cogitation. In paradise, fortunately, on this side of the universe, there is a lot of time to overthink. In this aquarium of air, my think-tank of solitude, thank goodness I'm not in anyone's way, not eating up company time, figuratively speaking. There must exist, I'm sure, a citizen on the other side of the universe, one who understands the old-fashioned ways of genetic recombination, ancient transcription, and translation methods without editorial intrusions, and who aims to save us from our accidental selves. A savior of rogues, I imagine. Rippling as I relax on my waterbed, my mauve-colored arms spread open like a passionflower on the mattress, if you'll kindly forgive the indulgence of my reclining posture. I ponder the metaphysical nature of finitude and eternity, those spinning portals of the maker's imagination. How big is one compared to the other, anyway? Is there an

exposition or beginning, a crux or middle, and a denouement with a resolution or finale? Does the maker exist outside infinity or is it more accurate to say that the maker is unbounded by eternity, yet intrinsically eternal in character?

Here I am, caught in yet another loop. At the time of the second great flood, the citizens no longer believed in souls or an afterlife, abandoning the notion of a presence in the transcendent in favor of methodological atheism, grasping eternity as an empirical phenomenon. For instance, it's feasible to compute a sort of fiscal annuity in perpetuity, theoretically speaking. However, this investment is only eternal insofar as the borrower is willing and can afford to pay. The actual value is not infinite; I ramble and rumble on and on under the night's starry river of milk and to myself. Deal with it. An octopus is an octopus, and an octopus tagged by other names would still be an octopus. On the rosier side of things, at least you're not dismembered by the whittling knives of a seafood chef, your tenderized, charbroiled melonhead and curlicue arms not simmering in rosemary, garlic, thyme, and olive oil in a saucepan, about to be devoured alongside grilled baby octopuses in a red-and-white quinoa salad garnished with minced parsnips and fennel seeds.

Your beloved name is Emily, and you're not what's served for dinner.

Thank goodness I'm not a marbled slab of wagyu steak, not a tenderized loin chop or a soggy bag of duck giblets. Enough of the negative talk, I admonish myself. Obviously, the genes influencing an inherited compulsion for automatic thought repetition weren't knocked out of me; like free radicals roaming in our bodies at will, so do our compulsive negative thoughts, wreaking havoc on the psychological nuances of our inner lives, riding the hormonal tides of the body and the darkling imaginations of the subconscious alike. Free-radical scavengers like leafy kale, crudités, and dark-skinned berries

don't mitigate this negativity; only the free thought radicals and positivity advocates do. However, it does not hurt to add blueberries, blackberries, marionberries, radishes and carrots, and genetically modified, detoxifying chlorella boosted with vitamins A, B complex, C, D, and K.

The wilderness is no longer the wilderness, and a woman named Emily is no longer a singular personage; instead, thousands of women named Emily exist with the exact same or nearly the same genotype, even in the noggin of an octopus.

Snip, snip. How sharp are the scissors? Snip. Does it cut out single nucleotides in their pairs with accuracy? How do you assess the level of risk? Are the genetic pens truly safe enough for mass production? Will small errors be mass reproduced; what's the risk assessment? What about the genetic pens equipped with erasers? Are they truly safe enough for domestic use by citizens who wish to edit their own genes, or those of their gestating progeny? And so forth. Not surprisingly, the designer-gene pets are treated like royalty, brushed and bathed at a gene-therapy spa where their genomes are inspected for damage, then repaired using molecular scissors. Not blessed or privileged to receive gene therapies, rogues are tossed like bruised fruit tagged for jams and preserves—or to be more precise, blobs of protoplasm not worth preserving or dehydrating—into the black holes. When I ruminate on this too long, I start to feel sad, then a little angry; outraged, with nothing I can do except tuck myself—and my amorphous, overflowing lagoon of emotions—into a smooth glass jar for a couple hours, I wish I could cry. Instead, I ooze a pint of slime. I obviously wasn't edited for emotional self-regulation, at least, not to the extent that I can stop changing colors when I feel ruffled.

So I lie on my undulating bed—or it's my prostrate body undulating—while my skin changes colors from dusty rose to mauve and turquoise to scarlet, the papillae poking up like

pomegranate pips all over my mantle. This happens only when I'm truly provoked. Changing colors and pips simultaneously, I mean. I can't even open one of my nine toothless mouths to scream because I lack a set of vocal cords and windpipes. Don't have a blowhole like the dolphins and narwhals, and no beluga melon to generate bioacoustics. Nobody would hear me, anyway. Welcome to a masterpiece of failure, a mistake, a comedy of errors, a compendium of flaws. I complain bitterly, then instantly regret my words: autologophagy. You survived a singularity without the dreadful fate of spaghettification or getting smashed to subatomic smithereens.

Now you live in a laguna paradise, a lagoon on the edge of the universe where a spoonful of neutron dust would weigh more than a billion whales. There's no dystopic element in sight, except bouts of boredom in the ribbons of light filtered through a kelp forest, a form of psychological paralysis. This winding, molecular sentence unravels nanosecond upon nanosecond—a trance of elegant sentences, i.e. a sentrance—entranced without dotted lines as instructions, and without clear directions to tear along this fold or pull on this red tab after removing the perforated edges. Where's your positive outlook, I chide myself. Where's your litany of delights? You live in an octopodean paradise where you lack nothing, where everything is available for your sustenance and amusement, even shells and rocks the size of pomelos. You're in paradise, I admonish myself. How dare you entertain grumblings of boredom, your quibbling protestations and ingratitude?

In the primeval epoch of the antiquated talking cure, decades before the omnibus designed inhalable dust tailored to mitigate your genetic predisposition to anxiety and dysphoria, and before molecular scissors wielded by stardust editors trimmed our genes, there was a curious phenomenon of evolving psychologically into a new person after the death of a loved one, an arduous process of recovering from loss also

phrased, becoming a new person. Becoming. A new. Person. Not. An octopus. This psychological paradigm is now out of vogue on the right side of the universe, where newness and phenotypic expression are protean categories in a fluid sense: If you don't like brown hair and blue eyes, edit your genes to express, phenotypically, brown eyes and blue hair, easy as blueberry rhubarb pie. If you feel sad from the loss of a pet guinea pig who could fit into a tea pot, inhale a pinch of the smart dust to improve your positivity, dispel the spell of dysphoria. I've neither survived the deaths of beloveds nor changed into a second person, unless waking up as an octopus counts: Zoomorphism, not anthropomorphism. Even so, my octopodean identity is equivocal: I'm inwardly a human, outwardly an octopus. An alternative would be to change into either wholly a new octopus or new woman. However, what I've experienced is the opposite. Is this becoming a new hybrid person or transpecies organism, in a manner of speaking? Why not? Thought I was a woman, then woke up one day to realize that I'm an octopus. Referring to myself in the second person is not a far cry from actually becoming one, I suppose.

You're an octopus named Emily D.

D is for dystopia, so deal with it. On hindsight, the only bugaboo in this situation is how dull paradise is without the biomythical octopus monsters as chewy delicacies, sliced and tenderized *tako* octopuses to generate gastronomic melodrama on the high seas: to huck an igneous boulder at your melonhead while it swallows a shipmast or two, or cause a fatal whirlpool vortex by opening a giant tablecloth on the back of a giant paper nautilus. I can readily do without the interference of citizens and their pathological narcissism. I'd like a little more octopodean biomythopoeia, please. For example, where are the denizens of the deep who stalk their prey by changing colors on the seabed, their velveteen mantles pressed against coral reefs, or peeking out of undersea caves while turtles,

prawns, and fish swim nonchalantly past masked octoeyes, camouflaged like algae? Or how about octopuses the size of a jar of olives mischieviously hosing you with seawater for sheer amusement, just to see you shocked, then pushing off into the distance without an ounce of regret?

If you had access to the talking cure, or if you were an artist named Emily who designed paper cuttings or baked cakes as a reclusive form of occupational rehabilitation, you doubt that your situation would improve. However, you don't understand how to make art, or you struggle with knowing how. Pushing rocks around in a garden or crawling into glass jars as performance art, why or why not? The words, rock and art, shoved together in a phrase, send a marvelous thrill in your nerves, all nine of your brains. You're a vegetarian and don't eat animals, only mild plant-based foods and no sentient creatures that creep or crawl, none at all. No fish brains or swim bladders; plants don't bite unless they're carnivorous flytraps. In paradise, you enjoy all the olives you wish to eat in monotonously fair weather with a chance of showers, and live in an octopus palace on pink coral sand that looks like a postcard for a resort without the traffic and bare midriffs of designer-gene tourists with the illusion of flawless futures ahead of them. Trying not to feel sorry for your octopodean self, you envision an operetta starring an octopus as the prima donna. It's a comédie lyrique, a lyric comedy mixed with brief arias, a space opera as a comédie *mêlée d'ariettes*. On a side note, I'd like to say it's the prima donna within me, I guess, who conjures this vision. Personally, I have no ambitious desire to go on stage, as I get overstimulated by lights, big or small, diodes or not.

Besides, as a mute octopus, I have no voice whatsoever.

The crux of the tale is a frustrated diva who cannot hit a true soprano C two octaves above middle C, thanks to her genome's blueprint; she was designed to serve the Genzopolis

not as a diva but a data analyst to crunch numbers for the Genome Omnibus Database. Why is she angry, one might ask. Why not, I say. If you're a diva who can't hit a true soprano C, this disadvantage will doom you sooner or later. Is she a talented data analyst? No one will ever know. In this operetta, the flummoxed prima donna plays herself, an octopoid diva named Emily, an E for extraordinaire and a D for Diva, whose voice is a foghorn blowing inside her head, and she can't tolerate it. She dons a lacy octopus gown adorned with polyvinyl suction cups in the demure shapes of cherry blossoms and shows up at a gala to bewilder her fans, benefactors, and patrons with multi-armed flamboyance; divas are expected to flout convention, so the affluent socialites and philanthropists indulge her eccentric behaviors. At the gala, she plays a ditty using a nose-whistle whittled out of whalebone—yes, the same once infamously used for corsets—and blows with all her might, whee-wheeeeee. The whistle triggers a tinnitus fiercely ringing for several minutes in the audience's ears. The chandeliers in the opera house explode to smithereens, and dogs in the Genzopolis yowl with panic. This is a thwarted prima donna's revenge for her genetic limitations: don a garish octopus costume, borrow a nose-whistle, and shatter the chandeliers.

Now, designer citizens of the Genzopolis, please figure this one out yourselves, with your advanced expertise in bioacoustics and abstruse metaphysics of superluminal octopuses flying beyond the far reaches of your exosphere: dear citizens on the right side of the universe, please explain the phenomenon of an airborne octopus performing in an opera. Ridiculous, you say, this illusion is easily dismissed, right out of hand. It's more sleight-of-hand performance art than light opera. No, it's the theater of the absurd. There's only one act, and the prima donna whose name is Emily, who wears an octopus costume, and tweets the nose-whistle continuously.

Twee, tweeeee. Tweet until a velvet curtain falls with a boom. Goes without saying, the audience is very displeased. Boo, boo. Are genetically modified rotten tomatoes handy? Boo. No, the genetically modified tomatoes do not rot. Boo. The portly lady never sings, no gregarious barbers on balconies meddle as gossips, no magic flutes and bird-catchers mysteriously appear, and no jealous lovers spar each other atop parapets. There's no *deus ex machina* with a flying octopus. Instead, the libretto is littered with tacits, musical rests, and caesuras to portray the silent art of being a cephalopod. It's a mockery of so-called penny opera and performance art, or the reverse, performance art as a penny opera without words.

If I had access to resources, I'd design a microlexicon to assist those of us who've experienced the trauma of time travel through black holes. The microlexicon, like a specialized glossary, would aid us in remembering words we might miss due to memory loss caused by flying at the speed of light, if not also due to the sheer force of intense gravity. The words would aid our extraction of meaning from annihilating experiences like spaghettification in a massive gravitational field, where our bodily matter would get stretched out in noodles. This chapbook of words, a microlexicon, would include quotidian terms like a key and door. What is a key, for instance, and why not forget it? Why does anyone need a key? How does it work, and where does it go when it's not used? Next, what is a door? How does an octopus open a door? How does an octopus lock it, and who lives behind the door? What happens if you lose the key to this door? Do you and your chapbook get hurled into another universe?

If you lose the key to this door, ask for a copy.
How can a copy be made without an original or master?
Visit the locksmith, who'll take out the keyhole.
What if no more locksmiths exist in the universe?

If we reach that point, no one will worry about keys.
You asked about losing a key to this door.
If keys are lost, we won't need to know who we are.
Where we are, you mean.
That's a crisis.
Who said this was a crisis?

If I were a woman named Emily outwardly, not an octopus, I'd collect words for these microlexicons and collate their definitions into saddle-stitched fascicles or chapbooks to give away to friends for amusement, as jokes or riddles. What do you catch but never throw? A cold. What is the worst vegetable to have on a ship? A leek. What asks no questions but requires many answers? A door chime like the ones of yore, ding dong. What did the bee say to the flower? I love you, honey. When do astronauts eat their hoagies? Only at launch time, says the lexicon, adding, all sun and games. I have no feet, no hands, and no wings, yet I ascend the sky. What am I? Smoke of an engine that's burning oil. Please change the valve seals or replace the piston rings to prevent oil leakage, says the lexicographer, whose muffled voiceover is recorded in an audio chip.

What falls yet never breaks? Nightfall, proffers the microlexicon of riddles.

The underlying truth about many women's lives, of course, as allegorical octopuses, in a manner of speaking, begs the question, how do they manage to do so much? On both sides of the universe, women juggle more than what inflexible human arms could reasonably handle with children, pets, elderly first-degree relatives, maintaining an elegantly decorated home with a macrobiotic garden of beets and kohlrabi and radishes and red kale in the yard, cooking a little fleet of gourmet meals with gluten-free, nut-free, low potassium, low sugar, low fat, and dairy-free plates planned exactly a month

in advance; chauffeuring oneself and loved ones to and fro lessons like didgeridoo or other aerophones and drone pipes, gouache digital dabbling, mixed martial arts with indoor sky-diving, and skating on vanishing glaciers; not to mention flawless beauty as well as an unfading inner light. Eight arms aren't adequate to handle all these demands. No macroglossary or microlexicon is a mnemonic device with enough memory to capture everything one does, edited or not. Pondering this reeling monsoon of activity makes me want to squeeze into a jar for an hour or two, but it's too late at night to undertake an activity that requires more attention than I can spare. Should I open a jar of snails? Enjoy a spoonful of anchovy tapenade on an oyster cracker? I content myself with a gratitude list, expressing praises for this mode of being, no more.

> A strong roof over my head that doesn't leak in the rain.
> A rock garden to amuse myself when it's not raining.
> Ocean view with a thin layer of fog whirling, rising, falling.
> A sea of lost letters which I've visited only in dreams,
> where the missing nucleotides of flawed sequences go.
> Moonlight falling onto snails and moss in the rock garden.
> Olive trees on the other side of the universe, plus their olives.
> Elevenses, when we enjoy the habit of taking tea, if we do.
> Eight arms that taste and touch, each with a brain of its own.
> Little glass jars sitting in a row by the stove, filled with salt.
> Abandoned shells which remind me to live and let live.
> Space enough to include an eleventh item if it arises.

## 8 | WATER NOCTURNES AND MICROLEXICONS AT MIDNIGHT

Our octopus heroine weaves a bejeweled textile of codes. An improvised beatitude. Existential ruminations on her rogueness. The mystical fingerprints of the universe's maker.

## WATER NOCTURNES AND
## MICROLEXICONS AT MIDNIGHT

Near midnight, in a polychromatic dream of curling and coiling arms, I pick up the threads of my journey on the wrong side of the universe, weaving a code of my own design in the tickling spaces between shrouded worlds of wakefulness and slumber, a scriptorium of my own to generate an elaborate tapestry of genetic codes extending across the universe. It glows like fiber-optic cables buried in the seabed; it hums with the resonance of cable bridges swaying in the globally warmed wind currents. At least, that is my intent: don't know whether the codes will venture past my garden to the sea of lost letters. I'm not aware of any black holes riddling this lagoon, or how to summon fragrant portals to open like sky-pod doors on the other side of the universe. Why are those black holes fragrant, after all, lightly perfumed like rhododendrons, imparting doom while intoxicatingly irresistible? A maelstrom of perfume in tides upon the shoals of the universe, the diadem of faraway stars dropped in the hazy gauze of distance and time: a poet named Emily, who lived in a garden miles inland from a coast long before it was

drowned in the ocean, gazed up at the stars, then down at the houses at dusk, and called the lights *flambeaux*. However, it was another poet of green cockatoos and genetically unmodified oranges, not the first Emily, one who penned the line, *words of the fragrant portals, dimly starred.*

Where have our poets gone, dear Emily?

On the other side of the universe, I imagine the original Emily fixing her auburn hair in a knotted bun while a waning moon rises over her garden of amethyst hydrangea, intoxicating rhododendrons, and little pansies or violets. Her hairbrush and the papers on a cherrywood desk change to silver monochrome in the moonlight, and she's blown out the kerosene lamp an hour ago. The glass has cooled to the touch. The memory of a nocturnal moth flutters like a ghostly frock inside Emily's head, the papery moth at the window where a flame was burning in the lamp. How our short-lived wishes are like a flock of moths, she muses.

Do black holes impart the intoxicating fumes of raw mad honey as a proxy to the rhododendrons? Aren't the holes more apt to consume gaseous emanations due to their supermassive gravity? Are these love chronicles an absurd consequence of intoxication? Yes, in a maddening glory cloud of exploding stars, of nebulae and supernovae, the whole kit and caboodle of the universe flames with auburn hives of head-spinning mad honey. What is the neurotoxic odor of playful invention, of whimsically inverting an origami envelope? Or a flying octopus zooming at the speed of light, a wavelength punctuated by hiccups—the octopus, not the light, I mean? The textile weaves new beatitudes for things I love best, like microlexicons in a noggin powered by olives, for instance. No one is excluded from this textile because I don't know anybody; the sea urchins and starfish in the tide pools don't talk to me. With dire urgency in this dream, I must finish this beatific

weaving before daybreak, when it'll vaporize like dew on a cobweb in Emily's garden.

> Blessed is a recombinant tapestry woven
> vibrant as iridophores, chromatophores.
> Blessed are the round alkaline histones
> spooling around the clockface of time,
> colorful beads of chromosomes wound
> around each. Blessed is the chromatin
> which comprise the chromatids. Blessed
> are the chromatids which join together
> to form the chromosomes.

However, I won't finish this tapestry tonight. Flowering like marine fog over tide pools of filter-fed urchins and lazy starfish, the textile of dreams flows from one tip of my squishy arm to another, then trails the light over the threshold to the rock garden towards the sea, where the moon regards this side of the universe with a pale, unruffled gaze, sending its rays upon the equanimous features of my pet rocks around the lair. No lighthouses guide homecoming ships to harbor away from the shoals, and no keeper resides in it with his family, polishing the great lens of the lamp. There are no wayfaring ships, and therefore, no lighthouses. The moon looks like an antique coin on the waters, a countenance engraved without a sign of complaint or criticism as it has done for eons, its un-blinking monocle at once glaucous yet radiant in the night. As I wonder whether I'm a little in love with the waxing moon, the one whose shot glasses of tonic-colored light send me an ossan on a nightly basis, my skin pigments change instantly to the blushing hue of a berry. Yes, the word, metamorpho-sis, drifts out of my microlexicon. My limbs burst with the aplomb of blossoming cherry orchards and plum trees on the right side of the universe. While the blighted world glides into the spring equinox on its lone sojourn orbiting the sun, my

fused head and body morph into the colors of a muskmelon heavy with juice and slippery seeds, and my skin blushes in the shades of bougainvillea spilling its garlands of fuchsia and coralline.

As a rogue organism, I'm a bogus planet named Emily.

Blessed is the polychromatism of dragonflies winged by chitinous lace, of iridescent fig-eater beetles and seventeen-year cicadas, of star-nosed moles like the asterisks of kissing octopuses and pollen-caked bumblebees tumbling out of their hives. Blessed are the armored cockroaches of burnt umber, the fire ants carrying grains of rotten wood with their mandibles, and luna moths with the wingspan of a human hand adorned with ribbons. In the wilderness, the base pairs in our codes glow with promises of intelligent expression on the other side of the universe: a locust-eating prophet in the desert who finds water to herald one who is to come, an eidetic memory as well as a collective one for a storytelling group of people, a knack for new languages like xenoglossia, tongue papillae for tasting those languages in place of bodily goosebumps mimicking coral on the sea floor, the polychromatism of octopodean skin ranging from agave to mother-of-pearl and a lagoon of coral sand. This tapestry of codes illuminates more than the trials and tribulations of my rogue life as an octopus named Emily; rather, it explodes with artistry in the knotted cords of the eggs I would've woven in my lair if I were an octopus in the wild, cloistered together like jeweled knots in the warp and weft of this weaving, shining like drops of olive oil alight in votives.

In this dream, the maker's love touches my three hearts.

By a miracle, I am an original first edition, not a knock-off.

Quarantined in the realm of my melonhead without echoes or rhymes from a doting mother or gaggle of aunts, only my songs without sounds, why not navigate this bioexile in paradise as a rogue cricket instead of an octopus? If I were a

cricket, I'd chafe my skinny legs of chitin all night long to perform strident music—only a one-note chirp to most ears, yet a lyric serenade to the antennae of my intended beloved. Since I'm an accident, maybe the chitin is extra dense, therefore extra shrill. In fact, the sound is stridulation, almost a portmanteau of strident and adulation. As a cricket, I wouldn't have to haul myself across the garden on eight arms, or slather my skin copiously with non-comedogenic emollients after soaking in a hydrotherapy bath. A cricket's existence is far less insufferable than mine: I envy those arthropods who hide in the crannies of rocks or cracked earth with the ease of a star gliding behind a raincloud.

If not a cricket, then how about a lightning bug named Emily?

Yes, if only I were a firefly dotting the night with ellipses, a great-grandfly of the generation of flies engineered to watch the night hours as guiding lights of wisdom, a postdiluvian fly with bioluminescent skin and adorable nubs on my shoulders genetically altered to sprout wings. The night transliterates my older fly siblings into ellipses stuttering across the darkness, lesser stars in motion against the greater backdrop on the stage, a river of starry milk poured across the sky. As a nymph, I look up to my lamp-like sisters in the order of beetles as my genetic ancestors in this galaxy, the ones who pollinated magnolia groves with blossoms as big as lamps before the rise of honeybees.

If I'm no more than a rogue blob of protoplasm, there's nothing more than purposeless, disorganized sensations from one minute to the next. In my dreaming, since dreaming is a form of codification, as I weave a numinous textile of jeweled genetic codes, I work past the darkling hours of tides after midnight, knotting myself back into the warp and weft of this universe, the textile of stillness across the horizontal weft in motion, running over, under, and crosswise again in

repetitive and palindromic sequences; dreaming is a form of codification. Does it truly matter how I was knit outside anyone's womb, *ex vivo,* belonging to no one, without a kindred cephalopod in a flesh factory of odds and ends? Deleted from the archives of the Genome Omnibus Database, I claim no inheritance and no inheritors. With a set of rogue designer genes, I woke into this life as an octopus, a rogue one without kith or kin. Thanks to the limitations of this flesh suit of cells, I shall depart one day soon when my telomeres can no longer repair their worn tips with octopodean enzymes, abandoning my unraveled sentence of life for others to decipher, if not to salvage, then merely to satisfy their curiosity.

Blessed with a fragrance of the sea as it passes through the ages, the ballad of this rogue octopus recounts the conquests and misadventures of behemoths and leviathans alike, those monsters of the ancient days, extravagantly dulse-bearded and seaweed-dressed. In the myriad hues of this tapestry, I hum a mute hypolydian anthem from F to F, if you'll tolerate the F for Fecklessness, to denote the existential frustrations of a feckless, rogue octopus. The octopuses of the universe, rogue and wild alike, emerge from dens, lairs, and caves to sway with unspoken accord, changing their hues in a symphony of harmonized colors: cyan blue of their oceanic blood pulsing through three hearts, or skins wine red as the blood of beluga whales, then algal shades of green and bronze in the kelp forests.

I relish every hypnagogic minute of this ballad, which I dedicate to all the spawn named Emily in the universe, rogue or not.

Weaving this sequence of codes, I rise on a tidal wave of wings and foam; my body swells to a colossal size as the ocean gives birth to the world a second time. On this upsurge of renascent weather, my ink siphon opens up to the universe in praise of all manner of gleaming cephalopods and wriggling

whatnots in the sea, the meshes of goodness designed in the maker's workshop beyond the horizon as the global winds of history melt the retreating ice shelves and dwindling land masses. Zooming nearly at the speed of light, my swollen body yawns wider than the canyons and trenches of the abyssal deep where fish and mollusks barely rely on eyes to seek out their mates, where hydrothermal vents bubble like springs for heat-tolerant sea anemone to thrive yet enough to boil a tea kettle about three times over. My body is about to undergo spaghettification, wherein my cells elongate like noodles pulled under supermassive gravitational forces.

No one is truly accidental, I hum as a line of an improvised beatitude.

Blessed are the rogues who are not loved.
Blessed are the flaws in our bodies, each one.
Blessed are the blossoms dropping from trees.
Blessed is the oyster who sees the light of day.
Blessed is the woman who wakes as an octopus.
Blessed are the fragrant black holes, their perfume.
Blessed is this side of the universe, which is paradise.
Blessed are the bones summed to make a whole.

The joy of the maker's ink awash in my soul, I praise this world of all things midnight blue in the stairless mansions of the sea, and praise the maker for phosphorescence glistening in the bodies of squid in the nocturnal tide. Praise the maker for the algal blooming in waves rolling and breaking in the coves, and the bellies of firefly squid in their polka-dot bioluminescence, and the bobtail squid of luminous ooze in their dumpling bodies, too. Praise the maker for the octopuses of the wilderness, of nine brains and eight arms, the shy ones curled as if asleep. Praise the maker for the pods of dolphins and whales plying the depths of the sea above the benthos, fringed by eelgrass beds, with their sonar. Praise the maker for the angler fish and brittle stars in the lightless aphotic zone. Praise

the maker for graceful eelgrass and muddy microbialites. Praise the maker for the delicate mineral bones of radiolaria in undersea clouds nearly invisible to an unaided eye. Praise the maker for this side of the universe, where tidal pools serve as lesser mirrors of the moon's cool, steady gaze.

Praise the maker for designing the original Emily and copies of Emily in marvelous variations through the ages: Emily of the bobbins, Emily of the reels, Emily of the mantel photographs, Emily of the hanging wisteria, Emily of the wool shawls, Emily of the cocoons, Emily of the oceans, Emily of the heather, Emily of the darjeeling teas, Emily of the coffee beans, Emily of the aerial wires, Emily of the wine bottles, Emily of the engines, Emily of the glaciers, Emily of the hydroplanes, Emily of the sky pods, Emily of the silky finish, Emily of the cherry soils, Emily of the chocolate bonbons, Emily of the dark roasts, Emily of the adrenaline shots, Emily of the ginger lozenges, Emily of the green coconut curry, Emily of the spring rolls, Emily of the snickerdoodles, Emily of the world in a hazelnut, Emily of the upcycled woods, Emily of the billboards, Emily of the smithereens, Emily of the marquees, Emily of the buffoons, Emily of the cat-repellent potpourri, Emily of the aromatherapy, Emily of the cartoons, Emily of the vineyards, Emily of the rhymes, Emily of the reasons, Emily of the kits, Emily of the kaboodles, Emily of the right angles, Emily of the radiant angels, Emily of the gene pools, Emily of the bonanzas, Emily of the biodata, Emily of biogenesis, and Emily of biogenius.

I'm grateful to the mysterious maker who breathes renewed life into me, whose codes of origin serve as the material basis for every organism in the world, even my rogue genes. Although I've neither seen this maker's face nor entered the maker's abode, I speculate, does the maker dwell inside the glory-hole where I vanished? If there's a sail into oblivion, then there's a maker of the ship as well as a parent. Whose mystical hands designed the world, and what about the original codes, those spiral staircases of nucleotides shining like faraway fires, the minor stars in this minute space opera?

Did our left-handed chiral molecules emerge autonomously out of a carbonaceous brew, or right-handed proteins pop up in an organic broth, zapped by lightning? Who taught the mute oysters to loosen their liquid tongues of nacre around a spot of grit, or the thirsting olive tree to bear its green or black fruit in drought? The maker assembled these chiral molecules, not the stardust editors who follow scripts. Yes, the maker wove a left-winding genetic staircase of deoxyribonucleic acid, and the amino acids and sugars with right-handedness or left-handedness in their molecular structures, depending on the orientation of the enantiomers.

Clockwise or counter-clockwise, or like human hands, right and left, those molecules are not superimposable. If the molecules are rotated to face each other, however, they're unique mirror images, the mystical fingerprints of the maker shimmering on the edges of life.

I don't have any hands. No fingerprints. I curl the tips of my arms, which work almost as well as any fingers, forks, or forceps, touching and tasting my way through this side of the universe with a wet flush of chemoreceptors. Nocturnal rain, loose and silver as human senescence, falls out of the low-lying clouds over the sea. The rain enters my open window like a lyric poem brightly hammering its sounds and rhythms like a drum, tapping the sill and the floor of my abode. I don't sashay across the room to shut the window, but rather, let the water come in, dampening the walls. The night wind pushes a blustery curtain of rain towards my undulating waterbed as I inhale and exhale without snoring; neither nostrils nor a uvula nor a soft or hard palate in this octopodean body of breath. The rain of little mallets, drumming on my tricycling hearts, invites a phantasm of air and ocean, the lagoon of biogenesis. The rain is almost a friend who takes the form of liquid nocturnes, the melodious shapes of stratospheric water pooling and singing their litany of green notes in the rock garden.

Furtively, I glance at my tea cup on the sill, curling the tip of a shy yet inquisitive arm around its ear-shaped curve. The little cup

overflows with tea-flavored rain. For the tenth item on my gratitude list, I add my tea cup with the rosebud brushed on the side, the one which holds boiled water and bag of soaked chamomile flowers which I sip before going to sleep. Emily of the tannins. Emily of the chamomile tisane. Emily of the rosebuds. Emily of the sills. Emily of the hot chocolate. Emily of the gentle rains. Emily of the dandelion roots. Emily of the poppy seeds. Emily of the oaks. Emily of the summer thunderstorms. The twilight air is crisp, thanks to the cleansing out of the sky. Grateful for the misty night and its deft fingers of rain, I watch over this small place with a cranberry-colored mix of composure and sand-camouflaged assurance on this side of the universe. The wide algae leaf on my dresser lifts in the wind of the rainstorm, shivering in tacit approval with my sentiments, while the rain applauds its own robust perseverance through the post-midnight hours until the dawn.

> Raising my siphon, I ink the floor with this enigma
> *Leviathan makes the water boil with its commotion.*
> *It stirs the depths like a pot of ointment. The water*
> *glistens in its wake, making the sea look white.*
> *Nothing on earth is its equal, no other creature so fearless.*

Without fully grasping how or where these words arise, I know they resonate within me as more than immaterial echoes or memories, rather, more like a transcription of an ancient code long forgotten to us, yet assuredly designed by the maker of the universe.

## 9 | TRICYCLE OF HEARTS
### FLYING AT THE SPEED OF LIGHT

The art of a flying octopus. Mild bouts of aquaphobia. Flood, fire, and flight. An eschatological vision of the world. A case of nervous hiccups.

## TRICYCLE OF HEARTS
## FLYING AT THE SPEED OF LIGHT

In this episode of a space opera, I am a flying octopus. If I had an opportunity to recount my rogue tale of woe again, I wouldn't alter much, no pun intended. One morning, a day not apparently unlike any other, I woke up to the stark realization that I was no less than an octopus. Not a designer-gene citizen, not a person, not a woman, and not a human. By gum, a cephalopod, my dear sea stars. An octopus. Embracing my alterity, if that's what this space opera melodrama's about, doesn't necessarily mean I'm a more self-actualized creature than any other. Neither has it generated or cultivated megalomania, for which I'm grateful. Even if I do look like an octopus, the stardust editors of the omnibus knocked out any genes influencing megalomania, an effect of gene silencing. Imagine if I were an octopus afflicted with pathological narcissism; how insufferable would I appear to others around me. Fortunately, there is nobody. If you multiply megalomania by nine brains, then you'd have a monster of biomythical proportions, like the cloth-octopus who swallows ships whole, or the rock-hurling one also known to lurk in the cliffs as a giant red

spider. As a footnote in my runaway science fiction, make it a hairy, giant red spider of the rocks. I'd rather be your average joe, I guess, a generic flying octopus with hiccups, rather than an edited one with designer genes.

This is all to say, if I were to sum up the cosmic enchilada in one phrase, a woman wakes up one day on the wrong side of the universe and realizes she's an octopus. A tako, a polpo, a pulpo. Not an octopus in a woman's body, but rather, a female zipped into a bubble of octopus protoplasm. On the wrong side of the universe, no other cephalopods are discernible as far as her horizontal pupil can squint, not even a sea cucumber: no adorable baby octopuses, no hatchlings of frilled jelly sacs. No sea urchins, no sea horses, no sea anemone, nobody. Where are the dens of famished octopuses who lurk in the waters, awaiting bioluminescent squid and other cephalopods to drift unwittingly past their octoeyes? No mister octopus drifts into the picture, no sireebobby, and no molluskan pirate lingers on the horizon; only the moonlight, kissing the sea, befriends the octopus as a soul mate. In a huzzah of ideaphoria without pyrotechnics or pod-fuel, she zooms into orbit, gleaning what she can from the fields of time past and time future as a flying octopus.

Touch the sea, touch the sky without breathlessness.

Is the art of being an octopus mere surface and play, in other words, histrionics and masquerades, so to speak? Do sea cucumbers tumble in the surf? What about squid somersaulting through schooling parrot fish? And the nautilus in its papery spiral, will it dance a mambo or cha-cha-cha? In the third person, because she is an octopus, she couldn't care less. Goes without saying, despite a limited third point of view, she's wealthy, a flying bourgeoisie of an octopus with a waterbed in her chamber, a cache of bamboo spoons in her kitchen, a reading nook, a rock garden for her amusement, and a whole lagoon at her disposal, not to mention a

mysterious, if not miraculous, supply of all-you-can-eat olives and self-replenishing gorgonzola oyster crackers with a dash of shoyu, if she wishes. A smorgasbord of figs and pickled daikon, a razzle-dazzle pageant of papaya slices, in fact, and on rare occasions as a treat, a box of stroopwafels. Once banished from the bone-colored wards of the omnibus, now the rogue octopus collects bits of sea glass bleached and tumbled by the surf, then stores them in jars along with pearls. These mundane possessions, however, do not make her any less an octopus, no more than a handbag of silver dollars would make her equivalent, in currency, to the full moon.

For a season, the moonlight visits her lagoon in the ghostly shape of a mail courier with whom she is not obligated to make small talk, although he does listen, and who delivers letters—rejected gene sequences in a genre of poiesis—out of the sea. No one will fall in love with her because she's an octopus, even a flying octopus, and nobody else comes to see her. Fortunately, none of these dilemmas bothers the octopus, who has learned there's more to life than bemoaning one's bioexiled fate as an accident. In a nutshell, as the saying goes, this accordion of deckle-edge pages folded with care is an octopodean chronicle of love as the heroine sends the songs of her three hearts over the years: a song of hope, a doggerel of woe, and a ditty like a sadly broken music box with maroon octopus arms poking under a bejeweled lid. Without a word, she changes to the color of eggplant while pausing her breath without hiccups, then shifts to the red-violet color of plums. She lifts her ink siphon and doodles arrow-shot hearts and roller skates.

One heart, a futurologist, skates forward while gazing at the past
The second races wherever my wishes go, either wistful or
    unbridled.

The third is the crazy one in the broken music box, the one I
    watch
with octopus arms poking out of it instead of jewelry or a ballerina
twirling on roller skates, glued to a mirror shaped like a silver pear
or a human heart, our blighted world rotating on a tilted axis.

As the prickled night of stars approaches the pale morning, our modest-sized sun, one of a zillion inkspots in the universe, flares at a distance—atomic fusion blooming in a cosmos of floral aroma. I've got an urge to push myself out to the open sea beyond the lagoon, but dare not do so; not an amphibious barge or a modified baleen whale. I'm not designed in quite the same manner of an octopus in the wilderness, so my survival underwater isn't guaranteed. It isn't physiological, since I'm blessed with a waterproof suit of skin, but rather, psychological. Remember, my genes have run amok. My rogue genome, for some obscure reason, harbors gene sequences triggering bouts of aquaphobia, unlike the aforesaid wild octopuses who roam freely in the sea. Maybe my mild aquaphobia is due to a gene mutation of the original Emily's agoraphobia. No worries about a hydrotherapy bath in a tub, the nocturnal spring rain, or a glimpse of the ocean, but I don't relish the thought of spending hours submerged in a vast body of liquid hydrogen dioxide, even in lagoon solar-heated to a year-round average of seventy-two degrees, where I could get lost and not come back. The sea of lost letters, the sunk chains of long forgotten genes, doesn't offer any walkable maps for pedestrians of the present to visit the past. I suspect this fear is potentially due to my never having lived in the water, neither as a hatchling nor as a girl in a womb.

Yes, I blossomed in the bowels of a flesh factory, *ex vivo*.

Aside from the odysseys of flood, fire, and flight in my nightly dreams, do I wish to venture out to sea in the emerald

shadows of mermaids and postdiluvian seafarers reeling on wood berths, oceanographers diving in globes of air to gaze upon the benthos, and sea investigators with aqua lungs and rovers? What bliss to cradle a bed of oysters in my arms while each one soundlessly exudes drops of a microcrystalline essence around a grain of coral: oysters in the wilderness coat pearls at a rate slower than the motion of a clock's minute hand. In the benthic zone, oysters live as docile makers of beauty in their own right, even in the absence of a central nervous system and fine motor control. As an octopus, I wish my rogue genes were edited with a capacity for making pearls—I envy the oysters for their gift of design with minimal sentience, in my opinion. I ink my sundry memories all over the floor, on the limestone surfaces of my lair where microlexicons and fabulae are my verbal pearls in this sojourn by the sea.

On the other side of the universe, is there a lonesome Emily whose audible voice sweetly hums the ballad of a lost octopus? This is a fanciful method of saying that I, too, feel waves of nausea and heartache insofar as tales of woe ebb and flow under the stars. If I stayed at sea long enough, boating past the indiscernible curve of the horizon, maybe I'd travel far enough to reach the other side of the universe, if black holes don't pull me into their guts of intense gravitational fields, and get a glimpse what's going on out there, on the right side of the universe. Is anybody out there as we speak? Have the citizens experimented on each other to the extent that everyone's an accidental organism riddled by rogue genes, thereby normalizing the abnormal? Has the Genome Omnibus Database stashed enough data in its repository, i.e. the complete genome maps of every living species and especially the endangered but not one hundred percent of the extinct ones, and if so, can it use this responsibly; what is its compass for those decisions, the windrose of its bioethics for the use of biodata? Will the Genzopolis implode with biomolecular information overload?

Who ultimately regulates the editing, or is it driven solely by market bioforces? What other forces shape the lives of citizens on the right side of the universe?

Towards the early milk of dawn, my octoeye pupil widens with curiosity in the light, a milkiness with the tone of swamp milkweed, although I've neither tasted milkweed nor drunk mammalian milk on this wrong side of paradise. Were the landmasses of kindred species, the one with koalas and kangaroos and katydids, swallowed by swollen seas? Did the ocean truly arise like a cloth octopus and open up its damask maw to swallow it all in a few gulps, except for the intralpine valleys? How many introspective Emilys pinned rolled chignons of hair over their napes, tucking the chestnut buns upward and under like braided loaves of bread? And how many blew out their lamps, then touched with hungry fingers their handmade fascicles in the night, ruminating upon ways to preserve their eyesight before the advent of gene therapy for blindness? Or corticosteroid eyedrops for iritis and other ophthalmic inflammation?

As a flying octopus, my lyric cadence is a smooth legato riding a pulse, this beam of light stroking the rust-colored spores asleep in an aquarium of rocks and ferns, sheltered from the wind. With a tricycle of three hearts dreaming at lightspeed, I view the world from the exosphere as astronauts of yore would've seen it, a blue-green marble suspended like a bridal planet of veiled mists in a space opera without a traditional marriage plot. Whom will this vestal planet wed? No, instead, the inverted plot is multilinear, working against closure: One of my hearts looks forward with eager anticipation as the globe draws nigh, while my branchial hearts push glimmers of danger into my nervous system, recalling the fact that octopuses do not travel in outer space, even allegorical space, or a biomythopoeic one. There's not even an octopus constellation associated with a biomyth, besides; perhaps only

the sea-goat with the noggin of a goat and tail of a torpedo, and the sea-monster whale, and the flying fish.

Believe me, I don't mind missing a stellar outline of my melonhead in the stars; who covets the fame and glory when the maker has designed everything in the wilderness? As I orbit closer to the world, angling my pod over a ragged arch of alpine archipelagoes visible from the troposphere, I witness the bumpy mountain ranges obscured in bromine-colored haze, then the dots of settlements and little cooking fires in the valleys by the bomb shelters of yore, the domes, repurposed storm cellars, and round culverts. Where are the major continents, those landmasses drifting on the outer mantle? Did the sea levels rise to the base of the alps, as I feared? Did earthquakes demolish the seven continents, whose debris collapsed into the ocean? Was the ring of fire destroyed by raging volcanoes with blown-out calderas of ash? Why couldn't the world shield her own body from this destruction by her own inhabitants?

On my descent into the troposphere, I get nervous hiccups.

Foremost, with the bulk of original landmasses displaced or drowned, only the highest steppes and alpine peaks are inhabitable for the citizens who've settled in hangars and hovels of fuselage salvaged from the debris fields of wrecked sky pods on failed test runs for star system migration. Here, at the foothills of once the highest mountains of the world, the wealthiest designer citizens of the world live in dire poverty, hardly subsisting from grain to grain of genetically modified amaranth, millet, and buckwheat on the terraces. There is flood, fire, and famine. No more genetically modified vineyards on the coasts, no more fertile belts of bioengineered cash crops like spelt and corn. Famine rages in what's left of the world. For the time being, the ocean hurls its flagons of surf at the shorn faces of sea cliffs with a smashing force, a far

cry from the tranquil lagoons and archipelagoes predating the flood, while wildfires destroy the fields and orchards. Dare I say the weathered landscape is savage? A savagery bereft of pulchritude and politesse or even basic civilized polity meets the octoeye. As I lower myself out of the sky, descending closer to the world, what's more horrifying than the sight of a jagged landmass with the ghastly appearance of a necropolis? I witness bloody fields of carnage reminiscent of the days of yesteryear, when wars were fought by hand-to-hand combat instead of machines: fields haphazardly littered with cadavers stiffening with rigor mortis and rotting in mass open graves.

As I fly over the ravaged fields, I see gangrenous carcasses, flesh chunks flayed at the bone, ripped apart for their organs—heart, liver, lungs, kidney—or to allay hunger, then left to rot in the open air. No turf greens the earth, no flowers, and certainly no gardens. No humming bees dive into the skirts and bells of wildflowers, not even the little makers of cliff honey. The bees are long gone with nothing to pollinate, no milk or honey flowing out of the bosom of the world. The settlement is a festering necropolis where carcasses decay above the ground or in shallow foxholes, stinking in broad daylight, or else by bonfires where the citizens gather in groups to grab cooked meat. Flesh factories are shuttered, the pluripotent meat mills of yore, shut down; only the befouled ruins of rotting bones remain. Out of the foxholes, there's no rhyme or reason to the chaos. Where are red-spore, velvety ferns of love and old heartfelt grottoes of friendship? How about huddling together to guzzle modified wheatgrass, or shots of pineapple vodka infused with periwinkle extract? What about instruments of carved driftwood, lovingly honed and hewn by hand—the harp, lyre, and bamboo flute—and hospice care for the dying?

I wonder, how would an Emily conduct herself in a famine where the only flesh that creepeth upon the earth—whether

locusts or humans—was not only subject to extreme changes in weather, but the dire straits of deprivation: not even the shoes on one's soles to eat, or the guarantee of a grain of wheat, a bushel of dry upland rice, a flowering head of cabbage, a scarf of potatoes? Would a designer-gene Emily resort to committing taboo acts of incivility and cruelty, too? Would a variation of a cake-baking Emily actively engage in organ theft, autophagy, and cannibalism? Is she only a few gene sequences away from mixing batter for gingerbread to mauling someone to harvest their bone marrow?

In a context of scarcity, the new generations of genteel, designer-gene citizens regress to egregious conduct of a most repulsive kind, which I say even as an octopus without a jot of schooling or normative socialization. Uncannily, with a shudder of disgust, I instinctively recognize this behavior in the octopuses of the wild, whose aggressive rituals can mean ripping each other's guts and their flesh, mouth to mouth, orifice to orifice, exhibiting cannibalism and autophagy with a fury. An eye for an eye. Why the wild octopuses are genetically programmed to do this, I can't say. Did the maker originally intend any of this ruthless conduct? I doubt it; the fault is probably ours and not in the maker's stars, the bruised and battered fruit of unknown consequences. I put the tips of my arms up to my octoeyes to shield myself from this debauched butchery, outright revolting. I turn maroon as a dahlia, then indigo as an indignant midnight tulip. I'm an octopus: who am I to judge the citizens when my own kin is guilty of such conduct on the right side of the universe, in the shadow of my own rogue genome?

As I fly over the noxious heaps of defleshed, ruddle-colored bones, I marvel at the sight of designer-gene citizens with their flawless, freckle-free skin and eyes mauling each other on the face of the planet—or what's left of it after the sea levels rose—raging like monsters of turf and surf, destroying

each other on the shores of vanishing finger lakes and hill-ocks, grabbing their grisly body parts in fatal angles and choke holds, disgorging the deadly doses of tetrodotoxin—octopus venom, which I've never used—to paralyze their foes. The flesh factories are gone. This tableau vivant of carnage makes me forget my hiccups, to say the least. Have I flown to the right side of the universe, ironically? Is this what the future holds for our deluged Genzopolis and designer-gene citizens, who ignited gruesome bonfires of guts and gore in the valleys of slaughter? The citizens growl at each other without using the docile tongues of any language, vernacular or dead, resorting to grunts.

In a flash of my inner octoeye, I recognize some of the predatory traits of the nefarious blue-ringed octopus, smaller than a child's hand in the wilderness. The beleaguered citizens possess two arms, two legs, and a belly button, for instance; despite their use of projectile venom and other depraved habits like biting tooth-holes into other folks, however, they're not phenotypically expressed as cephalopods. The blue-ringed octopus is among the most deadly, if not the most toxic of octopuses, nearly bioengineered to extinction when its genes were copied and mistranscribed into humans, then retranscribed into the blue-ringed's spawn, a new generation of octopuses and deranged human copies: herein lies the consequences of tinkering with the wilderness.

If I could, I'd ask an Emily on the right side of the universe: What is beauty, and what is a beautiful life? Is beauty lodged in gene sequences coding the keratin in a stray hair caught in the boar bristles of your silver-backed brush? What if you and your black spice cake, chapbooks, and gardens amount to nothing more than rubbing your nose in the earth? Outwardly, the future citizens of the world resemble humans with chins and thumbs and earlobes, yet exhibit a craftier agility and cunning with the reflexes of venomous octopuses

lurking in the benthos. With a dearth of natural resources due to floods, the dissolution of families evokes a paradox of designer gene pools—everyone's related, yet no one's family— along with gene flow, where alleles in one population, say, those of octopuses, drift into another, for instance, a pool of people. The consequences of genetic flow, in this scenario, are magnified by the loss of the omnibus and its magistrate to keep the citizens in check.

Eat you, eat me, eat Emily, eat everybody alive under the sun.

Eat your spawn, your sisters, your aunties, your great uncles and little second cousins with the sticky hands, your kindred in the cold moonlight. The sight of all this depresses me tremendously, to say the least. Flying over a ramshackle settlement lit by little cooking fires, I see no one fit to ask questions or to explore solutions. Instead, cauldrons of boiled bone-broth sit outside hovels of palm fronds thatched with clay mud—where did they get these pots, I wonder—flesh pots of death, as the prophets of ancient days would warn us about. And where are the flesh factories and their bowels of deliquescent, designer-gene protoplasm? The dregs of death taint the pots of carnage, and it's not the toxic vines of a gourd as an ancient prophet warned in the divinely inspired arcana of sacred texts, long forgotten: what can we offer to atone for transgressions of this magnitude?

Genesis originates from the maker of life, who is love, not from us.

Without the maker, we annihilate ourselves. When an octopus in the wild feels highly stressed, drowning in the abyss of the interior, so to speak—in these nightmarish occurrences, she mysteriously inks the inner surfaces of her own wet cave of viscera—a phenomenon known as intramantle inking, sort of like endometriosis in human females but involving sepia ink, not menstrual blood. It's a type of cave writing no one will ever read, not even the octopus herself, yet she's the only one who gleans its message of despair, a sienna tattoo of grief inked on the walls of

her organs. This interior night, a festering wound of anguish, has no clotting agents to stop the blood or microneedles to cauterize the vessels. Bleeding drops of celestial ink, the milky river of stars drip their rays of light—thin strands of evanescence like ghostly mushrooms in the forest, mingled with moonbeams—into an inkwell of angst. I've never inked my innards before, yet this dark vision of a bizarrely dystopian future makes me wonder if the ailing planet, like a biomythic octopus of damask cloth, will open her body to a destitute world by locking the designer-gene inhabitants, dead or alive, in a vault of the night, inking her interior mantle.

With the archaic wings of love flown out the window, bloodthirsty aggression explodes with a fury. Despite the genes knocked out for mood swings and pathological narcissism, it's every citizen for oneself, regardless of genetic similarity. In each compound, a hill of bodies rots into the soil, thighbones and shinbones heaped in a tower next to it. When citizens feel hungry, they head for the tower of carcasses with swinging machetes, hack off a chunk of flesh studded with pearly maggots, and toss the remains onto the tower next to it. Fattened by the meat of degenerate genetic citizenry, the carrion birds circle overhead. Targets of hunger, the orphans—little abandoned children, boys and girls—are trussed up in broad daylight and vanish without a trace. Maybe they fell headlong into the black holes, stretched out into spaghetti noodles by the gravitational forces, then disappearing into singularities of infinite density? Are organs harvested if tissue copies aren't available? The citizens act out with nihilistic rage, devouring kith and kin with shrieking abandon.

Where is the angel of inspiration with a golden mandolin of praise, the angel of integrity with her silver-plated armor, the angel of candor with folios and fascicles, or the angel of information flipping her silicon mane of hair? Have the angels of the ancient days abandoned the citizens in their blighted civilization in the last days? The citizens of yore, who possessed a jot of common

good due to their pod-schooling as philanthropists, chose to risk the fates of wayfarers and extraterrestrial adventurers, letting go of the globe—this postdiluvian globe of rising seas—and repositioned their anthropocene maps and intergalactic atlases to the stars, migrating out of the solar system. Up and out is the new way, not down and under. One by one, in their exospatial collectives, they let go of the beloved yet battered planet like milkweed astronauts floating out their pods, journeying to another star system where they could mix and match their gene pools afresh for their flawless, disease-free futures. In this way, a segment of the genomes logged in the Genome Omnibus Database jumped ship, so to speak. No one knows whether the explorers settled extraterrestrial soil. Did they ever build hives of genetically modified cotton and maize, above-ground yams with edible skin delicate as rose petals, radial clockwork radishes, and glow-in-the-dark rutabagas? How about lavish microgardens of eggplant, chives, gourds, and asparagus? Did the sky pods of interstellar migrants explode, releasing their genetic data to the whims of random chance and radioactivity in the universe? Did it mutiny? In outer darkness, the fleecy stars engulfed the lesser lights of their souls; only the maker knows the end of their tarnished tale.

The generations who clung desperately to the planet in famine and flood survived by violating their ancestral taboos, augmented by mindless violence. My infamous first cousin in the wild, the poisonous blue-ringed octopus, would be appalled at their profligate use of venom. On the same hand, however, it's fascinating how the designer genes failed to improve the quality of citizenry overall, whose grotesqueries trigger the same frisson of horror I've experienced in nightmares: I face a spongy bed of seaweed, dandelion, and baby kale with morsels of bioluminescent fungus, tangy kumquat slices, and quinoa grains mingled with rice; upon closer examination, the bed of super-greens is garnished with the grilled arms of baby octopuses, their melonheads nestled among olives and anchovies. I shudder, wishing I'd

sprouted lids with lashes to shield my eyes. Instead, my flickering eyes stay open like those of a fish. This is nothing less than hyper-vigilance.

Wishing a supermassive black hole would suddenly yawn open and yank me away to the other side of the universe, I remember: I'm already there. Or here, rather. Am I on the right side of the universe? The wrong side? It's my alterity I see in a new light. Hug yourself, I say. Go ahead. Give yourself a hug today; you've got plenty of arms to do it. You're an octopus named Emily. Deal with it. That said, I'm grateful this adventure is only a figment of my imagination run a little wild. A figment of the dystopic future, a fragment of a nightmare. I do recognize that paradise isn't boring, even if a person wakes up one day as an octopus with no genetic value as a citizen, and if anything, this thought experiment has boosted my resolve to stick to a macro-biotic vegetarian diet of kelp. Yes, kelp will always do. A bowl of saffron bouillabaisse, not chicken soup or ox tail stew, will refresh my soul. Oysters are friends not fodder, not even an occasional delicacy for special celebrations, and cooking fires in my stove will never burn anyone who once was a nervous, sentient organ-ism, not even an oyster who cannot recount a story of her own making.

As for the rogue bananas in abundance on this island, I har-bor no ill will against any lifeforms, even bananas masquerading as berries. Believe me, rogue yet shamelessly humdrum are these innocuously modified bananas, insofar as I can't tell what's wrong other than an everlastingly yellow phosphorescence. Bowing and bending, endearingly coy in the sea wind, the banana fronds do no harm. No harm. They sway like canvas sails in the lagoon breeze, at peace with their own kind in the universe, a cosmos riddled with black holes wherein rogues vanish, i.e. the oddest of fruit like me. Modified banana flesh is chock full of vitamin-rich, energizing complex carbohydrates, and their deluxe shade is

restorative; although I don't like their odor, texture, or mouthfeel, I am content to leave them alone.

In the milky light of the young morning, the bananas do not hold this against me. Like you, we are also rogues, the bananas murmur in their equable, non-verbal language, bowing in the wind. We mean no harm. We do no harm. No harm, Emily. Please use our creamy flesh to make banana leather, use our peels as skin grafts for burns, or harvest us for handbags and sandals. Our yellow is your yellow, say the bananas, and we do not live apart from you. Love and freely love, give and freely give, is our motto.

A firefly lifts its bulb into the sky, a winged bioluminescence among the winks of faraway stars. If only my rogue designer genes included a firefly's sequences of light; at least I'd glow in the dark while in flight, not drowning in a quagmire of amorphous emotions. If my rogue genes were muted for negative emotions or bitter memories, maybe I'd be less inclined to overthink matters, especially issues over which I had no control. If I were a firefly, I'd signal with ellipses, telegraphing nocturnal messages to friends who'll appear in the dark, those who recognize this code in the wilderness: greetings, luminous ones. No worries, I am coming to see you. Please don't wait for me. We're made of star dust, those invisible atoms of love. I shall meet you on the edge of a black hole with the fragrance of rhododendrons on the other side.

Don't forget. I am one of you, always, thanks to our gene pool.

## 10 | The Ultimate Hydrotherapy Spa

The fragrance of the universe, a mystery. A lamentation on autophagy, not to be confused with autologophagy. A gumbo of chromosomes. Hydrotherapy. A love letter to the maker. The magnum opus of a rogue.

# The Ultimate Hydrotherapy Spa

**N**eedless to say, I'm mortified by what I've witnessed in the aforesaid vision. Not the little wishes of fireflies, but rather, designer-gene citizens exhibiting regressed behaviors of the most depraved octopine activities. Even the blue-ringed octopus would feel ashamed. Didn't the omnibus know better than to modify octopus enzymes for direct use in citizens? What does an octopus do after witnessing this colony of dystopian chaos and waking up in a sparkling paradise, an octopia of abundance? With horizontal pupils dilated to wide rectangles in my weary eyes, I watch over the sea of lost letters while the fog rolls in as it has done countless times in the past. Voiceless with dysphonia, missing a larynx, I enumerate my blessings silently, awaiting the day when I can meet my maker. Nothing wrong with staying awake through the watches of the night; of course, I'm very nocturnal, up at all hours. Awaiting the day is a figure of speech, a metaphor for vigilance. The monotony of paradise, in a way, is a gift. Within a given routine, one knows exactly what to expect, and there's nothing to sabotage the enduring tranquility. It's a hydrotherapy spa in an octopodean utopia: Emilytopia.

# LOVE CHRONICLES OF THE OCTOPODES

The pleasure of naming places and things aside, what's an octopus to do after a mind-boggling dream of the future, a daunting revelation of a dystopia? Shall an octopus named Emily crawl into a dry sea cove at low tide, and wait for the high tide to drag her out? How depressing this sounds, forget it. Or crawl on eight arms into a rolltop desk and meditate on gratitude, listing the blessings in her life, silently and without interruption: the moonlight, the undulating kelp forest, the glass jars, the circular hands of the sea wind rinsing, cleansing the night? A vitreous wrinkle in her vision shifts lithely in a reflex; she changes her myriad hues from green to eggplant to grenadine back to emerald and then bluish like the shadows of lactose-reduced skim milk poured in a tea cup, or blushing like non-radiogenic cloudberry cream with a drop of liquid stevia leaf in it. One might witness a change in the way she arranges objects in her domestic spaces—jars this way, the abalone shells that way—or in her mute relationship, if one could even call it relational, with a ghostly mailman who arrives with the moonlight.

In a morning bath, her body is surprisingly phosphorescent, a likely indicator of unstable nuclei emitting radiation. Emily glows like a radiogenic black radish. Or maybe it was something I drank, now forgotten? From what, radiopharmaceuticals on the other side of the universe? Traces of nuclear medicine in the water? Maybe I'm paranoid, Emily concludes. Hypervigilant, she corrects herself. She says, obviously, I'm an octopus irradiated by free-floating anxiety, more than free radicals, and chronically inflamed by post-traumatic stress. The neurotic symptoms manifest with hiccups, periodically. There isn't a detectable trace of radioactive material in this room, but she believes an invigorating round of saltwater hydrotherapy might help. The tub, however, has no jets, no filters. Dissolved sea minerals of chloride, sodium, and magnesium will have to do the trick, heated one by one by the kettleful on the little

stove. In a puff of steam, the octopus sighs profoundly, then raises her siphon to ink the walls of the room.

> I wish to compose a song about the radiolarians—
> the beauty of their micro-symmetry, mineral matrices
> like snowflakes without black holes in a benthic zone
> floating down after their little deaths in radiolarian mud
> changing into radiolarite, the sediment in sea cliffs
> singing with glassy chalcedonite, flecked with chalk—
> following what I've glimpsed of a future dystopia,
> it'd be preferable if the diseased globe were devoured
> or conquered by the clouds of undersea radiolarians
> with warm-water protozoa, squid, and octopuses.

On the other side of the universe, an Emily opens a box of shells, driftwood, and stones gathered from the beach she once visited as a girl with her family. A lace-trimmed sun bonnet lies on her bed, a bleached frock hangs from one of the posts, and bundle of purple heather tied with thread leans against her collection of books. Dipping her quill in an inkwell, she scribbles, *God* and *light* and *hymn* and *wave.*

As I lower myself into this bath spa of electrolytes, the relaxing effects of vasodilation take effect mercifully. The mineral water stimulates the immune system and diminishes the negative symptoms of stress, triggering the release of endorphins while blue blood murmurs through my system. I float, wiggling my arms and opening my soft mouths, releasing the tension from the night's rigors of dreaming. My coppery blood pressure drops with pauses between the diastole and systole of three pulsing hearts. I don't suffer from hypertension, but the cumulative effect of overthinking with nine brains and three hearts is stressful, a form of information overload, I suppose. It's a lot of synchronous detail to process, not to mention whatever imagery, stashed in my melonhead of wily neurons, firing up in my visual cortex. If I were a beluga whale, would

I need a hydrotherapy spa, as well, or would I benefit from a higher capacity for emotional self-regulation? What fun to sport a melon-sized wad of fat atop my head, or rather, inside my noggin, a fatty blob operating not as an adipose buffer against the cold like an earmuff, but rather, for echolocation. To see where things are in front of you underwater, use your wireless sonar to gauge their shapes. If only I could express polymorphism and change into one zoological form, then another, plus more. In this tub, I ponder the incidents which could've elapsed in a parallel life as a woman named Emily or even a beluga whale, herbivorous iguana, or algae-infused sloth named Emily.

With only a pair of arms and not eight, a woman named Emily wearing a wool pea-coat, grasps a cloth-bound monograph about octopuses in her left. No, wait a minute, a bouquet of star-gazer lilies grasped by the fingers of her left fist, and a stamped valentine in her right. She's on her way to the post office as one of thousands whose heels will tap the sidewalk that designated hour of the morning, where she'll drop the valentine in a mail slot. Nope, she hasn't checked the address of the recipient, though. Let's say the recipient is a beloved niece who lives far away, who moved inland short of a month or so ago, up into a valley in the alps to escape the steady rise of the seas, the neap tides which show minimal change between the high and the low tides, only during the quarter moons. This niece of thin shoulders and dainty arms, who wears a frock with lace on her neckline and sleeves of filigree spun by edited silkworms who spin jade-colored silk, never receives the valentine. It's misaddressed. This designer-gene woman named Emily, who lives on the right side of the universe, perfumed the pages with orange blossom essence. Goes without saying, in a worst-case type of scenario for natural disasters, those change-of-address requests lose their effectiveness, and the valentines fail to reach their destinations.

Even if you're on the right side of the universe, things might still go wrong. The wayward valentine sinks into a way station with other wet ephemera piled up to a battered roof upcycled from sky pod fuselage. The strokes of glue on an envelope flap, soaked with floodwaters, gently loosens the folds, and the postal stamp detaches, too. The ink pigments dissolve; the lace disintegrates. When the tides flood the bungalow, the lot, and the shed out back, fragments of the woman's memento to her niece surface in the moonlight with the sea of lost letters. In my mind's octoeye, the sea is lapis lazuli boosted by blue pigment, the royal color of jewelry boxes and illuminated manuscripts of the ancient days. Pleasing to the soul, I'd say, although I'd say less about the odor of the sea itself, of algae and bacteria in an upsurge of swells during a heat wave. The foaming waters rise without much fuss, the way a pool or aquarium fills with gushing dissonance, gallons rushing every second; mute thunder, rather, not unlike listening to the roar of a cliffside waterfall at a safe distance, or witnessing its reverberation through a pair of binoculars.

The iodine odor of the sea, however, is astringent today, although there's nothing discernibly amiss. Don't have a clue if the aroma is due to pulped fibers in the disintegrating pages of the ocean, or some other alchemy of genes mixed with algal saline. It's not quite a stinking, reeking odor like a durian fruit; what does it resemble? Black mission figs ripening on a window sill, a hand-mill grinding coffee beans? Fancifully, I guess it reeks like cacao eau de parfum, in other words, chocolate alcohol, i.e. theobromine with a xanthine stroke of danger. I could sink my whole melonhead into a tureen of this perfume, intoxicated by its aroma, musky and earthy-sweet on a single whiff, then luxuriate in the darker notes of chocolate ginger ganache with undertones of cardamom spice and pistachios or cabbage roses in a tea garden. My dear heavenly stars of the sea, I could rave on and on about this forever. The valentine,

along with the other lost ones, is never read, yet its inked face is engulfed with a blue fragrance of the sea, the inexorable perfume of its bathymetry of submerged chromosomes.

On hindsight, it's irrelevant to decipher the missing letters if their fragrant pages offer access to their contents; in other words, if the sweetness or bitterness of their dispatches are distinguishable through an olfactory sense, decipherable through molecular fragrances, then decoding them by the usual means is no longer necessary: put away the dehydrators and ultraviolet lights, the microfiche and magnification with color filters; use the filtering screens for shadow hand-puppets instead, and ink solvents for another project. As for the genetic spawn named Emily on the other side of the universe, one I could've been if designer genes were spliced properly and my genome accurately edited, the spawn are utterly oblivious to me. And the original Emily never knew who I am, no matter how many telepathic memorandums I transmit in the wee hours of the night into her cloudy jar of dreams.

Neither do I know whether any Emily exists for certain, and whether the original Emily actually did, either. Who knows? As an Emily with octopodean enzymes, she could've pursued the career of a stardust editor, orchestrating nine genome projects in synchrony if she had nine brains in sum, or even better, as an oenologist who could taste nine wines simultaneously, discerning the robust years versus mature years of syrah and sauternes; years of chablis, zinfandels, pinot noir, and oaky reds in decline; cabernets and merlots in their peak years. What about the ice wines pressed from chardonnay frozen in the vineyards after the first frost, or the fruity muscatels leaving a buttery glow on the tongue? With a ganglion in each hand, she could easily handle nine vintages at once, no pun intended. Yet at the back of her mind is a nagging sense of doubt. Outwardly a woman named Emily, inwardly an octopus, i.e. the opposite of my predicament. She wonders

aloud, what does an octopus know about vintages, anyway? The octopodean oenologist distrusts her own judgment, even while a finger curls around the rim of a glass, savoring the velvety drops of wine.

I see this other Emily in my mind's octoeye, an aperture or rift into the other side of the universe wafting rhododendron perfume—the intoxicating dream of mad honey, I'll remind you—in a pod of imagination. Gracefully, as if safely enclosed in a bubble, I start falling over a canyon in the earth, my shadow widening over this mile-wide fissure in a desert whose subterranean murals, when lit by the sun rising above the horizon, sets the arroyo walls aflame in plumes of ginger. Introspective, hair twisted up and knotted in a bun, the woman named Emily is oblivious to any rift in the universe, arranging her perennial violet cuttings on the counter, filling a fishbowl with water where the cuttings will propagate roots from the leafy petioles. Using moist, soil-loving fingers, Emily will transplant the violets to the clay pots on her sills where afternoon light comes in like a church, and prays the cuttings will survive and helps them along by talking to them. Finally, she whispers a short blessing so they'll take root in the earth, that is to say, when it was fertile enough to sustain diverse lifeforms; now I don't know for certain.

Emily's violet perfume wafts gently across the universe as I wake in the morning, shortly after dawn the color of a kumquat. The benediction of the violets touches my skin as I lie on my waterbed with octoeyes open, waiting for the sea breeze to warm up with the fragrance of honeysuckle and plumeria, and another day to commence. This melonhead, dewy with nocturnal transparencies and rusty stardust, drags a bit; exhausted by these visions, my blue-rimmed tricycle of three hearts creaks like a rocking chair, if you'll excuse the poorly mixed metaphor, before facing a new day, when I'll drop the kelp hat on my noggin and scoot outside to take stroll in the

rock garden, or tuck myself carefully into a jar and vanish, at least, for an hour. Quarantined in a round, glass room, who would want to do anything else? Not a rogue, least of all this one. Who will redeem the lost hours of hiccups in a lagoon, even if it is paradise? Only the maker knows the answer. In the genesis of mysteries woven by the maker, an unedited, worthy lamb will be the universal sacrifice once and for all, for the rogues and designer-gene citizens alike. Maybe this lamb has appeared to us already; like a flyby asteroid missing the moon, we've missed it by a mile as our battered planet hurtles into a foreseeable future, haplessly fractured and blighted in the outer darkness of our transgressions, minor or not.

The futurologist of my three hearts beats resolutely in darkness.

One day, in a dystopic future of dyspepsia, if I visit the sea of lost letters face-to-face and not only in fantasy, will the gumbo of chromosomes unravel their jumbled, clandestine grievances, or will I get a bellyache from a noxious flood of biodata and the destroying fire of nonexistent bioethics? Will I see the letters emerge like credits rolling at the end of a cellulose acetate dream of silver salts, presenting the sea of lost letters to tourists as a map cave? In the film, a camera eye slowly pans a dark, claustrophobic space; in a shot-reverse-shot from a shadowed door frame, genome maps flutter in unrolled rags underwater. In the gloaming, an eight-armed figure arises in sharp relief against a spotlight, exploring this undersea cave of lost maps with her flexible limbs. An octopus? If so, what is she doing in this space opera, a melodrama of undersea wanderings and star system migration?

Ladies and gentle genes, my hydrophilic ability to attract water draws all the molecules of dihydrogen oxide to my soul like a tsunami rolling in reverse; with the flickering of a reel in reverse, the whole ocean withdraws into every cell of my existence, the heat-tolerant starfish and krill and urchins siphoned

into this motley aquarium, leaving only the ribs of shipwrecks and rusted submarines, the seaweed-tangled hair of drowned seafarers and of course, the long chains of lost letters fluttering in the darkness. With the sea waters of the world absorbed into my reservoir of coppery blue blood, I expand to the size of a mid-range planet, ballooning in outer space until I reach the height of the blue-fringed stars far beyond the exosphere of any flying octopus except me, the first one headed for the ringing music of the celestial spheres on the other side of the universe.

In the film, I'm not drowning or asphyxiating, you see.

Not underwater apnea, fortunately, neither am I the mermaid who dissolves into foam after breaking the octopus jar, dying of heartache and dancing on knives. If I wrote the fairy tale, I'd be the octopus named Emily who returns from the ocean and refuses to moor in a putative marriage with a prince. Yes, this Emily decides bipedal locomotion in fairy-tale kingdoms are a load of crock. The palace on the sea cliffs, perched on the ledge of the world, will one day wash out with the rising tides. In shades of anemone blue wedded to my skin, the sea hours change in gradations of tone like the harmonies of a nocturne, alternating from glaucous and ice-blue, faded denim to indigo, alice blue with cyan juxtaposed to violet, powder blue and turquoise, iris to midnight, asters and sapphires shot through with ultramarine or turquoise, majorelle with flecks of phthalo, cornflower streaked with periwinkle, forget-me-not and peacock blue. In this aquarium of a body, I billow out with the galactic blue-blackness of a burning exosphere with faraway stars spectrally shifted, rays shortened for those suns careening towards us rather than away from us—those distant star-fires once serving as navigational sky maps when pods dropped into the sea after flaring white-hot on reentry, before the massive waters gathered in a corner of

the world, then flooded the entire planet up to the foothills of the alps.

As I swell, the iridophores in my skin go transparent with a tinted sheen like a one-way scrim, then the chromato-phores shift to midnight blue-on-black with a slenderness of moonlight turning like a marble of swirled, petaled glass, rotating luminously within me, its opaque petals opening and parting shyly inside, filtering the starlight of reminiscence. Hypothetically, there could be no end to this expansion, and I could go on and on without any barriers to stop me. Except, of course, my own gravity in outer space, which gradually pulls my limbs back into an aggregate ball of parts, then a knot of atoms. Who am I in this conundrum? No longer an octopus in my own right, with nine brains transformed into the shapes of nebulae and supernovae ejecting gas and star-dust, and bursts of nucleosynthesis where new stars are born, the grand, unified cosmos is essentially an octopus beyond my absolute being, a radial blossom of animate, uncoiling, multi-foliate petals: a cephalopod galore under blue-ringed stars and geysers of newness. It's an octopus named Emily, I say, who resides at the heart of the universe, an omnivore pulsating like a raw jewel by the maker's hand. Or the universe is an octopus who holds her own vortex of biodata together—algal, fungal, or gaseous matter alike, so our world doesn't explode.

The sea of lost letters might never surrender its aphotic zone of archives, or unlike the fragrant black holes, serve as portals to an octopodean paradise. With the onset of cannibal-ism in a future dystopia, a common good may no longer exist on the other side of the universe, with yesteryear destroyed by floodwaters and by the designer-gene citizens. Should I call it an operating system, or at minimum, an orderly inventory of ephemera? How can I, when I haven't deciphered them myself, only tasted their contents by their aroma? All I can say is, this biochronicle of love, unraveled sentence by sentence, is

coaxed out of me by a power sweeping through my blood like a coppery wave when I least expect it, while a tricycle of three hearts pedals in a rhythm which originates from the maker. Accident or not, our mystical dialogue might go something like this.

> Do you know who I am?
> Pause. You're the maker.
> Do you know who you are?
> Pause. An octopus.
> You're beautiful.
> Pause. Am I?
> Yes, gorgeous.
> Pause. Thank you.

Inevitably, I shall go to the maker, the one who designed everything out of nothing and made it good. For now, however, I am an octopus in a small place. This is the life of solitude with which I must contend. Troubled by my dream visions, ill-equipped as an octopus to save the citizens of the future who've regressed to autophagy, I return to paradise on this side of the universe, saddened yet wiser from the revelation, and continue weaving a mystical tapestry that only the maker can read. It carries the fragrance of redolent black holes like rhododendrons bursting on a mountainside, a spray of roses with star-gazer lilies under a bridal veil, and the red wine poured at the bottom of a glass. It's my love letter to the maker, the magnum opus of my rogue life, or more humbly, a valentine; ultimately, it's about our futile attempts to save ourselves from ourselves, our flesh from our own flesh, and the virtues of assigning value to alterity. If we destroy the other, we destroy ourselves, and I suppose the maker might be very annoyed at us for doing so.

The world is on fire. The world is flooded.

The maker doesn't have to love us, or say anything to allay our ruffled egos to know this isn't right. What is beautiful, or what is just? What is the distinction between a world on fire, and a world that's flooded? On the beach, a tongue of foam pushes ashore, then withdraws into the bluest of cyan-blue recesses of the sea. Is there a giant cloth octopus lurking in its underwater lair? Who cares about biomythical sea monsters when there is no bread, no crops, and citizens edit themselves at flesh factories? A glittering trail of salt crusts my limestone floor, a consequence of my own neglect as I bathe in a tub of seawater without the presence of other sentient fauna in sight. The green folly of banana groves whispers to no one as I sweep halide minerals with a brush and pat the floor with my arms, ensuring no grains are left, then rinse my skin and moisturize my melonhead and limbs with hyaluronic acid and zinc oxide in a base of olive oil. Whereas I am tolerant of seawater with a low risk of drowning if I hold my head above the surface, I can't salt my body without the skin getting inflamed; the minerals must be washed off right away, or else I break out in an itchy rash.

In my mind's octoeye, I witness the opening of snow-flake-sized portals, those secret pathways to lagoons of rogue octopuses who survive black holes, gaps in the fabric of the universe. Each cephalopod, suspended in a pod of imagination, is a pear-drop jewel. A skin-blossom drenched in heady aroma. Floral, tender, and furled like peonies crazily bombastic with perfume. Each pod of the imagination is a roiling bubble of peacock blue, harboring a miniature octopus in a fragile liquid sphere, a million uniquely rogue octopuses in pods of fabulae pursing, billowing shapes and colors. Argonauts, in a sense, are explorers: pelagic octopuses and paper nautiluses like astronauts of yore in command modules back in the younger anthropocene days of our planet. Without shedding a tear of regret, I enter one of those pods to meet my maker on

this side of the universe in a shining cloud of light, and realize the maker is already here with me.

You're here, I say. You were with me all along, weren't you? As a spring breeze caresses my arms, I put drops of hyaluronic acid on them, lifting each limb, especially the shy one. Why didn't I know this the day before yesterday? All this time I spent waiting for you in a small place where I couldn't see your face, where I had no other spot for me to go, were you here all this time? Or have you just come from the other side of the universe? Do you know what is going on over there? Can you turn back the ancient hands of time? Have the citizens already regressed to unspeakable acts? If so, why are you letting them devour each other? How much time is left on the other side of the universe? The maker doesn't reply, which I suppose is the maker's prerogative.

> Let's cut to the chase, I say.
> Silence.
> Why didn't you undo these edits?
> Silence.
> I don't want to be an octopus.
> Silence.
> I don't want to be human, either.
> Silence.
> Why didn't you redo the wilderness?
> Silence.
> Why did you let the editing go haywire?
> Silence.
> What about the greenhouse gases?
> Silence.
> Why did you let the floodwaters rise?
> Silence.
> Am I talking to myself?
> Silence.

Can you hear me?
Silence.
Do you love me?
Silence.
What is my real name?
Silence.
Am I more than a number?
Silence.
Who are you?

My dear heavenly stars of alphabet soup, does this rude dialogue come across as pompous or outright preposterous for an octopus? Apologies to you, ladies and gentle genes, and to your ears as witnesses to shrouded enigmas. I can't explain this to my satisfaction, but in the maker's silence, I do sense an awesome presence like a dazzling flame I cannot touch, a globe alight in my blood like ball lightning. One who creates, sanctifies, purifies, and sustains life, the maker hides with me—yes, has also hidden me—in this small place, although the maker also dwells outside spacetime. In the maker's silence is love packaged in the shape of personhood, transiently realized in the flesh. I believe the maker witnesses the trials and tribulations of the ill-fated rogues, those bioexiled to live on the other side of the universe—on this side of things, I mean. From saltwater black pearls to fireflies and blue-ringed stars in the sky, I know the maker sees me as a fragment of a grand design whose unfolding plot and resolution are not yet divulged, yet originally coded in my genes as a blessed fingerprint of a divine presence, even within this blob of genes run amok.

Beloved, darling, beautiful one.

On this side of the universe, I don't expect to pick up a direct line to the maker. Am I nervous about the maker's assiduous silences, alternating with terms of endearment? I get the hiccups. Hello, maker of the universe, are you there?

I must confess that darling, gorgeous, and beloved are not words regularly used in my microlexicon. Do you know what this ninety-digit alphanumeric serial code says, more of a statement rather than a question. The maker who knows every hair on one's head—or papillae, if one doesn't have any hair follicles—wisely chooses not to reply or intervene at this very moment. I change from grenadine to emerald to blue skim milk and a water lily, the folded lotus on its pad. In a sense, my colors are wedded to the maker's creativity, one who not only sees but knows intimately every cell of this rogue body, even in the absence of words. A voice in dulcet tones, which I recognize as timeless wisdom itself, arises in my three hearts, echoing, *there are no accidents.* There are no accidents. There are no accidents. A fourth time: No accidents, my beloved. In the gap between the mineral waters of the hydrotherapy spa and the sea of lost letters, I've gradually embraced a new form of personhood without tears. The ferny vale of tears, missing from my body, flows within the great ocean of the maker's sky and sea, not out of glandular cells bathed in a pearly liquid of their own making. I don't cry, after all; my colors change, and my pupils narrow into horizontal lines, but I don't tear up.

Do I recall a brief season of tears on the other side of the universe, possibly when I first opened my eyes in the bowels of a flesh factory? Coming into existence or the reverse, entering a black hole, perhaps. Octopuses, as far I can tell, do not cry. However, in a flash, through drops of water stinging my octoeyes, I see the walls of the factory, the color of bone. I see the gloved hands of the stardust editors, moving while their mouths and throats made noises. Now my visual cortex summons hazy memories as if they're unfolding in real time: A freezing winter room, bone-colored walls, light-emitting diodes, and the fog of sensations I recall today as faraway reverberations, like the overhead buzz of airborne insects, signs of intelligent life other than mine? A wet butterfly pumps air

into its exquisitely unfolded wings—drying and stiffening like rice-glued kites in the sun—how is it that I'm flying around like an angel with an untroubled face, looking down upon my octopodean soul? What about the fragrant portals of the black holes where I disappear, crowded by an aroma of rhododendrons plucked from their boughs, the intoxicating mad honey couched in their nectar? The blue-ringed stars in their centuries-old motion of axial precession speed past me, faster and faster, and poof, I pop up on the other side of the universe.

In paradise, where the spring wind is unfailingly balmy, and the ocean bathed in a hint of algal bloom and seaweed, rain clouds gather on an azure horizon where no cloth octopuses, no hairy red spiders, and no giant seas cucumbers rear their biomythic heads, if you can refer to those brainless finales on echinoderms as heads. No fishing boats are seen, no buoys or floating isles of garbage, and no trace of a wilderness trimmed by molecular scissors. The lagoon is warm to the touch; the beach sand, everlastingly coral pink and soft to the head. It sticks to my arms whenever I poke it; then I rinse my whole body in kettlefuls of seawater. In my lair, everything is arranged in order, a small watery place where I will live out my days in serenity under the maker's grace. I figure out how to open the jars of gummy seaweed gelatin to slather onto my skin. I adore the hydrotherapy spa of my tub, not to mention my kelp hat. Although I forget it on my strolls from time to time, as well as the zinc oxide, I have yet to be sunburned. Is this a sign of grace? In all likelihood, the ultraviolet rays are filtered by the maker's hand which shields me, and my skin is edited to act as its own shield, too, a double gift of my rogue genes.

I disrobe myself of the desire to morph fully into a human woman: I take off my skin as an octopus, my rectangular pupils and multitude of chemoreceptors. I doff my melonhead like a ski hat in exchange for a cloud of thoughts. I detach

myself from a wish to grow breasts and a navel, to navigate life in a mammalian mode with uterine blood and a birth canal. I remove the fleshy sleeves of my beloved arms, the crook of my beak, the maddening crowd of mouths opening and shutting in response to hunger or curiosity. I slide out of my proto-plasm entirely, like a shy wish sliding out of a well, and keep only my nickname, Emily. I whisper my name by shaping my breath with wavelets of syllables—Emily and Emily, yes—into the universe. I lift the slippery suit of my body, anchoring my soul to its root, a mystical embrace flushed with life, and drop it upon the waters of the lagoon, where it vanishes.

At night, the sea of lost letters sends a loyal courier to my humble abode, an ossan of moonlight freely given out of the universe. Without operational mail systems on this side of the universe and entirely destroyed on the other side, and grounded fleets of cargo jets and sky pods flooded long ago, the mailman appears like a messenger angel or a seraph of paradise without the flashing sword. To guard me from what? The maker is my green shield. Maybe the angel is here to tell me about the arcana obscured within the sealed tongues of envelopes, never to speak about their subjects. I may never de-code the sequences of the drowned genes, which will never be legible to a common octoeye like mine, but whose smudged pages of nucleotide ciphers are known by the maker, whose hand ultimately ordered the atoms within me before any mo-lecular scissors edited my codes.

> Yes, I arrived on a shore without a list of instructions,
> yet the maker's invisible fingers arranged the atoms
> in this octopodean flesh, which contains a soul, a part
> floating to the maker after a body is shed in the sand
> like a husk of airborne seed. Octopus of blue blood,
> I say to myself, what is it that you sought in this life?
> Did the maker answer your questions as you gazed

at the fragrant portals of the sea? Do you understand from your dreams of witness that if we destroy others we destroy ourselves, and why this is so? Do you see the ghosts of this universe flitting in a sea of letters? Without a feathered plume or pair of wings, you rise like a warrior angel ascending a shaft of moonlight, waving goodbye as you speed past the heavenly stars to your maker, for whom exist no accidents of nature in an unedited wilderness flourishing in your equally wild heart-of-hearts on this side of the universe.

# Sources Consulted

Courage, Katherine Harmon. *Octopus! The Most Mysterious Creature in the Sea.* New York: Penguin, 2013.

Godfrey-Smith, Peter. *Other Minds: The Octopus, the Sea, and the Deep Origins of Consciousness.* Reprint Edition. New York: Farrar, Straus, and Giroux, 2017.

Montgomery, Sy. *The Soul of an Octopus.* New York: Atria Books, 2015.

*New Living Translation. Bible Gateway.* Accessed 5 March 2019. https://www.biblegateway.com/versions/New-Living-Translation-NLT-Bible/

The following works provided insights into the life and writings of Emily Dickinson, who partly inspired the fictional octopodean protagonist, Emily D, and her genetic copies, the other Emilys.

Dickinson, Emily. *The Collected Poems of Emily Dickinson.* New York: Barnes and Noble Classics, 2003.

Luce, William. *The Belle of Amherst.* Boston: Houghton Mifflin, 1976.

Oberhaus, Dorothy Huff. *Emily Dickinson's Fascicles: Method & Meaning.* University Park, Pennsylvania: The Pennsylvanian State University Press, 1983.

# Endnotes

## Chapter 1

Emily Dickinson, an octopus who resided in the Seattle aquarium, is described as "so shy she would squeeze her 25-pound body into a 3-inch space behind the backdrop of her tank" in this article by Lea Winerman: "An invertebrate with flair." *Science Watch*. American Psychological Association. June 2008. https://www.apa.org/monitor/2008/06/octopus

Perfluorocarbons serve as the basis for artificial blood plasma in a research study published by Suman Sarkar in the *Indian Journal of Critical Care Medicine*. 2008 July-September 12(3): 140-144. https://www.ncbi.nlm.nih.gov/pmc/articles/PMC2738310/

Wilderness of nights: alludes to Poem 269 ("Wild Nights") by Emily Dickinson.

Good morning: alludes to Poem 425 ("Good morning, midnight") by Emily Dickinson; also the title name of a novel by Jean Rhys.

In the agnostic epoch depicted in this novel, the Genome Omnibus Database is a giant database of the world's genomes with acronym G.O.D. It is a fictional repository partly based on the real-life Gene Expression Omnibus. Read more: "Genome Expression Omnibus" located at https://www.ncbi.nlm.nih.gov/geo/

Hoyt, Alia. "Do People and Bananas Really Share the Same DNA?" *How Stuff Works*. 4 November 2019. https://science.howstuffworks.com/life/genetic/people-bananas-share-dna.htm

The technology of using molecular scissors to snip strands of DNA refers to CRISPR, an acronym for clustered regularly interspaced short

palindromic repeats, in turn shorthand for CRISPR-Cas9. Emmanuelle Charpentier and Jennifer Doudna received the 2020 Nobel Prize in Chemistry for their work on CRISPR-Cas9. The enzyme that acts like a pair of molecular scissors is Cas9 or CRISPR-associated 9. *IDT: Integrated DNA Technologies.* Accessed 5 March 2019. https://www.idtdna.com/

According to Katherine Harmon Courage's *Octopus! The Most Mysterious Creature in the Sea,* the octopodean enzyme for editing genetic material is especially precise. She refers to the research of Joshua Rosenthal, of the University of Puerto Rico's Institute for Neurobiology: "Some diseases, such as some types of cystic fibrosis, are caused by a single genetic point mutation. Because these conditions are triggered by an incorrect sequence in the genetic code, they have long been the target of gene therapy. For this remedy, a healthy genetic sequence is fed into an inactivated virus that then can infiltrate a patient's cells, providing a correct copy of the gene. But this is simply adding another copy. 'If you could *change* that A back to G in the RNA, you could cure the disease,' Rosenthal says. Currently he and his team are trying to learn from the octopus's RNA-editing trick how to manipulate the editing enzymes. 'If you can make this happen, it will give you a lot more power than traditional gene therapy," he says. One of the researchers in his lab, Maria Fernanda Montiel, is working on finding a way to redirect RNA editing to locations that we would want to alter to cure human diseases. Rosenthal reassures me that instead of injecting octopus enzymes, they would start with the human version and work backward 'to manipulate it to behave like the octopus one does in a certain context.' This would make it more readily accepted by the human body as well as by the Food and Drug Administration. 'The enzyme that does the editing is structurally quite similar' to ours; the octopus has just tweaked theirs a bit, he says. 'So figuring out that turning, how their activity is slightly changed, is important' " (81).

Additionally, the following article in *Nature* reports the findings of using a new type of molecular scissors called "prime editing," which is more exact than CRISPR and can be used "to insert various tags and epitopes precisely into target loci." Anzalone, Andrew V. and Randolph, Peyton B., et al. "Search-and-replace genome editing without double-strand breaks or donor DNA." *Nature.* 21 October 2019. https://www.nature.com/articles/s41586-019-1711-4

With regard to "prime editing," Fyodor Urnov, a geneticist at the University of California, Berkeley notes: "'Gene editing, like many technologies, can, in principle, be put to nefarious use. Prime editing in that regard does not pose an added danger to the planet,' Urnov says. 'That said, now is not the time for a sense of false security, but rather added vigilance.'" Stein, Rob. "Scientists Create New, More Powerful Technique to Edit Genes." 21 October 2019. https://www.npr.org/sections/health-shots/2019/10/21/771266879/scientists-create-new-more-powerful-technique-to-edit-genes

Chial, Heidi. "Rare Genetic Disorders: Learning about Genetic Disease through Gene Mapping, SNPs, and Microarray Data." 2008. *Nature Education* 1 (1): 192. https://www.nature.com/scitable/topicpage/rare-genetic-disorders-learning-about-genetic-disease-979

Dumé, Belle. "Black Hole Hologram Appears in a Graphene Flake." *Physics World*. 30 July 2018. https://physicsworld.com/a/black-hole-hologram-appears-in-a-graphene-flake/

Kirk, Harrison. "If you travel through a black hole, where do you go?" Ancient Code. 27 September 2019. https://www.ancient-code.com/if-you-travel-through-a-black-hole-where-do-you-go/

"The Many Plurals of Octopus." *Merriam-Webster Usage Notes*. Accessed 5 March 2019. https://www.merriam-webster.com/words-at-play/the-many-plurals-of-octopus-octopi-octopuses-octopodes

"The Melon Heads of Michigan." Urban Myths. *Reddit*. https://www.reddit.com/r/UrbanMyths/comments/ang7cr/the_melon_heads_of_michigan/

Scutti, Susan and Yoko Wakatsuki. "The real reason people rent middle-aged men in Japan." *CNN*. 3 August 2018. https://www.cnn.com/2018/08/02/health/ossan-renting-middle-aged-men-in-japan-intl/index.html

Wehner, Mike. "Scientists turn house plant into air purifier by adding rabbit DNA." 20 December 2018. *New York Post*. https://nypost.com/2018/12/20/scientists-turn-houseplant-into-air-purifier-by-using-rabbit-dna/

## Chapter 2

Joseph, Michael. "26 Types of Olives." 23 September 2018. *Nutrition Advance.* https://www.nutritionadvance.com/types-of-olives/

Dew-snail: alludes to Poem 149 by Emily Dickinson. In the poem, Dickinson compares her attempts at predicting the snail's route to a 19th Century astronomer, Urbain Jean Joseph Le Verrier, who predicted the physical existence of Neptune through calculations. https://www.britannica.com/biography/Urbain-Jean-Joseph-Le-Verrier

Temple, Emily. "Now You Too Can Bake Like Emily Dickinson This Holiday Season." *Lit Hub.* 8 December 2017. https://lithub.com/now-you-too-can-bake-like-emily-dickinson-this-holiday-season/

## Chapter 3

Read more about the banana's botanical classification as an herb and a berry, plus its similarity to the human genome: Abbes, Barbara. Edited by Annaliese Griffin. Produced by Tori Smith. "Bananas: Quartz Obsession." *Quartz.* 12 November 2019. https://qz.com/emails/quartz-obsession/1747047/

The frigates and mermaids in the basement of the sea allude to poem 656 by Emily Dickinson.

Dean, Lindsey Kristine and Heather R. Sparks. "Water Creatures from Japanese Mythology and Folklore." *Guerilla Cartography.* 22 March 2019. https://www.guerrillacartography.org/2017/01/10/8-water-creatures-from-japanese-mythology-and-folklore/

Denise Levertov penned these lines: *You have come to the shore. There are no instructions...what I experience when I'm writing a poem is close to prayer.*

McKirdy, Euan and Junko Ogura. "Creature from the Deep Surfaces in Japanese Harbor." *CNN World.* 28 December 2015. https://www.cnn.com/2015/12/28/asia/toyama-japan-giant-squid/index.html

## Chapter 4

"Emily Dickinson's Health." Emily Dickinson Museum. Amherst, Massachusetts. Accessed 14 September 2019. https://www.emilydickinsonmuseum.org/emily-dickinson/biography/special-topics/emily-dickinsons-health/

McKenzie, Sheena. "Gigantic hole two-thirds the size of Manhattan discovered in Antarctic glacier." *CNN.* Accessed 31 January 2019. https://www.cnn.com/2019/01/31/health/antarctic-glacier-cavity-nasa-intl/index.html

Pappas, Stephanie. "Your Dreams May Come from These Two Genes." *Live Science.* 29 August 2018. https://www.livescience.com/63459-dream-genes-rem-sleep.html

Scoles, Sarah. "It's Sentient: Meet the classified artificial brain being developed by US intelligence programs." *The Verge.* 31 July 2019. https://www.theverge.com

## Chapter 5

Gardner, R.C. and A. J. Howarth, et al. "The complete nucleotide sequence of an infectious clone of cauliflower mosaic virus by M13mp7 shotgun sequencing." *Nucleic Acids Research.* 1981 June 25. Volume 9 (12): 2871-2888. https://www.ncbi.nlm.nih.gov/pmc/articles/PMC326899/

"Takotsubo cardiomyopathy (broken-heart syndrome)." *Harvard Health Publishing: Harvard Women's Health Watch.* 2 April 2018.

## Chapter 6

Anderson, R.C., J.B. Wood, and R.A. Byrne. "Octopus Senescence: The beginning of the end." *Journal of Applied Animal Welfare Science* 5 (4): 275-83. 2002. https://www.ncbi.nlm.nih.gov/pubmed/16221078

"Cream: Order this test on MyVGL." *Veterinary Genetics Laboratory.* U.C. Davis Veterinary Medicine. Accessed 5 March 2019. https://www.vgl.ucdavis.edu/services/horse/cream.php

## Chapter 7

Kelland, Kate. "CRISPR DNA editing can cause risky collateral DNA damage." 16 July 2018. *Reuters.* https://www.reuters.com/article/us-health-genes-crispr/crispr-gene-editing-can-cause-risky-collateral-dna-damage-study-idUSKBN1K61YT

"Kids Riddles." *Riddles.* Accessed 5 March 2019. https://www.riddles.com/kids-riddles

Wathen, Jordan. "How to calculate the present value of a perpetual annuity." 22 June 2016. *The Motley Fool.* https://www.fool.com/investing/2016/06/22/how-to-calculate-the-present-value-of-a-perpetual.aspx

## Chapter 8

"All Things Bright and Beautiful" is an Anglican hymn by Cecil Frances Alexander, an Irish hymnodist and poet who was married to the clergyman, William Alexander. https://www.irishtimes.com/opinion/all-things-bright-and-beautiful-an-irishwoman-s-diary-on-cecil-frances-alexander-1.3535009

*Leviathan makes the water boil with its commotion...* is quoted from Job 42:31, *New Living Translation.*

Olins, Heather Craig. "Photosynthesis vs. Chemosynthesis." 31 May 2013. *Blog: The Alien Worlds of Hydrothermal Vents.* Harvard University. http://sitn.hms.harvard.edu/flash/2013/the-alien-worlds-of-hydrothermal-vents-2/

## Chapter 9

Bennett, Heather and Ronald B. Toll. Intramantle Inking: A Stress Behavior in *Octopus bimaculoides* (Mollusca: Cephalopoda). *Journal of the American Association for Laboratory Animal Science* 50 (6): 943-45. 2011 November. https://www.ncbi.nlm.nih.gov/pmc/articles/PMC3228935/

"Death in the pot" is an allusion to 2 Kings 4:38-41, when the prophet Elisha returns to Gilgal and discovers a raging famine there. Part of the tragedy of this advanced yet dystopic world of gene-editing is that the Old and New Testaments are shelved arcana that nobody reads. The designer-gene citizens harbor a vaguely agnostic but not a personalized understanding of God's love letters. Their vast body of knowledge is technical and empirical—there is only this earthbound life in the flesh, no soul or afterlife.

"Genetic Mapping." National Human Genome Institute. 21 October 2015. https://www.genome.gov/10000715/genetic-mapping-fact-sheet/

Octopus cannibalism is described on p. 195 and p. 244 of *The Soul of an Octopus* by Sy Montgomery.

## Chapter 10

The fragrant portals allude to famous lines in the poem, "The Idea of Order at Key West" by Wallace Stevens: "The maker's rage to order words of the sea, / Words of the fragrant portals, dimly-starred, / And of ourselves and of our origins...."

Karen An-hwei Lee lives in greater Chicago. She is the author of the novels *The Maze of Transparencies* and *Sonata in K*, both from Ellipsis Press. Several of her recent poetry collections are *Duress* (Cascade Books), *Rose is a Verb: Neo-Georgics* (Slant Books), *Phyla of Joy* (Tupelo Press), and *In Medias Res* (Sarabande Books).

ellipsis
• • •
press